Dear Reader,

They say that people are the same all over. Whether it's a small village on the sea, a mining town nestled in the mountains, or a whistle-stop along the Western plains, we all share the same hopes and dreams. We work, we play, we laugh, we cry—and, of course, we fall in love . . .

It is this universal experience that we at Jove Books have tried to capture in a heartwarming series of novels. We've asked our most gifted authors to write their own story of American romance, set in a town as distinct and vivid as the people who live there. Each writer chose a special time and place close to their hearts. They filled the towns with charming, unforgettable characters—then added that spark of romance. We think you'll find the combination absolutely delightful.

You might even recognize *your* town. Because true love lives in *every* town . . .

Welcome to *Our Town*.

Sincerely,

Leslie Gelbman
Editor-in-Chief

⚭ OUR · TOWN ⚭

BECKONING SHORE

DEWANNA PACE

JOVE BOOKS, NEW YORK

BECKONING SHORE

A Jove Book / published by arrangement with
the author

PRINTING HISTORY
Jove edition / June 1997

The Putnam Berkley World Wide Web site address is
http://www.berkley.com

ISBN: 0-515-12101-0

A JOVE BOOK®
Jove Books are published by The Berkley Publishing Group,
200 Madison Avenue, New York, New York 10016.
JOVE and the "J" design are trademarks
belonging to Jove Publications, Inc.

PRINTED IN THE UNITED STATES OF AMERICA

10 9 8 7 6 5 4 3 2 1

This book is dedicated to my friend and
writing cohort,

Jodi Koumalats,
a.k.a. Jodi Thomas.

You applauded my efforts;
you encouraged me to persist;
most of all, you never quit believing in me.

Acknowledgments

Many thanks to Muriella Powell at the Biloxi Library
for her invaluable help with interlibrary loans of
my needed research books and maps.

My heartiest appreciation is extended to
Kjetil and Mary Mjolhus
for verifying the Norwegian vocabulary.
Takke du.

To Art, John, and Katie at the Amarillo Public Library
Central Branch Reference Desk,
countless thanks for all those answers
to questions I posed
throughout this and many other novels I've written.
I wonder if my name is listed on the library's redial button?

Author's Note

Many coastal towns celebrated a blessing of the fleet before each shrimp season. Biloxi's didn't occur until later than the time frame depicted in this novel. However, the seaports along the Gulf of Mexico, known as the Six Sisters, always celebrated the coming of the tourist season. Much later, the Queen of the Mardi Gras festival was known as Ixolib, which is Biloxi spelled backward. I decided to take a bit of literary license and play "what if...."

What if the town had a special festival that celebrated the tourist season? What if this festival were the forerunner of the now-famous Biloxi Blessing of the Fleet that occurs the first week of June? What if there were three little girls who desperately wanted a new mother and aspired to win the title of Little Princess, the inspiration for Ixolib?

And what if there were one special man and one special woman who would fall in love and be changed forever by all these "what ifs?"

BECKONING SHORE

❖ 1 ❖

MEREDITH STANFIELD WALKED along the promenade, quickly examining and declining the oysters, menhaden, and red snapper offered by the gulf merchants. An eight-foot-wide planked sidewalk ran the entire front of downtown Biloxi, leaving no beach to traverse before reaching the sea and ending the annoyance of sandy shoes. The promenade allowed an unrivaled daily parade of fashion that most beachfront resorts could not boast, and made visitors believe that the town emerged from the sea itself. The rich scent of black Mississippi soil blended with the fragrance of magnolia, azalea, and sweet gum trees to ease the salt-laden odor of the bounty that Biloxi Bay offered up from its depths—a sweet, heavy scent that made Meredith dizzy with yearning.

If only something different would happen today... anything to get her out of this endless rut she'd carved for herself. Even the lively conversations and vigorous bartering among the people who inhabited the fish market could not intrigue her today.

She tried to keep her mind on the task at hand—to find a good batch of shrimp for the dinner party her mother would host tonight. But her gaze kept rushing past the grand houses that lined the beachfront, each with its own wharf, to focus on the children darting into the surf where the long curve of the shoreline became nothing but white, sandy beach.

Though a moist breeze made the shopping venture more bearable, the heat of a feverish rendezvous with summer loomed over the narrow twenty-five-mile peninsula. Spanish moss hung like gray, tattered shawls from branches, making the crepe myrtle and sweet gum trees look like ladies traipsing to the shore hand in hand. How Meredith longed to tear away her shoes, lift her hem, and join the children as the gulf rushed white and strong, frothing up the beach to leave it the brown color of softly moving crawfish claws. Oh, to be so carefree, so playful, so unmindful of the terror the sea could strike at any moment.

Rather than her shoes, Meredith took off her gloves and stuffed them in the pocket of her black merino skirt, grateful for the chance to let her hands cool.

"Miss Merry, we'd best be making our purchases and returning. Your mother will be concerned if you're late, and I have a few things to finish up myself before the guests arrive."

"Of course, Winnie." Meredith suppressed the urge to shudder each time the gentle ebb and flow of the gulf caused the pier beneath her feet to sway. "You go on back to the house. Tell Mother I'll be right along. Oh, and—" She faced the elderly woman who had been their housekeeper for as long as she could remember. "—make certain you don't tire yourself. If Savannah changes her mind about wearing the violet dress, I laid out several gowns on *my* bed just in case. She'll find the appropriate accessories that go with the dress—slippers, gloves, jewelry—lying near each choice."

Meredith leaned over and kissed Winifred on the cheek. "I knew she'd be flustered at the last minute, and I don't want her causing you to be the same."

The gray-haired woman gripped Meredith gently by the shoulders. "Don't offer her the silver-blue one. No one but you has the eyes to wear it. Promise?"

With a quick nod, Meredith fought back a sharp sting

of grief that instantly brimmed in her eyes. "I w-wouldn't anyway. You know it's the one Papa bought the day he . . . well, that day."

"Dear child." Winnie hugged her gently. "I wish there were some way I could make his and Phillip's passing easier for you."

Relishing the comfort in her housekeeper's arms, Meredith realized Winifred Bascom was more a mother to her than Angeline Stanfield had ever even attempted to be. "You have. You *do*, Winnie. Every day you help make my life a little easier." She backed away and wiped the tear that fell unbidden down her cheek. "And I appreciate you for it."

"Well, somebody has to, Merry. Your mother and Savannah seem concerned only for their own well-being." Disapproval etched Winifred's normally gentle features and disgust filled her tone. "I know I shouldn't talk about your mother this way, but she is my cousin, and I've never been one to mince words."

"No, you haven't." Winifred was a distant cousin of her mother's who had come to live with them years ago. Her father had asked her to be governess and housekeeper, deciding that her ethics and good breeding would be the proper example for his daughters. To this day, Meredith knew that her beloved friend and mentor hid some mysterious secret from her past. But Winnie had never chosen to share it, and respect kept Meredith from asking. However, she would be there if the woman ever needed a confidant.

"They put too much on your shoulders. Meredith do this, Meredith do that," Winifred criticized softly. "You'd think they didn't have their own two arms and their own wits to help themselves. You already manage the whole household and the company. A wise choice your father made, if you ask me."

The housekeeper sighed heavily. "At least the Stanfield fortune will survive in your capable hands. It's a good thing your father invested in timber and the railroad or we'd never have survived as well as we've managed. But you have too much responsibility, dear, and no time for yourself. It's quite unfair, and it infuriates me when I think of how they use your kind heart and gentle ways. I do declare, they're simply too lazy to do anything for themselves!''

''Don't assign me wings, Winnie. That's too hard to live up to. I'm far from innocent.'' *If only she knew how really wicked I've been, Mother and Savannah's bossiness would seem like a sand castle compared to the mountain of cruelty I've committed.* Meredith tried to lighten the mood. ''Besides, angels are supposed to be blond, and I'm a far sight from that.''

Winnie brushed back a wisp of the auburn hair that had escaped the heavy chignon Meredith wore at the base of her neck. ''A woman's temperament matching her hair color is purely a myth, Merry. Although, by the looks you're getting from some of the watermen, I should think the old adage about red might hold some truth. Red sky in the morning, better take warning. There's something different about you today, Merry. It's unlike you to brood.''

''Don't be silly. They're curious about the Stanfields, not me in particular. And I'm just feeling a bit restless— as we all are. The festival is only a few weeks away, and there's still so much to do. Everything must be perfect so we'll have the best season ever.''

The entire town counted on the preparations for the festival that launched the coming tourist and shrimp season. Their efforts seemed to foreshadow the level of success they could expect. Considered one of the Six Sisters—six resort areas along the Mississippi Sound where people escaped the heat, dust, insects, and open sewers of New Orleans—Biloxi often swelled to triple its population during the summer.

''Now, along with you, Winnie. Mother will be frantic if we're both late.''

''You never give yourself your due, Merry. You're quite lovely, when you want to be. The men are attracted to you, not your money.''

"Kind of you to say so, but untrue." Meredith heard shouts and turned to look up the wharf toward where her carriage waited. Three children of various ages ran as fast as they could, darting in and out of the crowd as if a pack of demons chased them. Two girls and one boy . . . no, three girls. The tallest actually wore boys' trousers, and the smallest had the back of her dress stuffed into her waistband to form makeshift pants as well. *The Cameron children!* Where was their father? Off again on some adventure to fill his coffers?

Compassion gripped Meredith's heart unexpectedly. She wondered if the trio ever missed Captain Quade as much as she missed the company of her father and fiancé. Though the two men had died years apart, the pain of loss stayed with her constantly. But the captain's absence was by choice!

Renewed anger filled her, making her doubly glad she had turned down the man's request to finance the refurbishing of the steamboat docks. Let him think she simply wanted to see Nolan Richards, a family friend, awarded the contract. In truth, she wanted no part in keeping Quade away from his family, which the project would surely do.

Winifred opened her parasol and angled it to ward off the sun. "I'll send the carriage back for you once I get home, Miss Merry."

"No need. I'll walk back. It's not that far."

"Your mother will disapprove."

"I'm sure you're right, Winnie. But I need this time alone desperately, I think. Just a little while."

"Your mother will be too busy with her hair to even know unless I tell her, so she'll not hear it from me."

Meredith waved her friend away, then turned to head for the shrimp stand at the end of the wharf. If Shanty Andrews didn't have good shrimp, there weren't any to be found. The Tennessee native prided herself on having a reputation for the best-quality seafood on the entire beach. Meredith should have known to look there first. But a part of her had wanted to dawdle at the wharf area—to tease the sea and strengthen her courage to face it.

Though she might be afraid of the mighty Gulf of Mexico, which ruled the lives and livelihood of Biloxi, she refused to let her fear go unchallenged. Someday, some way, Meredith knew there would be a reckoning between her and the ocean that had swept away the man she loved.

Discarded oyster shells strewn about the planked walkway became crushed underfoot, making her progress slow and a bit precarious. Though her focus should have been on the shell-littered path ahead of her, Meredith was fascinated by the long shelf of clouds on the distant horizon.

Would she ever be able to sail into the Mississippi Sound, out of sight of land and into that horizon? Or would she be like the pelicans, sitting like curiously carved knobs on the tops of the wooden pilings stretching out into the water, seemingly rooted to the last piece of resistance dry land offered? Would she ever overcome this fear and fascination with the sea?

"Out of the way, lady!"

"Coming through!"

"*Excuse* me, lady, I'm inna awful hurry."

Three small bodies rushed by Meredith like a gust of wind. She stumbled on her hem and started to fall, then reached out to grab for anything solid. Her parasol flew skyward. Her fingers clutched, latching on desperately. Something squishy, slimy, wiggly filled her grasp.

"Watch out there, gally-girl! Ye-in's gonna—!"

The shout came from above her in a voice thick with backwoods twang.

The warning came too late. Meredith landed on her knees with a jarring thud. Her palms splayed open, impacting with the promenade's planked flooring and cushioned only by the wad of shrimp she had unknowingly grabbed during her plunge. More shrimp rained down upon her head and shoulders as the living landslide she had set in motion continued to spill.

"Ouch!" she exclaimed as a splinter pierced her palm, reminding her that she had unwisely taken off her gloves earlier. Now, her hands would smell like fish for the rest of the day.

"Look what ye-ins done to poor Miss Meredith! Best apologize immediately and help her up." The nasal twang of the Tennessee hill country made the admonishment shrill as a tugboat's whistle, and the well-rounded woman came from around the stand that had housed the shrimp.

Meredith glanced up and accepted the offered hand. Her savior was none other than Shanty Andrews, famous in Biloxi for her unusual hair. The patchwork mop of curls looked as though God had decided to quilt the woman's tresses instead of color them.

"I'll pay for these shrimp, Shanty. Every one of them." Meredith discovered that three more pairs of hands stood ready to rescue her. One dusted the crushed shells from Meredith's knees. Another offered the lost parasol. The smallest tugged on her hem, then quickly deposited a fistful of shrimp into Meredith's hand.

"You can wash them off. They're still real good." The freckle-faced child smiled, her front teeth missing.

Meredith smiled back at the red-haired youngster.

"Got anything to say to Miss Meredith, gally-girls?" Though only four feet tall herself, Shanty towered like a giant over the children with her fists balled on her hips and wearing a stern expression.

The tiny girl's grin vanished. Her eyes rounded in apology. "I'm sorry, Miss Meredith, for making you fall. I didn't mean to."

"Apology accepted."

The smile returned, even broader now. This one would grow up to be a heartbreaker, Meredith predicted, wanting to offer the tiny beauty a hug.

Shanty introduced the child. "That's Miranda Cameron, Cap'n Quade's youngest."

"We've met before . . . briefly, but I'm afraid to say I've forgotten your names."

"That's all right. I forget names too when I'm in church," Miranda informed them, then giggled, "except Dooley Duckworth's."

"Her name is *Randy*," announced the strawberry-blond, who appeared to be about eleven years old and ready to shed the plumpness of youth. "I'm Alex, the oldest."

"Alexandra," Shanty countered. "She tends to be in charge of things."

"And you?" Wasn't the middle child's name similar to Savannah's? Meredith held out her uninjured hand to the tall, slim girl who wore trousers and seemed to be a couple of years younger than Alex despite her greater height.

"She's Samantha. She's nine. Sam's kinda quiet . . . sometimes. I talk for both of us mostly. But when it's real important, she talks a lot."

Dimples on either side of Randy's smile seemed to bracket Meredith's heart. The white muslin dress could have passed for an angel's robe if it hadn't been pulled up into the makeshift trousers. Meredith laughed at the girl's ingenuity. No one could criticize her for wearing inappropriate clothing. How often had Meredith dreamed of having a daughter just like her?

Samantha accepted Meredith's hand and shook it gently. "I would curtsy, ma'am, but I don't want to offer one until I learn to do it right. Alex hasn't taught me—"

"Shhh!" Alex glared at her sister defiantly.

"Nobody's s'posed to know, remember?" Randy's brows formed a V over her jade-green eyes as she tried to whisper, but her vibrant tone defeated that purpose.

"Know what?" Shanty asked. "What are ye-ins up to now . . . and where's Miss Applegate? Have ye chased off another governess?"

"We didn't exactly chase her away," Samantha attempted to explain.

"We was going to," Randy interjected. "Alex said so. Said if we got rid of her, we could use the money Papa pays her to—"

"Hush up, Randy," Alex scolded.

"Best tell me the truth, gally-girls." Shanty thumbed

back toward the gulf. " 'Cause it'll be worse on ye-ins if your pa sails in and learns it later.''

Alex looked at each of her sisters. Samantha nodded vigorously, but Randy shrugged her shoulders and started playing with one of the flounces on Meredith's dress. "I guess you're right, but don't be too angry with us, Miss Shanty. Miss Applegate wasn't very nice, and she wasn't honest either.''

"Hold off there, gally-girl. I gotta get this here splinter out of Miss Stanfield's hand.''

"No, that's quite all right. I can wait until I get home," Meredith protested.

"Ye won't do no such of a kind. I got just the thing to take care of that, and it won't take me two thumps of a toad's toe to fix it. Sit yourself down on that stool over there, and I'll grab my needle. Ye won't feel nothing.''

Meredith did as she was told and soon found her palm under Shanty Andrews's quick administrations. While she worked, Shanty told Alex to get on with her confessing.

"Well, you see . . . it was like this. Me and Sam and Randy decided we wanted to learn how to be pretty and smart and know all that fancy stuff we're supposed to know for our coming-out parties.''

"And we want to try out for Little Princess too." Randy rocked back on the heels of her slippers, excitement lighting her eyes. "I think I got a real chance, don't you?" She turned this way and that, showing both sides of her dimpled profile.

"You certainly do," Meredith complimented.

"I think she does too." Samantha ruffled her little sister's hair affectionately. "But someone from Miss Winkle's Finishing School or St. Joseph's Academy for Young Ladies always wins the crown.''

Every girl in Biloxi, at some point in her life, hoped to win the coveted title during the festival held the first week of June. The winner represented the township at many balls, soirées, and serenades during the summer. From young to old, the titles of Little Princess for the young girls and Sea Princess for the ladies was a feather in anyone's bonnet. Every female wanted the citizenry to consider her the Biloxian most treasured for her graciousness, beauty, and kindness to the community. To have a standing invitation to *any* social function was the competition's true appeal.

Yet it wasn't the yearning for the Little Princess title that bothered Meredith. The children's need to be taught etiquette for *any* reason captured her concern. Was their father neglecting their needs?

Everyone in Biloxi knew how deeply Quade Cameron grieved over the death of his wife, Katherine. Losing the only loves of their lives was one experience Meredith and the captain shared. But it had been five years since Katherine Cameron's death. Not having a mother to teach them how to become proper ladies, while having a father who constantly worked himself to forget his grief, must have made the tiny trio's lives terribly lonely and limited.

"I thought I could enroll in Miss Winkle's Finishing School and learn everything in a month. Then I could teach it to Sam and Randy." Sincerity darkened Alex's expressive eyes, which were only a shade lighter than Randy's. "Father was gone with the rest of the festival committee up to St. Louis, so we couldn't ask him if it would be all right to use the money. Since it belonged to us, we didn't think he would mind . . . very much."

"Mind what?" Meredith and Shanty asked in unison, smiling at each other's curiosity.

"That we used some of the emergency fund money he's been saving for an important occasion. It was our money 'cause he said it was. So we weren't stealing it."

Alex paused, searching each adult face as if she might receive a reprimand. Finding none, she continued, "We told Miss Applegate he wanted me to enroll and that he intended to pay the remainder of the fee when he returned."

"It was only a tiny fib." Samantha glanced at her older sister for reassurance. "Papa would pay if we asked him to."

Alex nodded, sending a visible wave of relief washing through the slim child.

"But Papa's late in coming home," Samantha continued, "and Miss Winkle won't let Alex return to school without more money. We didn't have much of our emergency fund left, but with Miss Applegate's wages, there would have been enough."

Shanty removed the splinter. "Done! Pour a little comfrey on it, and it'll be better come morning."

"Thank you." Despite the lateness of the hour, Meredith was too intrigued to leave without hearing the rest of the children's story.

"I didn't learn even half of what I need to know," Alex complained. "And Father hasn't returned from St. Louis yet."

"That's why we decided to let Miss Applegate go and use her wages to keep Alex in school." Samantha looked a bit nervous, as if she weren't telling the complete truth. She wouldn't meet either woman's gaze. "But Miss Applegate had already gone and taken the rest of the money with her."

Meredith was appalled. Stealing—from children, no less! Naomi Applegate would receive a visit tomorrow. The woman had best never ask for her help again! To think only a year ago, she'd given the woman a good reference.

"How did ye-ins plan to convince her to leave?" Shanty linked her arms across her ample breasts. "Crawfish in her sheets? Crabs in her shoes?"

Meredith's toes curled in reaction. Suddenly, she realized these little darlings had easily convinced her they were the wronged parties in this drama. But how did they rid themselves of unwanted governesses who were *not* guilty of stealing? Another view of the girls took seed and rooted itself in her mind. Were the daughters as tempestuous as the captain?

Randy giggled, putting both hands over her mouth to keep from laughing aloud. Her eyes lit with mirth. "We was gonna put a snapping turtle in her pantaloons."

"Randy!" Alex and Sam complained in unison. "You weren't supposed to tell!"

Tiny red brows arched. "Well, we planned to. And Miss Shanty said we better tell the truth, or Papa's gonna be awful mad. And, we don't want Miss Shanty mad at us, or nobody'll take care of us till he comes back."

"*I'll* take care of us." Alexandra lifted her chin arrogantly. "Like I always do."

"Papa will be madder than a snapping turtle himself if he comes home and finds out we didn't get someone to watch us after Miss Applegate left." Samantha plunged her hands into her pockets and stared at her feet. "Besides, you don't cook so good."

"I'm hungry." Randy glanced at the two adults as if to see which of them would be the first to fulfill her wishes. "Will one of you cook for us? It's Miss Opal's day off."

Shanty set her patchwork curls into motion, shaking them vigorously. "I'll fix ye young'uns something to eat all right, but I can't keep ye. I done promised Gizelda I'd go to N'Orleans with her and pick up the new decorations for our shops."

The woman looked apologetically at Meredith. "She booked passage for us at Pass Christian months ago, so I can't disappoint her, now can I?" Shanty's frown eased. "But I could step in next week if the cap'n still ain't returned. Ye're plumb out of luck if ye-ins are counting on me for this week. Miss Merry, how 'bout ye?"

"Me?" Meredith looked at the expectant faces and found their eagerness a bit daunting. "What about Miss Opal?"

"She's our housekeeper . . . some of the times," Samantha informed. "She'll cook for us on the days she cleans, but Papa would want someone else to watch us. Miss Opal is—" The nine-year-old hesitated. "Well, she's near-blind."

"Being half blind don't make her shortsighted. She'll help you corral them young'uns when she's around. But Sam's right. The cap'n'll want a sharp-eyed chaperon keeping an eye out for his little hurricanes.''

What do I know of caring for children? Meredith wondered as Shanty stared at her expectantly. Didn't she have her own family to look after? Furthermore, after her refusal of the loan, their father disliked her immensely. ''I c-couldn't,'' she insisted. ''I have a household to run. A business to see to.''

Even as Meredith refused, she knew the business wouldn't falter in a week while Shanty was away, and Winifred was more capable of running the Stanfield household than she. But images of snapping turtles among the folds of her pantaloons reminded her that her lack of experience with raising children might cause utter chaos.

''Don'tcha ever get tired of the same old dawn-to-dark duties? Add a little spice to your gumbo, gally-girl.''

The recent restlessness that had consumed Meredith made her stop and listen closely to what Shanty said. She stared out at the gulley boats shrimping the shallow waters near the chain of barrier islands twelve miles offshore— a common sight in the gulf. Too common for comfort today. Perhaps taking care of the children *would* offer the change of pace Meredith needed. It couldn't be that much different from caring for her family, and might at least provide a break in the monotony of her days.

''Please, Miss Meredith? I'm 'fraid to eat Alex's cooking.''

Randy's sweet voice softened Meredith's heart with decision. She nodded but hid her smile so Alex wouldn't be offended. ''All right. I'll be your governess but only until Shanty can replace me. Hopefully, your father will be back soon.''

The trio reacted instantly—Randy with bouncing exuberance, Samantha with a shy smile, and Alex with a sigh of relief.

''Where ye gonna do this governessing?'' Shanty started straightening her shrimp, salvaging what still could be sold. Disapproving seagulls protested raucously. ''Their place or your'n?''

The thought had never occurred to Meredith. ''I presume Stanfield House.'' Her mother and sister would no doubt object to having children in the house, so perhaps the captain's quarters should not be totally out of the question. That, however, would require Meredith's family to do for themselves for a few days. That option certainly had its appeal.

''It's best to stay with them at their quarters. They'll be more comfortable in their own surroundings, and a houseful of young'uns when one ain't used to them can make a woman mealy-mouthed contrary.''

Meredith was uncertain that living at the captain's house wouldn't leave *her* ''mealy-mouthed contrary.'' She was tempted to take back her agreement. He was too disturbingly male, too ruggedly handsome, too commanding in personality not to have left his personal imprint upon the place where he dwelled. Quade Cameron had filled her office last month with his sheer presence, and his image had lingered long after angry words forced him from her door. How could she ever spend time in his home and not feel unnerved by the essence of such a vibrant man?

''I don't know if staying at the Cameron house is such a wise thing to do after all,'' she admitted, wondering if she should take the girls with her to the dinner party at her home despite their need for fresh clothing. Perhaps she could find something for each of them among the dresses Savannah had worn only once but refused to donate to charity. They'd been saved in the attic for ages, which now seemed a blessing because there would be all sorts of sizes to choose from.

''What could it hurt?'' Shanty Andrews assured her.

''The captain might return before you get back,'' Meredith countered.

''That's a fact, but he'll be proud ye stayed with his children.''

''He'll boot me out on my ear.''

''Not Papa,'' Samantha whispered softly. ''He'll be glad to see you, Miss Stanfield. He's told me he wants to get to know you real well.''

Surprise filled Meredith at the nine-year-old's remark. "When did he say that?"

"Last month."

Curiosity filled Shanty's face. "He said he paid ye a call. Care to tell me why?"

Business matters were between Meredith and her customers. "I'm sorry. I'm not at liberty to say, if he hasn't already told you."

"Oh, he told me what went on, but I wasn't sure I believed him. I wanted to hear it outta ye-in's own mouth."

Wondering if the woman was baiting her, Meredith sidestepped the remark. "What did he tell you?"

"That ye turned him down flatter than a lily pad when he asked ye to loan him the extra money he needs. Ye didn't, did ye?"

"I'm afraid it was necessary."

Sam nodded. "That's when my papa said he was going to get to know you. Better than you know yourself, he said. *After* you told him no."

Meredith fought off the memory of the captain's angry words and the irritation glazing his eyes a lighter shade of green. "That doesn't make sense. He gave me the impression he never cared to see me again."

"I see ye've got a lot to learn about the cap'n, Miss Meredith." Shanty chuckled. "Tell the man something's impossible, and he'll kill himself trying to prove ye wrong. Ye got him stirred up now. Best ye get ready for the brew to boil, gally-girl. Quade Cameron ain't no quitter. If ye're gonna back out of watching his young'uns, now's the time to do it. Some old salt along the wharf'll take 'em in. We all stretch our nets to make sure they're safe and sassy whilst the cap'n's seafaring."

"No, I said I'd be their governess, and I mean to keep my word." Regardless of what kind of plans Captain Quade made to change her mind. She couldn't worry about a man who *might* show up. She had to take care of the here and now. She accepted for Alex, Sam, and Randy's sakes.

Once again, Meredith found herself rushing in to fix things for someone—three someones—who needed help, when the truth was she had no idea where to begin to repair her *own* life.

"Miss Meredith?"

Randy tugged on Meredith's dress, drawing her away from her somber thoughts. "Yes?"

"Do you wanna get married?"

Startled by the unusually personal question, Meredith fought off a blush. "I suppose all of us want to someday, sweet. Why do you ask?"

"Just in case Papa wants to get to know you real, real, real good. Good enough to be my new mama."

"Shhh!" Alex hissed against the raised finger lifted immediately to her lips.

"You *for sure* wasn't supposed to tell no one *that!*" Sam whispered.

Randy's mouth formed a tiny O.

Meredith found herself suddenly feeling faint. And to think she'd been worried only about snapping turtles in her pantaloons! It seemed the Cameron children had their own plans in the making. Was she now about to become their bait—the lure the children were planning to use to reel in their shark of a father?

Their tiny fingers tangled in hers like nets as they enticed Meredith away from the pier and her doldrums.

❖ 2 ❖

THE FIRST THING Quade Cameron planned to do when he stepped ashore was to head to the candy shop and buy a stick of peppermint for each of his little ladies. He'd been gone longer than the month he'd intended and missed their lively chatter and spontaneous hugs. Though the gulf was his livelihood, his daughters were his life. Five weeks was a terribly long time to go without seeing them.

Yori Svengsen, the giant Norwegian who had been Quade's friend since childhood, emerged from his shucking house and moved to the end of the wharf ready to catch the line. The robust, bronze-skinned seaman waved his cap and offered a hearty welcome.

"*Velkommen*, Captain Quade! Come ashore!"

A flock of white-breasted sandpipers that were pecking along the water's edge scattered at the Norwegian's loud call, leaving behind chipped and disorderly shells—some empty, others that took hurried short walks to a safer section of the shoreline.

"Seen my blossoms?"

"Not in a few days, I am thinking." Yori's massive arms swiftly tied the line and secured the boat. "But then we've all been busy swabbing the pier and polishing up our shacks for the festival. Not much time to visit with the little ones. Check with Miss Shanty. Maybe they are together, *ja*?''

''Or wonder of all wonders, they might actually still be with Miss Applegate.''

''Their governess?''

''Their *most recent* warden.''

''I believe this is not so.''

''Why am I not surprised?''

Both men laughed. The Cameron siblings were loved by all the watermen and women along the promenade, but everyone knew that their father allowed them leniencies not often granted to most children. They were a handful at times, but a loving handful to Quade.

''How go the preparations?'' Quade dusted his seaman's cap on one pants leg and raked his fingers through the hair at his right temple. Without a strand of rawhide to bind its length, the tawny mass fell inches past his shoulders. He nestled the cap back into place.

''Slow. But now that you're here, things will get done.'' The shucker fell into step beside Quade, matching him stride for long-legged stride. ''Let your hair grow any longer and they'll start calling you Cap'n Rapunzel, *ja*?'' Yori teased. ''Planning on being crowned Sea Princess?''

Any other man would be more cautious than to tease Quade in such a manner, but the two men knew Yori's jovial banter was given in good humor and meant no harm. Quade offered him a mock glare.

''I see Banker Winkle and Elise have set up the kissing booth again this year. What's he charging this time? A penny?''

''*Ja.* But he'd make more if he charged everyone who had *already* kissed his daughter, I am thinking.'' Yori jabbed Quade with his elbow.

Quade tipped the brim of his cap, nodding a brief acknowledgment to the pair as he and Yori passed the stand decorated with colorful ribbons and hearts cut from lace. The voluptuous dark-haired young lady standing next to the banker flicked her fan flirtatiously in front of her face and offered a wave with her unoccupied hand.

Yori waved back, causing Quade to return the jab.

Banker Winkle, the stout man with his hands clasped behind his back, turned from his inspection of the booth. "So the committee has returned, Cameron."

"We have."

"Did you get enough fireworks?"

"I think the citizens will be pleased."

"That's good to hear. We've all been a bit sluggish in our enthusiasm. Everything's behind schedule. Not good tidings, I fear. Not at all. When we saw that you were delayed in returning, everyone feared our efforts were for naught. Why break our backs hurrying to have the floats ready and the mainfare decorated if the committee could not get home in time with the fireworks?"

Though Quade offered the man a smile, his eyes narrowed into slits. "I said I'd have them on time. When have I ever gone back on my word?"

"Never," Yori defended him.

"Where are they then?" Banker Winkle looked past Quade and stared at the pirogue he'd rowed ashore. "Surely, you brought more than *that* could carry."

"The main ship is anchored at Ship Island." Quade watched as the banker stared at the lee of the northwest end of the island. It was the only natural deep-water harbor along the entire length of the shallow Mississippi Sound. The walls of the half moon–shaped Union garrison that had been erected on the island twelve years ago were imposing even from this distance.

"We don't want any accidents like before. I've left them in good hands. We'll bring them over a skiffload at a time. But first, I want to visit with my children. I haven't seen them in more than a month. I take tonight for my family, Winkle. Tomorrow, you and the town council can depend on me to honor my word."

"Where you headed, Yori?" Elise's tone held a sense of breathless huskiness that would have seduced a more gullible man.

"To Shanty's shack."

"She and that Gypsy woman went to New Orleans a

few days ago. In fact, I believe they'll be back soon. They were to be gone less than a week.''

''Are my children with her?'' Though uneasiness flared inside Quade, he shook off the feeling as foolish. He knew what the answer would be even before the banker's daughter gave it.

''No. She and the gypsy left by themselves.''

''They're probably with Miss Applegate, after all,'' Yori attempted to reassure him. ''We'll go check the warehouse and see if they're in your quarters. Shanty wouldn't go anywhere without the girls being well cared for. She loves them like her own grandchildren, *ja*?''

Quade instantly set a wharf-eating pace.

''Captain Cameron! Yoo-hoo, Captain!'' Elise bustled along behind him, trying in vain to catch up with his longer strides. ''Your children aren't at your quarters either.''

Quade stopped and allowed her to reach him. He waited patiently as she fanned herself elaborately and attempted to catch her breath.

''They've been staying at Miss Stanfield's house for nearly a week now. She took the poor dears in when that horrid Miss Applegate flew the coop, so to speak. Very generous of Miss Meredith, don't you think?''

''*Very.*'' Quade arched his brows in surprise.

''Now, Cap'n, remember your temper.'' Yori untied his long white apron so it wouldn't hinder his ability to run if necessary to keep up with Quade's gait.

''I'm remembering it quite well, Yori.'' Quade paced. ''What the hell is that woman doing with my girls?'' With the sound of dismay exiting Elise's lips, he realized the company he shared. ''Do forgive my crudeness, Miss Winkle.''

''I didn't mean to distress you, Captain Cameron.'' Elise's dark eyes widened in exaggerated sympathy.

''You haven't at all, Miss Winkle. I merely find myself concerned that my children are not in the same care in which I had left them. May I escort you back to your father?''

"Allow me, Elise." Yori offered his arm to the woman and nodded toward town. "You go on and see what has happened to the blossoms, *ja?*"

Quade forced himself not to run down the promenade. He couldn't care less whose attention he drew, but he needed time to gather his thoughts. Why had Meredith Stanfield stepped in and taken charge of his children while he was gone? Was this some kind of warped revenge for that day in her office when he'd told her all her benevolent kindnesses were just a front so she could hide from life?

"Ahoy, Cap'n. Why are you stewing so fiercely?"

Glancing up, Quade offered an indulgent, if brief, smile. "Got business that can't wait, One-Eye. I'll get back to you later. Save a sip for me."

The peg-legged, one-eyed man stood from his perch on a piling and tipped the jug marked with a skull and crossbones to his lips. He wiped away the lingering remnants of the jug's contents as it darkened the edges of his mouth. "Aye, that I will, me bucko. It'll make a man of you. Grow hair on your toes, 'twill. Brewing up a ballyhoo of a batch for the festival, I am. When you can slow your gait down a naut or two, come back and we'll swap some yarns."

"Later, Thomas. I will later." Quade hated ignoring the man, but One-Eyed Thomas was a notorious story-teller, embellishing tales to suit his mood and stretching them as long as anyone could keep an ear willing to listen. Quade didn't have time for a seaman's song; he needed the reality of his children back in his warehouse quarters where they belonged, not in the mighty Stanfields' palatial home.

Quade considered hailing a hansom but decided the walk would help vent his anger. He'd have time to calm the thoughts racing through his head and seek reason. Two streets away from the beachfront businesses and homes, he turned the corner into a lane known coastwide as Plantation Row.

Mansions with white marble columns offered shady porches rising above gently sloping lawns. Biloxi's finest citizens had found these estates peaceful havens from the difficult five years of Reconstruction the rest of the South had suffered. The strong roots of the ever-fragrant white-blossomed magnolia trees shaded the lane with silvery blue-green leaves. They looked soft at a glance but were strong and leathery to the touch, enabling them to endure harsh conflict and great change.

He knew the people who lived here well, for this place had once been part of his life too. A life he no longer desired. A life from which he intended to protect his children. Though he tried not to look, his eyes could not resist the strong pull of memories beckoning to him from the fourth house on the sun-dappled boulevard.

Belle Raven! Its columned grandeur seemed more magnificent than that of any other house on Plantation Row. Ivy climbed to the second-story veranda, covering the gleaming peach-tinted marble with a blanket of green. A sadness emanated from the stately house, a loneliness Quade could feel from the street. Even the limbs of the massive live oaks forming a horseshoe around Belle Raven twisted downward, as if it took too much effort to grow toward sunlight.

Someday you'll be happy again, Quade promised, allowing himself to hope as he hadn't in five long years. The house had been built out of love. Love for Katherine. Now it stood there, cold and empty stone, a replica of his heart. One day, Belle Raven would warm again when Alex, Samantha, or even little Randy had a family of her own and brought happiness inside its walls. Perhaps someday he could hope the same would happen to him.

"Hold on, Cap'n! We can't keep up."

Quade turned and was surprised to see not only One-Eyed Thomas, but Yori beside him acting as a human crutch. "Why are the two of you following me?"

"These newly Yoo-nited States of America is a free country. We can walk where we have a mind to, *ja*?"

"Aye. And we've a mind to walk right behind you, bucko," Thomas offered for good measure.

"Walk anywhere you want, but stay out of my business."

One-Eyed Thomas winked his good eye at Yori. "Are we doing anything but enjoying a stroll down Plantation Row? And a lovely lane 'tis."

"Go back to the wharf, will you?"

"And miss this? Not in my lifetime I ain't, laddie." The jug bouncing against One-Eyed Thomas's peg leg added a steady *thump-click, thump-click* to his venturesome gait. "Besides, they may be your wee ones, but they're our joy. We want to make sure they're all right."

"Fine, but don't invite yourself in." Quade waved them back as he walked to the huge ornate door that graced the colonnaded Stanfield House and gave its knocker three hard raps.

Moments passed as he awaited the appearance of the houseman. The door swung open, revealing a somber-faced black man dressed in an immaculately tailored black frock coat and trousers. The severe color was challenged only by the whiteness of the man's gloves.

The servant bowed low. "Good evening, Captain Cameron. Shall I announce you? Or would you care to wait in the parlor with a glass of whiskey? The Stanfields are dining at the moment."

Quade nodded his greeting to the servant who'd been a part of the Stanfield household for as long as he'd known the family. Pomender never aged, nor did the formality of his British upbringing. He'd looked the same thirteen years ago as he did this very day. "Please announce me, Pomender. I'd like Miss Meredith especially to know I'm here."

The servant half bowed and motioned Quade forward. "Please follow me."

The hall opened into a grand ballroom that could easily host hundreds of guests. Two staircases swept from the second-story landing, gracefully curving to either side of the ballroom. Crystal tinkled above him. Light from the lamps placed at intervals reflected from the exquisite

prisms and enhanced the beauty of the imported chande-
lier.

Quade turned his head from the sight, blinking away a
memory of his Katherine laughing with Savannah Stanfield. Many years ago, she had moved down this grand
staircase, the light causing the harvest gold of her hair to
resemble a halo. Quade had been the proudest fourteen-
year-old in all of Biloxi that night—in all of the South
for that matter. But that was a lifetime ago, when he had
been but a foolish boy and deeply in love. He pulled at
his collar, feeling as though he were being suffocated by
the past. He had to get out of here.

"This way, sir."

Unaware that he had stopped and was staring, Quade
shook off the past and moved toward the two oak doors
to the left of the farther staircase. "Are they in the formal
dining hall?"

"Yes. Excuse me, sir, while I announce your arrival."

The servant opened one of the elaborately carved doors
and quietly slipped inside. Though certain he was crossing
the boundary of good manners, once again Quade moved
to keep the door from being totally closed. He had no
idea of what scheme Meredith Stanfield planned concerning his children, but he did not intend to leave here without them. He would make certain she did not refuse his
company.

"Captain Quade Cameron to see you, *madame*."

The sound of someone gasping and something clanking
against china—a spoon or fork perhaps?—assured Quade
that the Stanfields were unprepared for his visit. Not waiting for further introduction, he boldly stepped into the
room.

"Forgive me, Widow Stanfield, for intruding upon your
meal, but I would like a word with your daughter." Quade
bowed in deference to the owner of Stanfield House. He
acknowledged her older daughter by offering a nod of
greeting, then immediately focused his gaze upon the au-
burn-haired vixen sitting at the opposite end of the table
with his three children. But he couldn't intimidate the

woman with the expression he'd practiced on the way
here, for his little ladies were not the patient sort and
demanded to be heard first.

"Papa, you're home!" Randy's voice squealed.

"Father, I thought you'd *never* return." Criticism
seemed to battle with relief in Alex's less exuberant greeting.

"Papa, how I've missed you."

He smiled as Randy nearly tilted her chair over as she
raced from the table and hugged his leg. "Hello, Muffin,"
he teased, lifting her into his arms and waiting until the
tiny arms locked themselves around his neck. He leaned
forward and rubbed noses with her, eliciting giggles that
made him chuckle in response.

Sam walked shyly to his side. He encircled her with
one arm, pulling her closer. "I missed you, too, Samantha
Rachelle."

His middle child hugged him back, warming his heart
and almost . . . almost . . . making him forget why he was
here.

"Will you forgive me for staying away too long, General?" His daughter sat rigidly upright against her chair,
having yet to make a move toward him.

Alex scooted the dumplings around on her plate, as if
they were barges being pulled down the Mississippi.
"You promised you would be back last week."

"Yes, I did, but one of the committee members became
ill. You wouldn't have wanted us to return until he was
well enough to travel, would you?"

"I suppose not, Father."

"Then come here and welcome me home. I have a
present for you. Perhaps it will help you forgive me."

"I don't need a present, Father. I forgive you."

"She's just being noble, Papa," Samantha admitted,
her eyes rounded in apology. "We've done something
awful. She wants you to feel guilty so you won't be so
angry with us."

"I do not."

"Do so."

"May I break the tie, Papa?" Receiving a nod, Randy leaned into his ear and whispered, "Do too."

"Do not," Alex repeated, shooting her sibling a wait-till-I-get-you-alone glare.

Angeline Stanfield rose from the head of the long, lace-covered table. Her dark hair and gray eyes framed a porcelain-pale complexion that made her royal bearing appear even more regal. "Please, children. I'm quite sure your father has had a long and arduous journey. Perhaps the captain will join us, then both you and he can return to your home before the hour gets much later."

"Please do." The older sister's tone left nothing to the imagination.

"Savannah!" Meredith admonished.

"I did not mean it like that." Embarrassment stained the brunette's cheeks a becoming shade of rose. Her eyes thinned into hazel slits, glaring at her sister. "Really, I didn't, Captain Cameron. I meant . . . please join us."

"No offense taken, Miss Stanfield, but I think it's best I gather my brood and we take our leave." Instantly deciding to postpone confronting Meredith until tomorrow, when the children were not in attendance, he half bowed and nodded a brief good-bye. "Thank you for your kind hospitality toward my daughters, Widow Stanfield. I hope they have been on their best behavior."

"We have, Papa," Samantha assured him.

"Well . . . I been on my almost-best," Randy confessed, offering an impish smile.

Meredith rose from the table and placed her linen napkin on her plate. Her gaze met his directly, making him aware of her almond-shaped eyes and long, sooty lashes.

"If you'll be kind enough to wait, it will only take me a moment to gather my things."

"And where, may I ask, are you going this time of evening?" Savannah challenged her sister.

"To Captain Quade's quarters, of course."

"You're what?" Surprise and suspicion battled in equal measure within Quade.

Savannah's mouth gaped open. "You can't mean that,

of course. The captain is home now. He can care for the brat—the brave little darlings himself.''

Angeline Stanfield nearly melted back into her chair. "Think of the scandal, Meredith. No one will believe that you've offered your services as governess to the children. For what purpose? You certainly don't need the money. It doesn't make sense that Biloxi's wealthiest belle will be staying under the roof of an unmarried man—widower that he is. You will disgrace your father and bring shame upon the Stanfield name."

Determination braced Meredith's shoulders and directed the stubborn lift of her chin. "Father would expect me to keep my word to Shanty and the children. I really don't care what anyone else thinks. If they're that narrow-minded, they need to look at themselves . . . not me." In a softer tone, she added, "It's only for a few more days, Mother; then Shanty can take over."

Meredith quickly explained to Quade the events leading to her temporary guardianship of his daughters. "I'm not certain what you've been told."

Suspicion eased into a grudging respect. Quade admired Meredith for wanting to honor her word. The fact that she could not be swayed by the tide of scandal that often festered in the strict Southern society in which they had been raised spoke for her courage.

The truth was, he didn't have time to look for a new governess and still complete preparations for the festival. Every planter, businessman, waterman, and woman in Biloxi joined forces to decorate their homes and businesses for the coming tourist season. They planned events to entice the visitors to stay and enjoy this seaside resort rather than others along the coast. The township expected Quade to see that no effort was duplicated and all would be ready by the opening day of the weeklong celebration.

A glance at his children said they seemed no worse for wear, and Meredith had stated that she would no longer be involved after Shanty returned. What had Elise said? A few more days and Shanty would be back.

He took a long, estimating look at Meredith Stanfield,

finding her prettier than he'd noticed before, though she'd never been what any man would call plain.

"But what about us?" Savannah whined, enlisting her mother's aid with constant looks. "How are we to finish decorating the house before the festival? I haven't even chosen which dress I'm going to wear, and Mother needs help selecting the flower arrangements. You're the only one who—"

Quade watched Meredith lean over and quietly lift the glass off the lamp that lit her end of the table. She bent to blow out the flame dancing lively on the wick, but paused, leaving every detail of her intriguing face illuminated. A full generous mouth smiled easily. Tiny laugh lines hinted that the good nature extended to her silver-blue eyes. Though she enjoyed high cheekbones and porcelain skin like her older sister's, Meredith's bone structure was more angular. She would never be a beauty in classic terms, but it was a face full of character. One that a man could not look at just once. A face that it would take an artist years of study to capture on canvas.

"I shudder to think that the two of you can't make a decision without me. Winifred can manage quite nicely, I should think," Meredith said. "At the moment, I'm needed elsewhere. It's time you relied on yourselves, and I must honor my promise to the Cameron children. Therefore, I'm going."

"Talk sense to her, Captain Cameron," Savannah insisted. "She—"

"She'll be going with us." Quade's matter-of-fact statement cut off Savannah's protest and surprised the hell out of him.

"Yeah!" Randy exclaimed, bobbing up and down in his arms.

"Can we wear these dresses home?" Samantha looked at Meredith expectantly, fingering the layered flounces of the silk dress she wore.

"You can have that dress, sweet. Savannah has a dozen others where that came from."

"Mother?!" Savannah protested.

"We hope you enjoy the dresses, children," Angeline Stanfield returned graciously, her expression forbidding any further argument.

Quade tuned out the exuberant chatter of his children, the protests of the elder Stanfield daughter, and the curious beating of his heart when he realized Meredith was staring intently at him.

He didn't know *why* he'd agreed to allow her full rein of his little ladies for the time being. Was it because she would free him from the responsibility of hiring another governess until his obligations to the committee were completed? Was it the fact that he'd determined long ago to get to know this woman in the hopes of changing her mind about the loan?

Or . . . was there yet another reason he wanted Meredith Stanfield near him? A reason that swam frantically around in his brain like a tired swimmer fighting to reach a distant, beckoning shore. A reason, Quade Cameron swore to himself, he would never allow to surface.

❖ 3 ❖

Meredith LAY ON her back, staring out at the moon that rose over the Biloxi harbor. The windows lining the southern wall of the two-story warehouse gave a panoramic view of the night sky blanketing the Mississippi Sound. The curious restlessness she had managed to hold at bay during the day seemed to intensify that night while she waited for sleep to overtake her. She yearned for something to fill the void of happiness always just beyond her reach.

Tonight had been eventful, to say the least. She'd expected Quade Cameron to be anything but pleasant about her taking charge of his children. Perhaps tomorrow would bring second thoughts. But he'd looked tired to the point of exhaustion and probably needed sleep more desperately than he did a confrontation.

Feeling a bit awkward about the whole situation, Meredith wondered whether her time with the children would alter the joy it had been so far. The captain's presence had filled the dining hall of Stanfield House with masculinity and unquestioning love for his children—two very becoming qualities that lured her mind away from the duties at hand and made her acutely aware of him as a man.

Thank goodness Quade had elected to spend the night

on his boat. She suspected his real reason for doing so had nothing to do with wanting to keep a watchful eye on the shipment of fireworks and everything to do with not wanting to sleep under the same roof that she did. A wave of guilt washed over Meredith as she realized he undoubtedly longed for the comfort of his own bed after so many weeks away from home.

Rambunctious little Randy nestled deeper against Meredith, hugging her as if she were a favored cuddly doll. Meredith caressed a strand of the child's red tresses, admiring its silken texture and marveling at how easily the six-year-old had come to trust her.

No matter where they had slept during the past few nights, whether at Stanfield House or the Camerons' warehouse quarters, Randy had crept softly to Meredith's bed to snuggle in and be held. She would surely miss the children when Shanty took over the governessing.

Needing to stretch, Meredith gently slid away from Randy, took her pillow, and laid it next to the sleeping child. As she hoped, Randy nestled against it and settled back into deep slumber. After tucking the covers around the tiny shoulders, she brushed back a wisp of hair that had fallen into the cherubic face, then leaned over to gently press a kiss upon her forehead. "Sleep tight, little one," she whispered, amazed at the affection that had blossomed in her heart five days ago and continued to flourish.

Grabbing her ivory chambray wrapper, draped over the bed's footboard, Meredith laced it together over her nightgown and picked up her slippers. She crept past the fourposter bed where Alex and Samantha slept soundly. Both lay turned in the same direction with one arm angled high over each head and a leg lifted as if they were choreographed to the same dream tune. Certain that all was safe and secure, Meredith decided it would not be remiss of her to enjoy a bit of fresh air and perform her nightly ritual.

Spending time in the children's home had given her enough recollection of the layout. She managed to dodge the various pieces of furniture and shadows, making her escape from the warehouse more easily than expected and without stubbing a bare toe. Once outside, Meredith put on her slippers and hurried to the other end of the promenade. A glance backward assured her that all was quiet on the beachfront . . . for now. Night hours were brief along the shoreline. Fishermen would rise long before dawn and head out into the shallows to tong for oysters and cast their shrimping nets.

When she reached Shanty's shack, she raced down the slanted walkway to the soft sand gleaming whitish-pink in the full moon. Stripping her feet of the slippers now, she placed the slippers beneath the promenade.

Her toes sank into sand and wiggled as the softness oozed between them. Heat from the afternoon lingered, making the sand warm and soothing. Meredith strolled to the water's edge and stared at its gentle ebb and flow, finding the gulf's peaceful motion calming. The tide brought waves further up the shore, teasing her, wetting the tips of her toes. Meredith retreated a step, remembering the sea's deceptive tranquility.

Don't show your fear. Meredith gathered her courage, reminding herself that she'd done this many a night and tonight was no different. She would dare to challenge the mighty gulf by wading a little farther than last night and the one before it. But first . . .

A delighted giggle escaped her as she reached between her ankles for the back of her nightgown and wrapper. Pulling them forward, she tucked the hem into the belted cord she had tied around her waist. The makeshift pants allowed the air to flow freely against her legs. The fact that she could walk more easily made her envious of the six-year-old who could use the style during the hotter hours of the day.

"Dare I?" she wondered aloud, gazing out into the moonlit water, yearning to experience what the children did when they fearlessly frolicked in the surf.

Closing her eyes, she imagined herself rushing to meet the incoming waves, skipping out into the surf at breakneck speed and laughing joyously. Instead, her heart began to race. Her pulse beat a helter-skelter rhythm in her throat, behind her knees, throbbing down to the ends of her toes. Perspiration dampened the roots of her hair as she attempted to calm the wave of anxiety rushing through her.

You're stronger than this, Meredith. Don't let it defeat you. You can't live with this fear forever.

Taking courage in hand, Meredith took a deep breath and ran toward the gulf. She rushed several yards into the water, but it wasn't until the surf raced past her and started to ebb that she imagined the intangible pull of the current. A tidal wave of terror washed through her, taunting her with a feeling of being drawn outward and under. Meredith stumbled. She screamed, felt herself falling.

Her bottom hit the warm moist sand, soaking her gown to the waist. Another wave drenched her, splashing her shoulders and face as if the sea had slapped her. Frightened beyond terror, Meredith slapped back at the surf with one hand, using the other one for leverage as she back-crawled to the shore. Great sobs tore from her throat, but the waves kept coming, endlessly battering her senses.

Suddenly, two hands locked beneath her arms and lifted her upward. She turned, burying her face in an oak-carved chest, bare except for a soft mat of goldish-red hair that triangled downward in the magnificent slope of his torso. She anchored her arms around the muscular expanse of the man's shoulders, holding on as if he were a lifeline.

''P-please help me,'' she managed to whisper between sobs. He raised her out of the surf and into his strong arms, cradling her as if she were a child. Powerful strides carried her ashore.

Her trembling would not subside.

''You're safe now.''

Every fiber of Meredith's body stiffened as she recognized Quade Cameron's vibrant tone. Her breasts molded against his chest, their peaks straining against her sodden clothing. Embarrassment swept through her, sending added heat to her skin beneath his palm, which pressed

against her bare thigh. Her hands unlinked from around
his neck. Her body jutted backward as she silently insisted
upon standing.

"Th-thank you. I'm afraid I slipped and couldn't regain
my balance. I don't know why I overreacted." She stared
at her bare feet, aware that his own gaze was examining
her slowly from head to toe. Gooseflesh rose in the wake
of his gaze, stirring strange new sensations in her that
were almost too overwhelming to contain. Her knees
threatened to buckle.

"You need to sit."

"Yes," she breathed. At his merest touch, the blood
coursing through her elbow suddenly tingled with an increased current.

Quade guided her to the slanted walkway leading from
the wharf and helped her sit. He stood a short distance
away, his legs spread apart as if he had taken a defensive
stance to face an opponent.

Hair the color of burnished wheat dipped below his
shoulders to his collarbone. The angle of his arms, as he
clasped his hands together behind his back, defined the
granite-carved sinews of a man who thrived on physical
labor. The moon shone on the lower half of his face, leaving his eyes in shadow. Yet she felt his gaze upon her,
sensed that he was watching her every breath.

Unnerved by the bone-searching intensity of his hidden
appraisal, she attempted to turn away. But the sight of
him was far too compelling. The strong chest she'd felt
only moments ago slimmed to an admirable washboard-
patterned abdomen and muscular thighs. The black cos-
sacks he wore ended abruptly at knee-high boots, giving
him the look of a pirate . . . sprung from the frothy sea
itself.

A sigh escaped her, rising from a depth untouched by
exhaustion. He moved closer, gently took her hand, and
helped her stand. His lips were but inches from her own.

"You'd best go in with the children. They'll be up
early."

"I know." She lingered where she stood, resisting an

impulse to close the distance between them and satisfy
the craving to taste his lips.

What foolishness! Meredith suspected one step closer
and she would be lost in the spell the night had woven,
in the sound of the gentle lapping surf, in the glow of
moonlight upon the sand. The compelling presence of this
man drew her as if he were rainfall and she parched earth.

She started up the walkway, grateful that the strength
had returned to her legs. Quade fell into step beside her.

"Why are you doing this, Miss Stanfield? Is this some
form of revenge for that day in your office?"

"Doing what?"

"Tempting me."

Indignation flared within her, halting her escape. "If I
recall, I had no inkling you were here." Meredith glared
at him, hoping he could see every ounce of her anger in
the moonlight. But he was partially right, wasn't he?
She'd wanted him to notice her, hoped he would think
her pretty. Yet she hadn't deliberately set out to seduce
him. "Do you think me so scheming that I would resort
to scandal?"

"I don't know you well enough to answer that."

His features defined themselves more intensely, though
she didn't detect even the slightest movement. "I'm told
you've already plotted that particular course, getting to
know me *well*."

"From whom?" When he received no answer, he
shrugged. "No matter. The truth has never harmed me. I
happen to believe the best way to change anyone's mind
is to discover all there is to learn about her. I want to
change yours, so I intend to know you—" A smile lit his
face, flashing white in the moonlit shadows. "—and well,
as you said."

She wasn't about to tell Quade that his own daughter
had revealed his threat. "Only one man has ever attempted that, and he's dead."

"I've learned to respect rough seas and survived the
worst of them, Miss Stanfield." Quade's callused hand
covered hers, stopping her progress. He imprisoned her

fingers between his own and the muscle over his heart. "I thrive on challenge."

She looked into his stormy gaze and saw a hunger in the emerald depths that was so raw she would surely be devoured in the wake of his need. The night seemed to suck in its breath. All sound stopped. Even the surf swept out to sea and paused. He was indeed challenging her, but to what? To change her mind about the loan? Surely no man would dare resort to such lengths to win access to her bank account.

Adventure beckoned her like a siren's song, hinting that this might be the answer that would quell her restlessness of late. It lured Meredith into an uncharacteristic bravado. "Then plot your course, Quade Cameron. You'll find *this* sea more difficult to navigate than any other you've ever sailed."

"And what if that course leads me to your bed, *Miss* Meredith? Will I discover hidden treasures there? Virgin territory?" he taunted.

"Perhaps you'll find yourself run aground, Captain," Meredith returned, hoping the moonlight didn't illuminate the swell of her breasts beneath her wet garments, for her nipples had peaked once more at the challenge of his words. "I'm not sure that that overinflated vessel you call an ego could ever find passage through the shallow channels of a Stanfield's heart. That *is* how you think of me, isn't it? As shallow? Heartless?"

Quade looked into the depths of her silver-blue eyes. His fingers longed to map the path from her mouth, to her throat, to regions beyond. He watched as a droplet of water did so. "I think of you as the governess of my children at the moment. It's your saving grace, *madame,* but you haven't yet named your price."

"I'm a Stanfield, remember? What could I possibly want that I don't already have?" She asked the question of herself as much as of him.

"I don't know," he responded with a shrug of his magnificent shoulders.

"Then, sir, right now you know me as well as I do myself." Meredith hid her frustration beneath a sigh. "I'm afraid at the moment we've both entered uncharted waters."

❖ 4 ❖

THE PUNGENT SMELLS of strong coffee and early cries from hungry seabirds flying outside the warehouse windows woke Meredith. Morning had come all too soon, and there was much to do. Remnants of sleep lingered, urging her to ignore obligations for the day and snuggle closer to the small child who nestled against her. A wave of dissatisfaction washed over Meredith as the feel of the strong arms she'd been dreaming of eluded her.

"Miss Merry, are you awake?"

The sleepy softness of Randy's tiny voice brought a smile to Meredith's lips. The child's whisper brushed warmly against her arm. "No, Pumpkin, I'm not."

"Then would you help me wake up? I wanna be the first to kiss Papa good morning."

Sleep drifted away, leaving in its wake a certain melancholy. How many times as a child had she rushed into her own father's arms, knowing when he greeted her with a hug and a kiss that nothing felt too difficult to conquer and everything seemed possible? Meredith blinked back the tears that instantly welled from the treasured memories. Though her father had been dead less than a year, her love for him sprang from an eternal well.

Allowing two fingers to walk slowly up Randy's arm, Meredith deliberately lowered her voice and coaxed the six-year-old into percolating giggles. "Slowly he walks, step-by-step, inch by inch. Tickle Turtle turns thisaway and thataway and back thisaway, but he can't decide whichaway to go. What should poor Tickle Turtle do?"

Randy squealed so sharply that Meredith placed a warning finger over her lips to quiet the child's anticipation. But Randy's laughter was so contagious that Meredith's "Shhhh" sounded more like someone's saw blade run amok.

"She's too big for that baby game," informed a child's voice from the other side of the room. The sound of covers being thrown back and feet sliding into slippers warned that Alexandra and Samantha were now awake.

"Am not," Randy countered, tickling Meredith behind the right ear just the way *she* wanted to be tickled.

To the child's delight, Meredith squirmed and retaliated, eliciting victory in Randy's jade eyes. She stuck her tongue out at her older sister.

Alexandra's gaze focused on the ceiling, then back at her sibling as if seeking the strength to endure. "You know when Father's finished with his coffee, he's gonna work with the committee. We won't see him till tonight. I thought you were going to ask him if we could . . . you know . . ."

Randy's tongue disappeared instantly. She rolled out of the bed, landing with a muffled *plunk* among the covers that slid with her.

"Your father's already up?" Meredith had assumed that Opal, not the captain, made the delicious-smelling coffee. The captain's housekeeper came by every other day to keep the quarters cleaned and the pantry stocked. Opal had met Meredith's pleas that she take over the governessing duties as well as her cleaning with steadfast refusal. She said there wasn't enough money in the South to persuade her to keep up with those children twenty-four hours a day. The girls were active and sometimes argumentative with each other, but so far had done nothing Meredith found worthy of such dread.

Hurriedly dressing, she realized that the first light of

dawn already shone through the windows. How unlike her to oversleep! Normally, she would have already had breakfast and reviewed the day's calendar of events. What an impression to make on the captain's first morning back!

"He usually comes and kisses me awake," Randy said, untangling herself from the quilt. "Right here and here . . . and here." She pointed to each eye and her nose, then grabbed the dress she'd worn yesterday and draped it over her head. "I was gonna wait until I kissed him, *then* I was gonna ask him. You know Papa never says no if I ask him with a kiss."

Meredith shook her head and pulled out a peach-colored frock from the armoire. "Wear this instead, Pumpkin. A lady always wears something clean and fresh each day."

Whatever the children had in mind, one thing was clear—the youngest Cameron knew how to manipulate her father, and the older two put her up to it.

If only she could leave off these layers upon layers of petticoats, Meredith thought. Perhaps Samantha had the right idea about dressing in less confining garments. Meredith's fingers fumbled as she hurried. "Did you know it's unfair to persuade your father by offering him a kiss?"

"Why?" Randy turned her back to Meredith. "Would you button me, please?"

"Because you don't just be nice to someone in order to get something in return," Samantha informed, slipping into the boyish garments Meredith envied. The trousers only accentuated her slimness. The nine-year-old glanced at herself in the oval mirror that rose over the dresser, stopping only long enough to brush down flyaway strands that had dislodged from yesterday's braids.

"If it works, why not?" Alexandra shrugged. "It's better to get what you want now, because you might not be able to later."

The matter-of-factness about the eleven-year-old's statement disturbed Meredith. Where had the girl learned to be such a realist? Meredith returned her attention to her own grooming. "But you should never do so at someone else's expense," she gently countered. "Manipulating your father into granting your wishes is costing you his trust."

"But we can't help *man*-ipulating Papa, he's not a lady," Randy said.

Meredith bit back a smile. Randy had no idea how true a statement she had made. While in the darling girl's company, most men, Meredith had noticed, tended to fulfill Randy's every wish. Not that she blamed them. The child knew how to thaw every chilled chamber of her heart. "Come, Samantha, and let me redo your hair."

Samantha allowed Meredith ready access to the thick, whitish-blond mass. Her own coiffure would simply have to wait. "Another lesson to remember. Even if you wear the same style, always comb and brush your hair each morning. If you don't, the rest of your day will seem to be as rough as your hair looks."

Samantha lifted one hand to cover her smile. Meredith wished the captain's middle child felt less unsure of herself and would show the world the charm she so readily offered to anyone who took the time to notice. "Why are you laughing?" she asked, urging Sam to share her sense of humor.

"I-I was just thinking if that was so, then Miss Shanty must always have mixed-up days."

Even Alex joined in the laughter. "Did you ever see anyone with so many different colors of hair?" She laughed so hard that her nose honked like a northbound goose.

"Like her mama painted it all whichaway," Randy added.

Samantha swung about, her eyes rounding in dismay. "Do you think her feelings would be hurt if she knew we were talking about her . . . oh, sorry." She faced the opposite direction and allowed Meredith to finish the rebraiding. "Do you think she colors her hair?"

"Nobody would look like that on purpose," Alex said

haughtily, glancing at herself in the mirror. The expression that crossed her face left no doubt that she, at least, was pleased with her reflection.

"Well, I think she looks different . . . kind of special," Samantha interjected, instantly defensive.

"Girls, I hear you up and around." The resonant tone of Quade Cameron's voice interrupted Sam's defense of the shrimp-shop owner. "Wake Miss Stanfield if she isn't already, then ask her to come down to breakfast. Tell her I'd like to speak with her before I leave for the day."

"I'm already—" Meredith realized she was yelling back at him and stopped. A glance at Samantha assured her the girl was completely dressed. Randy was finishing the last button on her shoe, and Alex . . . well, Alex needed no assistance. The captain's eldest daughter was stubbornly efficient. All the children could muster inspection and pass. A condition *she* sorely lacked.

"Yet another lesson. Don't shout at each other from room to room," Meredith reminded in a hushed tone. "Genteel people present their replies either in person or through a messenger. Alex, will you please inform your father I'll be right down? First, I must see that the beds are made since it's not Opal's day to clean." *And make certain my hair looks a bit more presentable.*

The dampness of her hair brought back heated memories of being cradled in Quade Cameron's arms last night, her clothes sodden and clinging, his presence masculine and beguiling. Never had she been made more aware of how much she was lacking as a woman. A quick study of her reflection confirmed there was little she could do about the mediocrity of her features.

"Oh, and tell Miss Stanfield that I need her to come down as soon as possible," the captain added. "The bed-making can wait until I'm gone. I don't have time to waste on such frivolities this morning."

Three small sets of eyes stared at the rumpled covers, focused on Meredith, then glanced at the stairway leading down from the loft. She'd made a point of insisting that they leave their room tidy on the days Opal didn't work.

It was such a small battle, but one that might escalate into something much larger if she allowed it to. It was his home and his beds, and she supposed he had a right to decide when they were made. "Since he's been gone for so long and won't get to see you most of the day, we'll wait to straighten the room," she said between clenched teeth. "Tell your father I'll be right down."

"Thank you for joining us, Miss Stanfield." The captain motioned her to a chair at the opposite end of the table from his own.

Seeing him in morning light reminded Meredith of how he filled a room with his presence and offered another shade of green to the eyes that mesmerized her with their intensity.

A large vase filled with magnolia blossoms graced the table, forming a fragrant centerpiece that partially obstructed her view. Though she could no longer see him clearly, his every nuance had etched itself into her mind, disturbing her now as it had her sleep long after midnight.

"I hope you'll forgive us for starting without you, but the children's breakfast would have been cold by now."

Meredith's cheeks tightened with a blush. She would make certain she never gave him cause to complain again, even if he disguised it as an apology. "I'm sorry it took me—"

"Yes, of course. Now if we may, I would like to discuss the girls' plans for the day. Now that their grooming has been seen to and breakfast is almost finished, you may allow them to straighten their room." He glanced out the window that gave a panoramic view of the bay. "High tide should last another hour or so. If the girls want to visit one of the bathhouses, it would be better to do so before the bed-making. I'd rather they didn't swim this morning—"

"Ahh, Papa, why can't we?" Randy's lower lip pouted as she instantly rested her chin on both fists.

Meredith waited, expecting him to inform them of last night's misadventure in the surf and the fact that they had no proper chaperon to supervise their swimming activities.

"I would rather you waited until I could enjoy that bit of merriment with you blossoms. Is that too selfish of me to ask?"

The children's faces lit expectantly. Randy's hands unfisted, and she became buoyant in her enthusiasm. "Could we swim tonight, Papa? In the moonlight, when it's so pretty?"

"Yes, Muffin." He flashed them all a disarming smile and winked at Meredith. "Perhaps Miss Meredith will see fit to join us."

His playful challenge caused Meredith's pulse to vault into her throat like a dolphin soaring from the surface, only to plunge back into the murky depths of her fear. Would the children's presence help her face the terror she experienced at the shoreline? If her mind was on watching them, would she be less afraid?

"P-perhaps," she answered, uncertain if her willingness to try was purely an effort to overcome the stranglehold the gulf held on her or a desire to share a pleasant moment of companionship with this alluring man and his offspring.

Quade nodded in approval. "Good. Then visiting the bathhouse should be sufficient for this morning."

The bathing boxes that had been built at the end of each wharf, whether private or public, were rectangular affairs consisting of cabbagewood enclosed in wooden lattice. Each provided a bench and allowed the waves to wash over the bather, while protecting him or her from being washed out to sea. Meredith looked forward to the visit, as it was one of the few ways she could enjoy the gulf and its motions without fear.

"Afterward, an hour of brisk walking along the beachfront should fill them with vigor. Then you should see that each of them reads a chapter from her favorite novel. I do not concur with the notion that the gentler sex be deprived of knowing and discussing literature. It's foolish to think that it taxes their mental capabilities. I find my daughters more clever than I at times, if the truth be known. After the reading, please have them . . .''

He paused long enough to take a breath before continuing on in a monotone that implied he had rehearsed this particular speech a hundred times or more. Just how many governesses *had* the children run off?

''—a tour of the soda shop seems appropriate for lunch, but Miranda will need a nap by two. Samantha and Alex may visit one of their friends until four, should they wish, then all three will take the evening meal with me at—''

''No, sir.'' Meredith could not believe the man had every second of the children's time mapped out as if it were waters he navigated and no veering from the charted course would be allowed.

''What?''

She jostled to the left, then to the right to catch a better glimpse of him. What she saw did not please her. His forehead was furrowed, irritation radiating from his gaze like a sun god whose anger had been kindled. ''I s-said, no, sir,'' Meredith stammered. Feeling far from brave, she still refused to let the captain see that the penetrating green of his eyes made her quake in her kid boots.

She deliberately straightened in her chair so the bouquet of flowers once again hid part of his face from view. The full impact of his assault upon her senses was more than she cared to deal with at the moment. ''These are *children*, Captain. They need spontaneity, not leashes. And if I am truly to be their governess, then I must insist on being allowed to restructure their schedule as I see fit. I will not lead them around like pampered pets. Groom them, feed and bathe them. Let them out to play until they are expected to return home. I cannot be a party to such behavior, Captain.''

An impatient smile quirked Quade's lips. ''Are you always this demonstrative with your employers, Miss Stanfield? No—'' He raised a palm to ward off her reply. ''—I forgot. You've never had an employer before, so you may be unaware of the proper etiquette that is most becoming to someone newly hired.''

The smile faded as quickly as it had appeared. ''For

that reason, I remind you, Miss Stanfield, that I am the children's father. You are their governess. Please see that my daughters are fed and have a nap so that their health will remain unchallenged by the summer heat while I'm occupied with the festival. Otherwise,'' he sighed as if conceding to her whimsy, ''you may teach them as you will. Now do we understand each other?''

''Yes, Captain, except—''

''Except what, Miss Stanfield?'' His tone had lost its patience.

She could feel him staring, burning a path through the flower stems. ''You did not hire me, Captain. I volunteered, remember?''

Challenge layered the distance that divided them. The girls glanced from parent to governess, their expressions full of dueling emotions: surprise, curiosity, guarded anticipation.

''Noted, Miss Stanfield.'' His voice took on a less somber tone. ''And lest I forget, thank you for taking the children in until Shanty returns. It was kind of you. Now unless you have further objections, I would like to enjoy the remainder of my breakfast with my girls. If there's anything else that needs my attention before I return this evening, you can reach me at—''

''That's not all.'' Meredith sat up straighter, eyeing each child to see if any of them would speak so she wouldn't have to.

Exasperation forced him to lean over and move the bouquet of magnolia blossoms that hid their faces from each other. ''What else is preying upon your thoughts and my valuable time this morning, Miss Stanfield?''

''Such lovely flowers,'' Meredith evaded, wondering if she had stepped over one boundary too many. ''Where did you find the rose-colored ones?''

''Papa fixes us breakfast and picks us some every morning so the table will be nice. Don't you, Papa?'' Samantha fingered one of the petals, drawing her father's attention from Meredith long enough to ease his stern expression. ''He says there's a special place where yellow and red and purple magnolias grow wild. But I think the white ones are pretty, too.''

A smile softened his features, making his eyes shine with sincerity. ''But you said the red are your favorite.''

Grateful for the child's peacemaking tactic, Meredith took the opportunity to plunge in with her request. ''The children want to attend Miss Winkle's Finishing School. And to try out for the Little Princess title.'' She gave each girl a go-ahead look, but none spoke up.

Meredith motioned to proceed, but Miranda shook her head vigorously, stubbornly refusing to take the opportunity. ''Randy especially feels she has a chance to win the title. It will be a wonderful experience for all of them.''

The trio's silence lingered. Their father leaned back and seemed to be considering Meredith's announcement. Finally, he enlisted his eldest's opinion. ''Is this true, Alex? Would you like to attend the finishing school?''

''Not any longer, Father. Miss Meredith can teach us what we need to know. You can see the difference already just since she's been with us these past few days.''

Samantha nodded enthusiastically. ''And she has such lovely manners, Papa. She could show us what to do to win the contest, I just know it. Everybody likes her. I know because I hear people talk about the nice things she does and all the people she helps. She could help *us*, Papa, if you let her.''

Heat fused itself up Meredith's neck, spilling onto her cheeks.

''Yeah, and she'd make a really good mama for somebody,'' Randy announced jubilantly. Her sisters shot angry looks that wiped the smile from her face. The child turned to Meredith, her eyes rounded and pleading. ''That is, if you want to get married and already have some daughters to start with.''

''Well, this is a new turn of events.'' Quade returned his fork to his plate and eyed each of his daughters. ''I'm not sure Miss Meredith is up to this particular challenge.''

When his gaze locked boldly with her own, the whole

world seemed to rush in at Meredith. Her throat constricted. The embarrassment that had heated her cheeks now skimmed over the surface of her entire body until she felt it bead along her hairline and the back of her neck. Her palms were slick and she laid down her fork lest it slip from her fingers. It was as if she heard an invisible clock *tick-tick-ticking* away and the time that sped by might somehow forever change her life.

"W-which challenge do you mean?" she stammered, attempting to regain her composure. "Helping them to win the Little Princess title?"

"Making somebody a really good mother—" His eyes darkened to mint. "—which generally means making somebody a good wife."

❖ 5 ❖

QUADE WATCHED YORI as the Norwegian rolled up
a rope, looping it over his palm and under his elbow me-
thodically until it formed a snakelike coil. Finally, the
sun-bronzed seaman tossed the coil onto the mountainous
pile built during their extended conversation. With the tidying up of Yori's shucking house almost complete,
Quade could count on his friend to join him in helping
others with their preparations.

"You seem a bit *forvirred* this morning, friend. Distracted," Yori translated before Quade could ask. "It
must be woman trouble, I am thinking."

With a laugh, Quade watched Yori work. "I do seem
to be surrounded by them more than most, don't I?" His
plans had been to seduce Meredith Stanfield to learn more
about her, not to insinuate that he was looking for a wife.
Yet the words had tumbled from his mouth as if they'd
taken on a life of their own—no doubt inspired by the
feel of her in his arms last night at the shore.

"Could be even more, if you cared to look." Yori
grabbed another rope and began to loop it, deliberately
flexing the muscles of his arms and chest to draw the
attention of women strolling down the promenade. Colorful parasols tilted at jaunty angles as several adventurous belles openly flirted with the two watermen.

"You need to stop, Svengsen. You'll be shark bait if one of those dandies decides you're paying too much attention to his sweetheart."

"I float good as the next man." Yori's laugh echoed over the pier. "Look at that little twist of petticoat there. No, I like the saucy one next to her. I think I am in *begjeer*."

"You're in *lust*, friend. That's got nothing to do with love."

"That's what I said." Yori's eyes disappeared into a squint of pure merriment. "I think I am in lust . . . *begjeer*. A man must first admire a woman before he can love her, *ja*?"

Yes, Quade admitted silently. Admiration renewed itself within him for the woman he had watched venture into the waves despite an obvious terror of the gulf. A woman of exceptional spirit, this Meredith Stanfield. A beauty that could not be defined in terms of classic bone structure or exotic features. Her curious appeal emanated from an inner radiance that drew him like a hunter of pearls to an oyster bed.

She'd been bold enough to face her fear, daring enough to challenge him for the sake of the children and impudent enough to deny the remaining funds he needed to restore the steamboat docks to their former glory. This spirited new governess might prove more heartache than help.

"The children need more than I can give them, Yori." Quade bent and picked up a large bread crust that littered the wharf, tossing it out into the bay. One of the seagulls that hovered overhead dove to scoop it up, then took to sea with the treasure. "They're growing into such little ladies, and I can't possibly teach them all that will be required of them. I've sheltered the girls from their mother's lifestyle for good reason, yet I worry one day they'll resent me for it."

"Miss Meredith is good-hearted and gets along well with the girls." Yori's blue-green eyes twinkled like the sunlight bouncing off the water's surface, but quickly darkened as he tried to ease Quade's concern. "She'll teach them what you cannot."

"But I don't want them to be all show and no stay."

"What makes you believe she is no stay? She's lived here all her life. Miss Meredith has never made me feel anything but proud to stand in her company. I always see her behind the serving lines at the charity booths. Not like her sister, Savannah, *ja*? That woman might suit a man's fancy by night, but by day she's as useless as a barnacle on his—"

"Are we talking about Meredith or her sister?"

"*Savannah*," Yori defined. "The woman is so infatuated with herself that a man feels he's intruding between her and the great love of her life." Yori laughed, trying to make light of the matter. "Ahh, but there are lots more just like her. That is the greatness of this Yoo-nited States." His hand took a broad wave, encompassing the whole of the promenade that paralleled the coastline. "There's plenty here for Big Yori Svengsen."

His words echoed over the water, drawing attention from passersby. "But Miss Meredith, she's nothing like her sister." Yori smiled at the onlookers and returned to the work at hand. "Pay attention. Watch her. You'll find she is friend to everyone from waterman to politician. Did she not donate the money for the fireworks this year? Miss Meredith is *all* stay and no show, I am thinking."

"You're portraying her as a saint." Quade was surprised by the irritation coloring his tone and wondered why he felt so exasperated by his friend's defense of the woman. Could it be that the thought that Yori had been watching her from a distance, and apparently for quite some time, didn't sit well with him?

"Maybe Miss Meredith is more firecracker than saint. A firecracker that has lit a certain fuse you'd rather *slokke, ja*?" Yori stamped his boot and rubbed the sole into the wharf as if putting out an unwanted flame.

"I always said you have a vivid imagination, Svengsen. Don't you have something better to do than examine my choice in governesses?"

"*Ja*, watch the lovely ladies in their ugly bathing costumes." He nodded toward the female tourists walking to the bathhouses in their muslin dresses.

The costumes were unsightly, high-necked, long-sleeved, and long-skirted. Quade tried to imagine Meredith in such a garment, but his mind lingered on the vision of her in last night's sleeping attire—a vision that had molded every transparent fiber of the cloth to the becoming swell of her breasts and hips, stirring long-denied needs within him. Yes, she was definitely a firecracker, but one he wouldn't allow to fizzle out on him as Katherine had.

"Firecracker or dud, I don't have time to search for another governess for the girls right now. I refuse to make a spur-of-the-moment choice without a thorough investigation into the next one's background. She must get along well with my children. The girls deserve someone who's willing to nurture them, not just earn a salary. They need someone who has the spirit to match them wit for wit, and if necessary, prank for prank. The next person I hire must last a lifetime . . . or at least until Miranda marries."

"Someone very much like Miss Stanfield, *ja?*"

Quade accepted his friend's teasing and freely admitted his good fortune. "Allowing the children to remain in her care until Shanty's return seems a logical choice. And they do enjoy being with her."

"So, it seems, does that Richards fellow."

"What does Nolan Richards have to do with—?" Quade turned toward town, instantly spotting the tall, dark-haired gentleman strolling down the boardwalk with Meredith and the children in tow. A pang of envy washed through Quade. He noted Meredith's arm linked through the Northerner's and the ease of her posture as she walked with the dandily dressed man. Richards's black knicker-length swimsuit, half-sleeved shirt, and red galluses might be all the rage back East, but here in the South the latest fashion in men's swimming styles seemed crude and ungentlemanly. Quade preferred to roll up his breeches and swim shirtless rather than submit to fashion's current tide.

"They say he's a family friend," Yori informed, offering Quade a rope. "Help me finish up here, and we can be on our way."

Quade grabbed the rope with gusto, discovering that the irritation that coiled in the pit of his stomach could be eased by keeping his hands busy. "Some friend. If he wins the bid to repair the docks, he'll make certain the port at Pass Christian fares better than Biloxi's. Mark my words. He's got ulterior motives he's keeping to himself." Quade quit working the rope and craned his neck to see which box the man, Meredith, and his children intended to use. "Will you look at that? Look, Yori. He's actually going to join them."

Quade took a step backward. "You'd think with all there is to do, the man would want to prove to the community how much he has their best interests at heart." With another step back, disapproval made Quade scowl. "You'd think he'd spend his time helping the rest of us get ready for—" The third step carried Quade into the brink.

Water filled his boots, churned around his head. Down he dropped, into the depths of an emotion he had not experienced in years. Letting the cold sting of the gulf wash over him, Quade asked himself if his feelings had been ignited by the sight of a man he despised, or—had they flamed from something far deeper? This was ridiculous. That's all he needed . . . to occupy his mind with something else.

As Quade sucked in a fresh breath of air, a round of applause broke out over the promenade. A Norwegian laugh hooted and hawed above all others.

"Quit your snickering, Svengsen, and lend me a hand," Quade growled, as the Norwegian bent at the waist and gripped his stomach in an effort to calm the uproar of laughter bellowing out over the wharf.

"Y-yist a minute, Captain. My b-belly . . . it's having a cramp, because my eyes have never seen a damper fuse, I am thinking."

"Yori Svengsen, if you don't get me the hell out of this water, I swear I'm gonna—"

"*Ja. Ja.* Yist a minute. Yist a minute." He couldn't move easily without pausing to stop and laugh. "I would not want you to shrivel up and disappoint the lady."

"Svengsen!"

Yori's brows daggered, yet his mouth refused to stop turning up at the corners. He motioned for some of the onlookers to move away so he could kneel closer to the point where Quade had fallen in. When he lowered himself and offered his hand, Yori attempted to keep a stern face but couldn't. "The water . . . it has soaked your sense of humor . . . I am *more than* thinking."

Latching onto the Norwegian's hand, Quade allowed himself to be pulled partially out of the water. But his friend was enjoying himself too much at Quade's expense. The impulse was too tempting to resist. With a forceful jerk, he yanked the unsuspecting seaman into the water, roaring with triumph as he realized he'd caught his friend off guard. But the Norwegian one-upped him and deliberately dove toward him, sending Quade sprawling backward into the breach.

Not one to be bested and relishing the opportunity to work off the tension of late, Quade grabbed the shucker and a water fight ensued. The two men wrestled like warring alligators, spinning over and over in the water, coming up for air only long enough to keep from drowning. Finally, they broke the surface at the same moment, reveling in the applause that erupted along the shoreline.

"A good swimmer you are, Quade Cameron," Yori complimented, slapping the captain on the back good-naturedly.

Quade nearly choked on the water he was about to spit from his mouth, almost going under again.

"But not such a good gator, I am thinking."

They laughed and reached for the edge of the wharf, each accepting a hand up from watermen standing in the crowd. Quade flopped onto the promenade, lying belly-down to catch his breath, feeling very much like a beached whale. While Yori managed to gain his land legs, the crowd moved back to make way for the Cameron children, who raced up demanding to see their father and his friend.

"Papa, are you dead?"

A wet strand of Quade's hair lifted from his eyes until he saw the precious sight of his youngest staring wide-eyed at him. She blinked, and he couldn't help but blink in response. "I'm fine, Muffin. Just extremely wet."

"See there, I told you so," Randy announced, letting the lock of hair fall so quickly that its tip stung his eye.

"You didn't have to tell me anything." Alexandra spoke from somewhere to his left. "*I* already knew. I wasn't the one who wanted to race over here and see if he was all right."

"She just wanted to make sure he and Mr. Svengsen were only playing." Samantha brushed the hair out of her father's eyes. "Isn't that so, Papa?"

"We were, indeed, Sammy."

"I should think you would set a better example than that, Captain."

The disapproving voice belonged to the woman standing above him. All he could see of her was the hem of her green muslin dress, yet he would recognize that readiness to challenge him anywhere. She'd set a precedent this morning, and now he supposed that every time they laid eyes on each other, the two of them would inevitably spar.

Still, he was a man who had learned to face the challenge. With slow precision, his gaze swept up the skirt that hid the long legs defined so acutely in last night's surf. Two fists balled at the becoming flare of hips that angled enticingly to a more-than-generous swell of bosom. But it was her expression that made him stand.

A battle of raging emotions etched her every feature. Anger, relief . . . fear? Her eyes were silver-blue pools transfixed on him, as if she were seeing not him but something or someone else. Her lips thinned into a grim line of anger as he reached out to brush away a tear that trickled down her cheek.

Did she believe him incapable of swimming? Had she almost drowned once, thus ingraining her with a terror of the gulf? His was a lifelong love of the sea. Quade swam like a dolphin and earned his living from the bay. Yet his antics seemed childish now, and he regretted causing her such distress.

"My apologies, Miss Stanfield. I allowed the balmy day and my friend's jovial nature to cloud my better judgment."

"Then you're quite all right?" The anger faded from her voice, leaving it soft and full of concern.

"Perfectly."

"Good. The children and I will be on our way now. We've changed our minds about the bathhouse and will dig clams after the tide ebbs."

Nolan Richards moved alongside her. His dark eyes mirrored his disappointment at her change of plans. "But you'll miss high tide. And it would be such a calming way to discuss—well, business matters."

Quade shook the water from his hair, deliberately dampening Nolan's bathing attire and his poor attempt at persuasion. "Oh, sorry, Richards."

Nolan flicked the bothersome beads of water from his suit as if they were pesky flies. "None the worse for the wear, Cameron."

An intangible rivalry erupted between the two men, making them glare at one another, both refusing to blink.

Meredith reached out and touched Nolan's arm, drawing his attention from Quade. "My duties are with the children until Miss Andrews returns. My decision about the bid can wait until then. The girls prefer to dig for clams, and we can talk while we dig. You're certainly welcome to grab a pail and join us."

Nolan's expression offered indulgence, though his words continued to plead his cause. "Aren't there far more important matters you should attend to?"

"As I told both you and Savannah this morning, Winifred is taking care of the needs at Stanfield House. Mr. Winkle will keep me informed of anything that should require my attention at the bank. And, no, quite frankly, nothing is as important to me this morning as sharing the joy of clamming with these children while also giving them a lesson in foraging for food if survival demands it. Please join us, or allow me to finish this discussion next week.''

That's telling him, Merry. Quade smiled as the man bid a hasty retreat.

Randy tugged on Meredith's skirt and looked up at her. ''Is that how you get rid of somebody you don't like, Miss Meredith?''

''Whatever gave you the idea I don't like Mr. Richards?'' Meredith asked as she stroked the six-year-old's hair.

Do you or don't you? Quade demanded silently, not liking this new bend to the conversation.

''Papa was frowning at him just like he is now, and Mr. Richards was frowning right back. And you kind of . . . well . . . you kind of frowned at them both. I know you're mad at Papa 'cause he's all wet, but Mr. Richards was dry and you still looked mean at him.''

''I don't like anyone telling me what I should do and when I should do it.'' Though the child deserved an answer, Meredith's narrow gaze pointed at the captain. ''Lesson number six: A lady must firmly and emphatically let a man know that he cannot demand from her anything she won't willingly do. No means *no*. Always remember that.''

''I will,'' all four Camerons replied in unison.

Lesson number seven, Quade decided, would be getting this woman to change her mind.

❖ 6 ❖

"I THINK IT'S a wonderful idea, Mr. López. And my answer is yes." Meredith accepted the twenty-year-old man's offer to carry the pail of clams she and the children had gathered. Time to put an end to this activity for a while. The sun beat down hot and balmy, making her skin prickle beneath the heated layers of muslin and petticoats.

"You won't regret this, *Señorita* Stanfield. I promise . . . all of Biloxi will benefit if my idea works."

"I believe you're right, Mr. López. If we can find a way to manufacture ice here instead of having it shipped from New England, think of the boon it will give all Six Sisters, not just Biloxians." The Spaniard's wavy blond hair, deep-set eyes, and black mustache gave him an unusual countenance, but his inventive mind intrigued her most.

Having ready access to ice could ease their ability to ship seafood by rail or steamboat to all points north, east, and west. More readily available ice would also add to the visitors' enjoyment of local beverages that helped ward off the sultry heat. The Spaniard's goal, if reached, would benefit everyone. Investing in his dream would be a wise move, no matter how long-range the investment.

He might be young, but he was a man of destiny. She

felt it in her bones. And Papa had always said, "Listen to your own instinct, Merry. Allow your mind to see what others blind themselves to. Trust your heart." And so she would with this newcomer to Biloxi. Though he had lived here only two years, the man already had the seaport's future at heart. That made him worth backing.

Just as Captain Cameron wanted to repair the steamboat docks? Meredith quickly quelled the condemning voice inside her and reminded herself she'd denied him the funds for reasons without condemnation.

"I would be honored if you call me Lazaro." The Spaniard half bowed. "It is a name handed down for generations. I bear it proudly."

"Lazaro." Meredith practiced it with a smile.

"Lazaro, Lazaro, Lazaro." Randy began a chant, using a stick to write his name in the mud. "He wants some money to borrow, to borrow, to borrow."

"Randy, that's not nice." Samantha ran up and put a hand over her younger sister's mouth to stop her chanting. Though muffled, Randy kept saying it, giggling as Samantha's hand moved up and down.

"He said Miss Meredith could call him that," Alex criticized, washing her hands in the wave ready to rush back out to sea, "not us."

"Please do me the honor as well, *Señorita* Alexandra. And you too, *Señoritas* Samantha and Miranda."

Meredith watched the eleven-year-old's face take on an expression of sheer awe.

Alexandra's cheeks turned rosy as her tone softened and she whispered, "Thank you, Lazaro."

The child on the verge of womanhood had just developed a considerable case of infatuation, a situation that deserved watching. Meredith told the children to gather their things and wash their hands. The Spaniard patiently waited until all was in order, then asked if he might walk them back to their quarters to further discuss the arrangements to be made.

"How long do you expect it will take to put your plan into effect?" Meredith asked, lifting Randy into her arms.

The child was having a difficult time keeping up with the group. As she settled the little girl against her left hip, she noticed that Randy's cheeks were tinged a deeper shade of pink than earlier, and her eyes drooped as if she were half asleep. Had she kept them out in the sun too long? A glance at Sam and Alex did not ease her concern.

Perhaps there was something to the schedule the captain had recited this morning. Limited play in the sun was logical, if not wise. But they'd all been having fun and enjoying Mr. López's company so much, she'd quite forgotten the time. A pang of hunger clenched her stomach, reminding Meredith it was long past lunchtime. The girls must be famished.

"I don't feel so good, Miss Meredith." Samantha grabbed her hand. "Could I walk beside you?"

"Of course, sweet. I think you'll feel much better, though, if we go home and get into something cool and clean. I'll fix us a light lunch, then we'll all take a nap until the afternoon cools off. Does that sound fun?"

The child nodded at her. Gratitude swept across her freckled features, making Meredith even more painfully aware of how bad Sam must be feeling. Her fingers felt moist and hot, hopefully just from working so hard at clamming rather than from any fever induced by the sun.

"May I walk beside you, Lazaro?" Alex placed the back of her hand against her forehead and slightly wavered on her feet. She let the hand drop halfway before reaching out to offer it to him. "I feel a bit faint."

"Let me assist you, *Señorita* Alexandra."

When he offered his hand, a smile broke out over her face before she realized that her exuberance at holding his hand contradicted the reason for doing so. "I think I'll be able to make it now." She sighed dramatically and deliberately leaned into the twenty-year-old.

Though only nine years divided their ages, the young man and child-woman were ages apart in personality. Meredith felt a pang of compassion for Alex. She knew too well the heartache of loving someone whose dreams would forever be foremost in his mind, forcing love always to remain a distant second.

Though Phillip had drowned six long years ago, their hope for a future together should have been put to rest long before the terrible tragedy that had swept him out to sea. Meredith had promised herself she would never again open her heart to a man who put work and goals before love and family. Never again would she let such a man rule her. The fact that she'd allowed just such a man's children to claim her heart in no way invited Quade Cameron into her life.

When he had said, "making somebody a really good mother generally means making somebody a good wife," why had her pulse raced rampantly and her heart eluded its regular beat? She wasn't one of those women who blushed at the mere sight of a man, nor did she swoon for *any* reason. Still, Quade Cameron's presence elicited primitive yearnings within her—yearnings that made her every pore hum with anticipation, expectation, and a need for sating.

The heat of the afternoon seemed to intensify in that moment, making Meredith slightly dizzy. Or was it thoughts of Quade Cameron that tilted her world so easily? Unwilling to acknowledge the latter, Meredith's strides became longer. "I don't mean to rush you, Lazaro, but the girls haven't eaten since breakfast, and I'm afraid they may all be suffering from too much sun. Would you mind putting off the rest of our discussion until another day?"

Concern filled his Latin features. He gently squeezed Alexandra's hand. "Of course not. Anything to better the *señoritas'* health."

Meredith liked Lazaro López more by the minute. And so, apparently, did Alexandra. She hoped Quade's eldest did not suffer a broken heart in the days or years to come, because, as Meredith well knew, sometimes a heart never mended.

Hurried steps took them from the shore and up the walkway leading to the promenade. They passed several grab netters tossing out their nets to fish for mullet in the shallows.

The water depth between the coastline and the Chandeleur Islands, which formed a barrier to the open sea, was less than twelve feet. But its strong currents easily swept life in and out of the bay at regular intervals. Tonging for oysters and netting mullet and shrimp brought a bounty of profit to Biloxians—a profit that could be increased tenfold if Lazaro's dream saw fruition. Everyone in the South was trying to recover from the war that had nearly destroyed them five years ago. Any idea to bring easier commerce was worth backing.

"There you are, Meredith. I've been trying to find you *everywhere*."

Savannah emerged from a shoo-fly near the Campbells' private wharf. She held a glass full of a sparkling green beverage. No matter how hard Meredith tried to greet Savannah warmly, she always felt a guarded reserve toward her sibling, a reserve she usually practiced during business hours.

Trying not to be critical, Meredith couldn't help but wonder if her mother knew that Savannah favored the alcoholic beverage served by the redheaded owner of the finest residence on the beachfront. The lattice gazebo encircling the large live oak allowed people to sit around and catch gulf breezes while escaping mosquitoes and flies—certainly a comfortable place in which to look *"everywhere."*

"I told you where I'd be, Savannah," Meredith quietly informed her, hoping she would not make a scene in front of Mr. López. "I don't have much time to visit with you now. The children haven't eaten yet. Perhaps you'd like to walk back with us."

A frown creased Savannah's forehead. "I need your help choosing a new pattern for our festival cake. Karena Smith said her King cake is shaped like a sea horse. Now everyone will think I *imitated* hers, for mercy's sake. And Jonietta is making conch-shell cupcakes. I simply can't think of a single design as impressive as theirs."

"What about a starfish?" A dozen ideas raced to Meredith's mind.

Savannah stamped her foot and pouted. "Oh, why can't I be the creative one, Merry, dear? It's quite unfair that you received more wits and I—" She smiled at Lazaro. "—unfortunately must deal with this bothersome beauty of mine."

"Have you any suggestions in mind?" Meredith's wits were tested by the sheer effort of quelling the solution *she* wanted to offer her sister. But her father had taught her to "Do unto others as you would have them do unto you." And that applied no matter what and how many times Savannah had done unto her.

"You know I'm of no real help, Merry. I was hoping you might just choose and let me visit later. While you're deciding, I can spend an hour or so with my new friend." Savannah held out her gloved hand toward the shoo-fly. A dark-haired gentleman emerged, half bowing in acknowledgment. "Come out and say hello, *mon amour*."

Her sister poured on the charm so thickly that Meredith thought she might jell where she stood.

"Good day, *mademoiselles*." He half-bowed. "*Monsieur*."

They all greeted the Frenchman.

"Hand me my bag, will you, Pierre?"

The Frenchman disappeared from view only to return again with a paisley carpetbag.

Savannah opened it and held up several pieces of parchment. "Here are a few recipes and a sketch or two."

The "few" looked more like twenty or thirty. It would take hours to pore over them and decide. Why had Savannah waited until now to determine the design and flavor to represent Stanfield House in the cake booth? Then again, why did Meredith think this year would be any different than past ones? Hoping Savannah might actually prepare for something ahead of schedule compared to asking a butterfly to quit flitting.

"All right, Savannah. I'll take them, but you'll have to come by tomorrow for my decision. The children's schedule is already running late. I really must be on my way.''

Savannah rushed to hand Meredith the bag, then noticed that Merry's hands were full with children. Exasperation instantly surged inside Meredith as distress etched her sister's lovely features. ''Unless it's heavy, give it to Alexandra. She has a hand not in use.''

Alexandra glared at Savannah. The elder Stanfield snatched her hand away lest she touch Quade's oldest daughter's fingers by accident.

''Thank you, Meredith. I'll be by in the morning, but no later. I really don't have any more time to spare, you know.''

Meredith knew her sister aimed to let the Frenchman believe she had bestowed stolen moments upon him. Why did she always allow Savannah to ask a favor, then demand that it be fulfilled to *her* specifications?

Meredith urged them toward the captain's quarters. Samantha's hand squeezed hers gently. Meredith glanced down to see sapphire eyes staring back at her.

''That's awfully nice of you, Miss Merry. I do nice things sometimes too, even when I don't want to. It's easier than arguing with my sisters. That doesn't mean I'm weak, does it, Miss Merry? Letting people get their way? Miss Applegate said I was, but I don't think so.''

''No, sweet, you're not.'' Meredith realized the child had just taught her a lesson. ''It's strong to be good to people who have no idea how to be good to others. If you keep doing it time and time again, perhaps one day they'll take notice and do the same for someone else. Passing goodness on to others is real strength, Samantha. Don't ever let anyone convince you differently.''

Minutes later, they bid Lazaro good-bye only to find Nolan Richards waiting at the captain's doorstep. Every fine hair rose on the nape of Meredith's neck, as it did when a shyster strode into her office believing he might swindle her out of her fortune. Yet her father had trusted this man completely.

Feeling disloyal to her father's memory, Meredith attempted a level of congeniality. ''Good afternoon, Mr.

Richards. I trust you haven't been waiting long?"

"Good afternoon, ladies. I hope your clamming went well." He tipped his hat, revealing hair the color of coal.

"It did. Now if you'll excuse us, we're all terribly exhausted, in need of food, and not in the best of temperaments. We do hope you'll accept our sincerest regrets and will come back to visit another time."

"Of course. I wouldn't think of interrupting when you're—"

Meredith gently set Randy down and linked the six-year-old's hand with Samantha's. "Help each other upstairs while I see Mr. Richards on his way." When both nodded, a pent-up sigh of relief rushed from Meredith's lips. She bent backward and pressed a hand against her spine to ease the ache that had developed from carrying the child up the promenade. No wonder mothers often looked exhausted.

Alexandra leaned her back against the outside wall of the warehouse, staring off into the distance. She clutched the bag as if waiting for a schooner to sail her to some faraway place. Meredith followed the girl's gaze and realized that the eleven-year-old studied Lazaro López's destination. First love in full bloom radiated from her mint-green eyes. A painful, poignant memory stirred that Meredith did not have the strength at the moment to linger upon. "It's time to go in, Alex. There will be other days."

Alexandra stared at Meredith, their gazes locking. For the first time, the child-woman allowed Meredith a glimpse at her vulnerability.

"Do you really think so, Miss Meredith?"

Meredith nodded, reaching out to anchor a wisp of strawberry-blond hair behind Alex's ear. "With every new day comes hope, Alex. And you need only a tiny shred of it to see you through anything."

The child catapulted herself into Meredith, wrapping her arms around Meredith's waist and hugging her tightly. Surprised by the normally stoic Alex, Meredith was uncertain what had inspired such a response. But she knew too well how desperately the child had needed hugs this past year, and there had been no one to offer them. She returned the hug and gently pressed a kiss atop Alexandra's head.

Alex lingered for just a moment, offering no words or explanation. Finally, she withdrew and blinked—once, twice—to hide the moisture that welled in her eyes.

"I g-guess I must be tired," she muttered, abruptly disappearing into the warehouse.

"Well, that was rather touching. You're really becoming quite the governess."

"What?" She'd forgotten Nolan's presence. His tone irritated her, rousing tactics she often used to dissuade an arrogant associate. It was none of his business whether she did the job well. In fact, he seemed to be making a lot of her business his own lately. Friend of the family or not, she refused to let him intrude upon her private affairs. "I like them very much. They're all wonderful little girls."

"In need of a mother?"

"I don't think that's any of our affair, do you?"

Nolan reached out to grab her hand. "Poor choice of words, Merry. I hope your relationship with Cameron won't come to that. *You* are my affair, if you'd just let yourself be."

Meredith pulled her hand away before he could clasp it firmly. "I'm terribly flattered, Nolan. Honestly. But as I told both you and Lindsay Littlefield—"

"Don't compare that dandy's sincerity to mine. We both know he's only out to marry your money, not you."

Just as you are out to win the bid for the steamboat docks, not to offer me marriage, she silently countered, but instead finished what she had meant to say before being interrupted. "I am a romantic, Nolan, who happens to believe in one man for every woman. The love of my life has come and gone, and now I must face this world alone until I greet him on a different shore. I promised myself I would only marry the one man I loved beyond all others. Unfortunately, that is not and will never be you. My heart buried itself at sea six years ago."

Nolan's eyes darkened to smoky ash. "I'm flesh and blood, Meredith." He pulled her to him despite her protest. "You can't keep a man from trying. I heard what you said to the child about maintaining hope."

She pressed her arms against the wall of his chest. Sadness surged through her, springing from a well so deep it felt as if it flooded every chamber of her heart. "A child needs to believe, Nolan. I'm a woman, fully grown."

"A fact I'm well aware of." His voice became husky, demanding. "The only way you're going to get rid of me, then, is to keep me so busy I can't court you." He allowed her to step away, then reached inside his frock coat and pulled out a collection of documents. "Will you read these at your leisure and try to get back to me with a decision? This festival business is stalling everything around here. That's all everyone's got on their minds. I must get moving on this project or go on to other opportunities."

Other *women*, she knew without saying. Accepting the papers, Meredith added them to the list of tasks she had yet to do before she could relax for the day. "I'll look them over."

"Soon?" Impatience marred his tone, though he tried to disguise it with an expression of anticipation.

"Very soon. Tomorrow," she announced, realizing that the sooner she read them, the sooner this pesky hornet would buzz somewhere or someone else.

"Don't let Captain Cameron see them, Merry. He would have the upper hand on a counteroffer."

"The captain isn't that sort of man," Meredith defended. "He may be many things, but he's certainly no eavesdropper or spy."

"Oh, no?" Nolan Richards pointed behind her. "Then why is he following you wherever you go today?"

Meredith swung around to see where he indicated. She scanned the group of people entering the bathhouse and thought for just a moment she saw a head—no, two— duck behind the structure. As she peered closer a cloud moved, offering momentary shade. Had the drifting cloud's silhouette on the latticework caused her eyes to play tricks on her? "Whyever would Quade Cameron trail me without letting me know his presence?"

Anger filled Nolan's hawklike features. "I don't know. Why don't you ask *him*?"

Weariness evaporated from Meredith, fueled by her own irritation at the man's insinuations. "No, better yet, tell me how do *you* know that he's been following us all day?"

"I . . . uh . . . was waiting until a moment I thought appropriate to talk business."

Though his answer was viable, she knew he lied. "I'm sure Captain Cameron merely checked on me to see how well I cared for his children." She hoped her comment was not at all true, because she'd done an extremely poor job of it today.

"Just beware of the man," Nolan warned when she turned to enter the warehouse. "His driving purpose is to make himself rich. You know how many fortunes he's lost and gained over the years. You've seen his bank—"

"The war cost many their financial security," she reminded him. "You and I were fortunate and should admire a man who doesn't allow defeat to keep him down time and time again."

"Yes, yes. I suppose. But think how easy it would be to gain and keep his next fortune if he marries the wealthiest belle on the coast."

She watched Nolan shade his eyes from the sun and wondered if he deliberately evaded her gaze. What was this man hiding? Worse, how would it affect the Stanfields?

"As you just stated, he is a man who will stop at nothing."

"That's not at all what I said. Don't twist my words to your purpose, Nolan. As you know, I'm well aware of the captain's past, and even more so of those whose interest is purely in my money."

She was through sparring with him and wanted Nolan to understand this in no uncertain terms. "Rest assured. Neither my heart nor my money is available for loan at the moment."

❖ 7 ❖

"BETTER CALL IT a day," Quade announced to the group of men painting the grandstand intended to house Mayor Henly and the visiting dignitaries during the festival. "Smell that?"

"*Ja*, me and every man here."

"No, not that, Yori. I mean the rain." Fighting off hunger proved difficult for Quade. He would go home to his own cooking instead of enjoying whatever Opal Ortega had prepared for the workers for supper. The woman's ability to cook was as widely appreciated as she was respected—for all she accomplished despite her near-blindness. There wasn't a finer chef and housekeeper in all of Mississippi, perhaps even in all the South.

This evening, Opal's iron skillet spewed out rich-smelling smoke as it fried something that conjured up images of golden crust, tender meat, and mouth-watering spices. "Take a look at that sky, Yori. We'd best put the paint away and throw a tarpaulin over the grandstand."

The sky darkened by the minute. Tree leaves turned an incandescent green in the shift of light, seeming to burn with emerald fire. A white wall of rain stretched across the horizon, swiftly advancing toward shore. The leaves began to dance, the huge limbs cross-whipping in crazy waves.

"It's only a spit, I am thinking. Won't last more than an hour or two." Yori and three other men grabbed hold of the huge canvas and tented it over four poles to keep it from touching the grandstand's roof. With an efficiency born of long practice, the men secured the makeshift tent over the freshly painted dais.

"Long enough to undo what we've done all day if this wind gets any worse," Quade informed his friend as the Norwegian rushed to collect tools and brushes.

"*Ja*. Worse."

Everyone there knew of the hell the two men refused to name. Each feared that a long-sunken titan might rise from the depths and batter the coast with wind and water-driven fury, bleeding Biloxi of human souls and alluvial sediment. *Hurricane*. The word struck terror in even the most stalwart seaman's heart.

"She's just being playful." Quade pointed to patches of blue sky that broke the curtain of white rain paralleling the horizon. The "she" he spoke of was revered by all—the mighty Gulf of Mexico. They relied on her for their very livelihoods, fearing and respecting her volatile mood swings. Today, their good fortune held. Biloxi could count its blessings.

One-Eyed Thomas offered Quade a drink from his jug. "Care to join me, Cap? It's one of me best batches. We can catch up on St. Louis."

Quade held up a restraining palm. "No thanks, Tom. I promised the girls I'd take them swimming, so I'd better head for home. They'll be eager to go, especially if it rains only enough to cool things off."

Yori bid the others good-bye and picked up the captain's fast-paced gait. "Do you think Miss Meredith saw us following her?"

"No." Quade hoped his friend understood all the reasons he had made certain that his tasks for the day took him to locations prime for observing the Stanfield heiress and his daughters. Did *he*, for that matter? "But I'm not sure Richards didn't. That snake is up to something, and

I want her and my daughters out of harm's way when the viper decides to strike.''

"She's beautiful, *ja*?"

To deny his attraction to Meredith suddenly seemed inane and pointless. The labors in the heat of the day and the frustration of the delay caused by the rain sapped Quade's ability to cloak his feelings. "*Ja*, Yori. She is that and then some."

"I am thinking, friend, that she may be the one to help you start living again. To bury the past."

A wonderful thought, but Quade had buried his hope for happiness and his anger at Katherine's betrayal in the coffin with her. Time had taught him that work was his only mistress and his children his only future.

Exhaustion settled over Quade, despite the rapidness of their strides. "It's been a long day," he told his good friend. *A long life*, he added silently as a deep sigh escaped him. "I think I'll take a walk before I head in." *Alone*, his tone insisted.

The Norwegian knew Quade well. "I know. I know. This is the point where you wander and brood, while Big Yori learns to keep his advice to himself." Laugh lines wrinkled at the edges of Yori's eyes, but his words held solemn concern. "Thomas and I plan to scorch supper together later. Join us when you quit stewing."

"Another time." Quade tried to lighten his mood by offering a wave of farewell, but gloom seemed to make even the air he breathed feel heavy. He rested one foot atop a raised piling, leaned an elbow on his knee and stared out into the vast horizon. His eyes closed, suddenly casting Quade adrift in a haze of memories.

The wind whipped tendrils of hair from the rawhide cord that held it back from his face. Despite the knowledge that the storm would last only briefly, the approaching tempest only served to darken his mood.

It was as if he walked in a dense mist, unsure of direction and void of landmarks. Yet something compelled him to move forward, hastening toward a destination not yet distinguishable or recognizable. Finally, he came to a barren tree standing near a columned manor house made of peach-tinted marble. Belle Raven? No live oaks encircled it. No ivy climbed its veranda. Still, a familiarity of the home struck a chord of recognition within him.

The branches of the tree were void of but a single magnolia of such singular captivation that he was forced to halt and admire its perfection. As he stared, a strong gust pummeled the tree, threatening to dislodge the flower from its roots. The sound of fragmenting wood splintered the air. The magnolia fell from its lofty height and landed in a mysterious surf forming beneath his feet.

All but the surf and the deep red bloom faded from sight; its perfume seeped into his every sense. It seemed to ebb with the tide, then return—staying just out of reach, taunting, teasing, changing each time he reached to touch its beauty. The blossom softened into lush auburn hair. Amid its thick mass, iced sapphires transformed into a pair of silver-blue eyes beckoning him to plunge into their fathoms. The surf took form and substance, defining a face full of character and spirit—perfection crafted by the almighty hand of creation itself.

Her eyes entranced him. Her lips formed a siren's song that enticed, seduced, beckoned him to believe.

"Just reach out to me, Quade. Tend me as you would the most fragrant of flowers. Hold me."

Quade's eyes opened as if from a trance. For a brief, haunting moment, he believed that Meredith Stanfield actually stood in front of him, offering all that he needed, dreamed . . . desired. His hand slowly returned to his side as he realized his fingers would surely have been pricked by the thorns she wore for protection. But protection from what? Everyone in Biloxi seemed to admire her.

And she seemed to have helped everyone except him. Her refusal to extend the funds he needed to rebuild the docks seemed unwarranted and unfair. He'd given his word that every dollar would not only be paid back but paid with interest. He'd even offered Belle Raven for collateral. Neither his children's heritage nor his word had been enough to change her mind.

How could he be envious of his children spending time with a spoiled, rich do-gooder with too much time on her hands? Hell, he'd probably lost more money than she'd inherited. And if not for the war . . .

Frustration drove Quade homeward, away from the strange attraction she stirred within him and toward a more satisfying answer to his quest. He must protect the township from Nolan Richards's plans—whatever they might be. From what he'd seen today, one of those plans was courting Meredith. Though that was none of his business, he could insist that it be delayed until Meredith no longer chaperoned his children.

The distance to his warehouse quarters passed easily. As he entered the darkened interior, an enticing aroma made his throat tighten in anticipation.

Everything seemed unusually quiet. The sense that someone was napping engulfed him. Bypassing the kitchen, he tiptoed upstairs. All three girls slept, their hair pinned up out of the way and their angelic faces slightly pink. Had they stayed out in the sun too long today? He would take up the matter with Miss Stanfield. A survey of the room revealed that their chaperon was not to be found. He placed a kiss on each sweet forehead then silently returned below.

A quick study of the warehouse's lower story offered no sign of Meredith. She must be in the kitchen, stirring up that wonderful smell. Despite the questions that drove Quade, he found it agreeable to come home to napping children and the pleasing aroma of food on the stove.

Quade opened the door that divided the kitchen from the sitting area and halted abruptly.

There, sound asleep with her cheek propped on one hand splayed flat against the table, sat Meredith Stanfield. Scattered about her were sea designs and recipes. Official-looking documents and papers had been neatly piled to her left. A dark stain of ink formed a glob at the end of the pen loosely held in her other hand. She'd apparently fallen asleep working.

All of the other emotions he felt toward this woman

evaporated as Quade took in the gentleness of her face, the curve of her slender neck, the rise and swell of her breasts as she breathed. The memory of her soft, wet body cradled in his arms fanned the fires she'd stirred within him last night. She had lured him with her vulnerability, tempted him with her softness, seduced him with her touch. Quade thought it had been only the enticement of two healthy bodies wet from exertion and inspired by the closeness necessary to lift her from the surf. But he stood a yard away from her now with only the memory of her touch to ignite the passion flaming so readily within him now.

Meredith's effect on him was total and complete—devastating. The fragrance of her perfume filled his soul. Her lovely curving form enticed him to carry her to a more comfortable resting place. Quade gently removed the pen from her fingers and threaded his arm around her waist, the other beneath her thighs. With a powerful yet gentle motion, Quade cradled her in his arms.

Her arms wrapped around his neck and, with a sigh, she nestled close against him as she had at the shore. Driven to distraction, he pondered whether he should attempt to carry her upstairs and risk waking the children or let her rest upon the cushioned davenport in the next room. Meredith moved against him. Warm breath tickled the base of his neck. His cheek turned toward the touch, only to feel her lips press gently against his skin. Gooseflesh rose in response, beading his spine like everwidening ripples upon the water.

Jagged lightning blinked through the windows, followed by heavy raindrops pattering on the roof. Errant breezes filled the room with the fresh smell of the storm. Quade strode softly to the davenport and sat, leaving Meredith cradled in his arms. Lightning bolts flashed across the broad expanse of the Mississippi Sound.

A strange sense of security washed through him as the storm enveloped the world beyond the windows. It had been a long time since he had lent softness to anyone but his children. A long time since he'd allowed himself to feel at ease in a woman's presence. A long time since he had ached to hold one in his arms and kiss her with every fiber of his being.

The raging winds outside and the arms encircling him with trust made it impossible to do anything but hold her and let her rest. He'd watched her all day, noticing how she cared for his children, dealt with her sister and Richards, and made time for Pomender who had obviously brought a message from home. From the mess on the table, it appeared Meredith Stanfield had taken on too many tasks and literally worn herself out. Respect dueled with sympathy inside him. She was indeed kind, but too helpful to the point of being self-sacrificing, it seemed.

Quade's fingers brushed the softly tangled curls from her nape.

A contented sigh escaped her.

His lips brushed her temple and pressed a kiss to her cheek. Memories of her beckoning to him, asking him to hold her, rushed vividly to mind.

Meredith turned her face, and he was truly lost. His mouth caressed hers in a long, tender, undemanding kiss that shaped and molded her lips to his.

Waiting for her to protest, Quade paused long enough to let her pull away if she wished. Instead, her fingers delved into the hair at the nape of his neck, and the kiss deepened. Craving the same touch, Quade tugged the pins loose from her hair and let his fingers slide through the luxuriant auburn tresses. Tenderly, he lifted her chin and gazed down into her bone-melting blue eyes.

"You're sweeter than the finest brandy," he whispered, suddenly aware of a thirst that had long needed quenching, achingly certain that only she could satisfy its craving.

His heart skipped a beat, then began to hammer as a smile sensually curved her mouth. Her eyes, though hooded, welcomed him without restraint. Slowly, deliberately, Quade pressed his lips on hers once again, kissing her long and lingeringly. His tongue flicked over her lips, teasing at first, then urgently insisting that she part them.

The moment she did, he tasted her deeply, intimately, exploring her inner sweetness while his hands pressed her closer in his embrace.

Wild sensations surged through him, leaving Quade trembling in their wake. The world tilted as he pressed her back against the davenport's seat and leaned over her. Only then did he see reluctance clear the smoky blue of her eyes.

She shook her head in feeble protest. "We can't . . . the children."

"Just one more," he whispered, his mouth silencing her, devouring the logic of her objection.

In fevered longing he groaned, crushing her tighter to the hard length of his body and drawing her tongue into his mouth . . . tasting, caressing, savoring. His world spun in an ever-quickening eddy, and he became drunk with desire.

Her breathy moan urged him to explore her earlobe, the sweet curve of her jaw, before kissing his way across her cheek. White-hot heat blazed along the slope of his shoulders and the granite sinews of his arms, as her fingers stroked and sought to thread themselves into his own.

His hands moved of their own volition, unfastening the top buttons of her muslin dress and seeking the soft swell beneath. The sound of feet padding across the floor upstairs penetrated Quade's passion-drugged senses, jerking him back to reality and away from a more intimate touch. Dazed by the consuming desire she'd stirred within him, he ended the kiss and shook his head.

"If we don't stop now," he murmured in a voice filled with as much regret as passion, "I won't promise I can stop at all." He reluctantly lifted his head.

Touching Meredith's cheek with a forefinger, he lightly traced the elegant slope of her nose, pressed a chaste kiss upon her lips and glanced to see if his children had started downstairs. Assured that his and Meredith's closeness was as yet undiscovered, he knew only one course of action would drain this fever from his bloodstream—shocking them both back into the cold, protective reality of their

guarded association. How desperately he needed that re-
moteness to douse the ardor inspired by Meredith Stanfield. The enemy's touch.

If only he'd found this passion with Katherine. . . . Perhaps he could have loved her enough to convince her to
stay. But he hadn't. He'd thought that building her a fine
home and giving her all she dreamed of showed his depth
of love for her. But his dedication to accumulating a fortune had only driven her into another man's arms. No
amount of wishing it were different would change the
facts.

The years since her passing had taught him that he and
Katherine had never truly loved one another. They were
enamored of the *idea* of love. But it would hurt too much
to lose the idea a second time. It hurt too much to believe
that the feelings between a man and a woman could last
a lifetime and beyond. Safety lay in closing off his heart
to that particular dream, in facing the reality that the kind
of love he wanted . . . no . . . *demanded* was for idealists,
dreamers, or yarnspinners.

He had to keep focused, for the girls' sake and for his
own. The preparations for the festival were exactly what
he needed to forget the temptation Meredith Stanfield
posed.

This was too dangerous a game to play. He had allowed
himself to get caught up in the net she cast. He needed
to dominate this situation, lest his ardor rage out of control. Quade offered a hand to help Meredith up just as
wind rattled the window and thunder echoed over the bay.

Footsteps raced down the stairs.

As if the heavens wanted to punctuate the storm that
would surely brew from his intended challenge, lightning
blinked and blinked again. The flash illuminated her di-
sheveled state and the loathing that his next words etched
across her face. "Has Richards won the bid for your affection as well as for repair of the docks?"

❖ 8 ❖

WHAT HAD STIRRED her to such lunacy? Imagine . . .
insinuating that she and Nolan were lovers! And kissing
Quade Cameron as if he were one! Meredith swung
around, turning her back to the captain and attempting to
straighten her hair before the children completely descended the stairs.

The last thing she remembered was stoking the stove
enough to allow the gumbo to simmer. Then she had taken
a second glance at the sketch that might please Savannah
the most. Tired from the long day, the cautious watching
of the children, and studying Savannah's and Nolan's
projects, Meredith's eyes had slowly drifted shut.

She had dreamed of floating on a wave toward land,
unafraid of the ebb and flow of the tide, unhindered by
the currents that rushed around her. Something golden
beckoned her from shore, called her name, reached out to
pluck her from the sea. She rushed toward that bright
beacon, sensing that it would somehow alter the pattern
of her existence and lead her into realms as yet unknown.
When that beacon took the form of the man who somehow stirred the yearnings she had thought were perma-
nently swept away, Meredith decided no harm could come
from indulging herself in a game of secret seduction.

But the man cradling her in his arms, ravishing her with

his kiss, was no figment of a dream. Quade Cameron was every indulgence she craved, every intoxicant she'd denied herself, the promise of every passion-filled night she'd longed to experience. An anchor of possibility in a life adrift with disillusionment.

Yet now his words had dashed that hope as quickly as it had surfaced, and she had allowed herself to be fooled.

Meredith's fingers still trembled with longing, and were unable to remain steady enough to repin her curls into place. Hurriedly, she fumbled with the top buttons of her dress, her cheeks heating with a blush at the memory of the intimacy she'd almost granted the captain.

She closed her eyes, took a deep breath, then faced the Camerons, attempting to focus all her attention on the three girls rather than the man whom she wanted to slap and kiss in the same instant. "That was a fine nap you took. I hope you're all well rested. I have gumbo cooked for supper, but if you're hungry now, I'll prepare—"

"I'm still full from lunch." Alexandra's complaint exited in a yawn. "Besides, it's not good to eat just before we go swimming."

Randy ran up and hugged her father's leg. "We still get to go, don't we, Papa? You said we could when you got home. We can, Papa, can't we?"

"It's *may we*," Alex scolded. "I told you the ladies at the finishing school say *may*, not *can*."

"*May* we, Papa?"

"The beach is so pretty when it rains," Samantha added, staring out the large window that presented a panoramic view of the Sound.

Quade lifted Randy into his arms and joined Samantha at the window. "Look at the waves, Muffin. They're cresting too full. Wait until the wind dies down a bit; then we'll go for a walk at least. We'll have to decide about the swimming after we see how long this blow's going to last."

The redheaded child kissed him on the cheek and stared at him with eyes round and pleading, turning on all her charm. "But you said we could, Papa. You promised."

He glanced at Meredith. Though she doubted *she* could have denied the child's request, Meredith offered him a look that said he'd gotten himself into this, and he shouldn't expect her to get him out of it.

He gave in. "A promise is a promise, isn't it?"

Incensed, Meredith couldn't contain her disapproval. If she were required to see to their safety and well-being, then he would definitely hear her say on the matter. "Surely you jest, Captain? You can't take a chance with the children's lives just to satisfy a pledge that was not well thought out when offered." Images flashed in her mind. Memories of Phillip vowing to return from the docks so they might resolve their disagreement. But he had lied. He never returned. Work had been more important to him than their courtship. "That's teaching the children to expect the unrealistic, encouraging false hope."

Sarcasm stained Alexandra's lips. "So what if the surf gets a bit rough? That's just one less of us you have to watch. Then each of us will have our own bed and—"

"Stop it! Don't ever let me hear such foolish words come out of your mouth again, Alexandra Cameron! Every life is precious. Every human being counts." Meredith stared at the family and realized that she was an outsider here and had no right to demand anything. No right to let her anger at *Quade's* words vent itself upon Alex's. She began to gather the few possessions she'd brought, mentally running through a list of potential governesses who might be worthy of watching the children. She would begin the interviews first thing in the morning.

"Don't leave."

A touch at her elbow stilled her hands. She was enveloped by the warmth emanating from Quade's fingertips, engulfed by the masculine fragrance of sunshine and labor exuding from his closeness, lured by the seduction in his voice. Was she so easily seduced that he suspected her of being attentive to any man's touch?

Randy leaned from her father's arms and wrapped a small hand around Meredith's neck. Pressing a kiss on her governess's head, she pleaded, "Don't be angry, Miss

Meredith. Alex says not-smart things sometimes.''

"Not-smart? You barnacle brain—''

"Alexandra!'' Though softly spoken, Quade's admonishment boomed as loudly as the thunder above the bay.

"Well, Father, she is sometimes. You don't know, you're gone too oft—well, you just don't hear her sometimes,'' Alex defended herself. "Besides, Shanty says the truth is always the smart thing to say, and you've always told us to listen to what Shanty tells us. What I said *is* the truth. If there were less of us to watch, Miss Meredith's job would be easier. Isn't that so?''

Meredith could still feel the strength of Quade's hand on her elbow, as if he truly didn't want to let her go. She tried to focus her attention on the escalating animosity between the children. Randy stuck her tongue out at Alex, but the eldest sibling remained unconcerned with her sister's antics. Instead, Alexandra stared expectantly at the captain for affirmation. Her eyes widened just long enough for Meredith to recognize the same vulnerability she'd seen earlier when Alex had thrown herself into Meredith's arms. The captain's answer held more weight than he might realize.

"It's always *seems* easier when there are less to consider.'' Quade tapped Randy's nose as his expression turned stern.

The pink tip of her tongue disappeared into her mouth and she whispered, "I'm sorry, Papa. I won't do it again.''

Alexandra looked crushed as she turned and stared out into the storm-filled sky.

"But this family never settles for easier,'' Quade reminded them, placing a comforting hand upon Alexandra's shoulder while he jostled Randy to a better position on his hip. "One person can be a handful, while three might be well-behaved. It depends upon the individual. Some are oysters, others are pearls. Personally, I'd rather have three little pearls rather than a bay full of oysters.''

"I know you're busy with the committee, Captain.'' Meredith wondered whether he noticed that the eleven-year-old looked as if she carried the weight of the world upon her shoulders. "So, I'll begin interviewing for a new governess in the morning." She wanted to be as far away as possible from him and the effect he had upon her.

"Whatever for, Miss Stanfield? Shanty should return tomorrow or the next day," he reminded. "Of course, if your other *duties* are that pressing, I'll order you a carriage for home immediately."

"The only *duty* that concerns me at the moment is to see that the children are not placed in harm's way." His innuendo charged the air between them as if a lightning bolt had struck inches away. Whether her and Nolan's relationship was anything more than a business acquaintance was none of Quade Cameron's concern. She would not stand here and bicker with him, no matter how well he attempted to hide his true meaning from the children. "I cannot in good conscience watch you sacrifice such precious gems to the whims of a watery fate."

"They're talking about us," Randy announced to her sisters, looking pleased with her cleverness.

Samantha held a finger up to her lips and shook her head to hush the child, but Alex was not to be bested.

"They're talking about a lot of things, barnacle brain. Us and Mr. Richards." Alex frowned at her father. "Why are you trying to drive her away from us?"

"I'm not driving her away, General." Surprise at his children's astuteness darkened his eyes. "She's choosing to leave." His attention directed itself at Meredith. "I don't intend to endanger my children, Miss Stanfield, but I will keep my promise to them. We'll just have to walk the beach until the storm subsides, *then* we'll swim. I was *about* to say, we will go swimming, even if it doesn't blow over until midnight. After all, a promise given should be a promise kept."

Had he read her thoughts so easily? Did he know that she needed to believe words were something more than an agreement on paper? That once spoken, they should be honored literally and emotionally? He was promising *her* something. She read the hidden vow darkening the sea-green depths of his eyes but was uncertain what he pledged. To discover whether she and Nolan were lovers? Her heart wanted to believe that he promised so much more, yet experience had taught her to expect less.

"Stay, Meredith. At least until Shanty returns. Join us at the shore."

He was reaching out to her, as he had in the dream. Plucking her from the sea . . . and her fear of it? Or was he merely hoping to detain her from access to his business rival?

"Papa can swim like a fish," Randy boasted. "And Alexandra too. But Sam and me, we like to find the shells that the waves leave behind."

"You should put them back so they can find their way home," Alexandra censured, "instead of making necklaces out of them."

Surprised at the compassion that spurred Alexandra's reproach, Meredith realized that deep currents ran within the youth—currents that might spring from a well of past hurt. She was too guarded in her father's company, yet needful of his regard. Getting to know Alexandra, and perhaps help her, was reason enough to stay. Making certain that the gulf never again stole someone she cared for provided the incentive to agree. Meredith set aside her anger with Quade's insinuations in order to help Alex.

"All right, Captain. You win. But just until Shanty returns. Then I'll visit the girls for an hour or two each day to help them prepare for the title, if that's acceptable to you."

"But Miss Merry, we *like* you staying with us," Randy complained. "We want you to stay forever and ever."

Samantha moved away from the window and sat on the chair farthest from the group, rubbing her hands over both arms as if she were bracing herself from the cold. She didn't utter a word. Her eyes stared down at her lap.

Meredith thought she saw tears and hurried over to kneel beside Sam. "I didn't say I wouldn't be back, Sammy. I'll visit every day." Her promise became a vow.

Samantha glanced up, blinking back the shimmer of

emotion that filled her blue eyes. "It won't be the same, Miss Meredith. You'll get busy and forget about us." She reached out tentatively, touched Meredith's hand, and pledged vehemently, "But I won't forget you . . . ever."

Compelled by the love welling in her heart for the three children, particularly for this child, Meredith wrapped her arms around Samantha and held her to her bosom. "Sweet Sam. So loving. So needing to be loved. Don't you know that I already do? Nothing will ever change that. Not time or distance or anything on this earth will ever change the fact that you are now a child of my heart."

Samantha threw her arms around Meredith and began to cry in earnest. But these were tears of joy, tears of discovery, tears of belonging.

"Me too, Miss Meredith?" Randy squirmed to get down. Her father released her, and the six-year-old rushed into the embrace both Sam and Meredith offered.

Meredith looked hopefully at Alexandra, but the eldest sister seemed unaffected. Finally, Alex strolled over and patted Samantha on the back, offering no words of reassurance and refusing to be included in the emotional outpouring. Meredith accepted Alex's guarded endorsement, hoping that one day the girl might trust her without reserve.

"Now that *that* is settled, why don't we go for a walk? I think it will do us all some good." Quade's tone was sharp.

Meredith was puzzled. He seemed angry at her. Did he disapprove of her confessing how much she'd grown to care for his children? Or had something else stirred his ire?

"I'll gather towels and a couple of lanterns," she informed him. Perhaps he wanted time alone with the children, and she was an unwanted presence. "And cover the gumbo so we can take it with us in the event anyone gets hungry."

"Forget the lanterns. The moon's full tonight. You'll be able to see for leagues." Quade stooped and handed Meredith the ribbon he'd taken from her hair. When their fingers touched, his lingered for an instant, then darted away.

''Well enough to follow someone if necessary?'' She stared him squarely in the eye, grateful that the opportunity had arisen to challenge him on the subject. How great his anger would become if he knew that Nolan had informed her about the captain's shadowing of her movements.

He acknowledged her cleverness. ''Well enough to waylay any distractions. Get the towels and cover the pot. I need to talk to the children for a moment, if you'll excuse us.''

''Of course.'' Meredith went into the kitchen to busy herself with tidying up the mess she'd left on the table. Though he seemed only to need a private moment with the girls, she couldn't shake the notion that he was angry with her. More than angry . . . furious about something. Could it be that the children wanted her near and admitted it openly?

Or was it that he wanted her too and refused to admit it to himself?

❖ 9 ❖

Darkness invaded the day, cloaking Biloxi with a blanket of stars and stirring delicate scents from flowering vines and lush foliage. Breezes trailing the storm offered a reprieve from the day's heat, keeping the rain-washed sand soft and cool beneath their bare feet.

Meredith felt almost at peace, walking hand in hand with Samantha along the beach. Quade and Randy strolled a few yards ahead, close enough to the surf to allow the waves to wash over Randy's feet and make her giggle. Alex walked in front of them all, as if it were her mission always to lead.

A pair of terns wheeled in wide circles beneath the clouds, riding upward on the currents of the storm, then gliding downward. With a laugh, Meredith drew attention to the birds' antics. When her neck cramped from watching too long, she discovered that Quade's attention was not upon the frolicsome flight but rather boldly measuring the length of her.

The muslin dress covered Meredith from neck to ankle, as did the bathing costumes worn by each of the girls. But his gaze seemed to strip away the layers of her clothing, warming her skin as if it were the sun taking the chill of winter from her bones.

A hand tugged upon her own, pulling Meredith toward

the water and breaking the spell Quade's look had cast upon her.

"Come on, Miss Meredith. Let's wade." Samantha let go of her hand and rushed into the surf. The child's knees bounced so high and her hands swung so wildly that she looked like a flamenco dancer.

"Be careful," Meredith called out, but the child had already ventured farther into the shallows than Meredith ever dared go. She watched Quade and Randy join her.

"Don't worry. They're good swimmers." Alex retraced her steps and halted beside Meredith. "We all are. Father taught us from the time we were two. He said a captain's daughter should know the sea well."

"Did he tell you of its dangers?" Meredith whispered before she thought. When she realized she might have caused a chord of fear within Alexandra, she attempted to correct her blunder. "What I meant was—"

"He told us never to go in alone without him . . . or at least with someone who can swim better than us, if that's what you mean. But he didn't want us to be afraid of the water." Her attention averted from her family to stare up at Meredith. "Is there anything you're frightened of, Miss Meredith?"

Your father, she wanted to say, but decided it was best to talk about fears she could define. "I prefer to enjoy the gulf from a distance. As a young girl, I swam in it constantly. The Sound was my home away from home. So much so that my father nicknamed me Mermaid. But that was years ago." *A lifetime and a love ago.*

"Are you afraid to get your hair wet?"

Meredith laughed, lifting a strand of hair still unbound by ribbon. "You don't think me that vain, do you?"

"Your sister is."

"I'm not Savannah."

"That's what I told Father a while ago."

Curiosity got the best of Meredith. The discussion that had taken place while she gathered towels had been lengthy. The girls seemed more awkward in her presence since leaving the Cameron quarters. "Why would he think I'm anything like Savannah?"

Alex reached down and picked up a seashell. When the next wave rushed in, she set the shell adrift.

"Why did he compare me to Savannah?" Meredith repeated, wondering if the child was deliberately ignoring her.

"He said that privileged people often take on projects out of charity and a sense of obligation to the community, but they'd really rather spend their time doing other things. Sort of like Miss Savannah wanting to be with that man named Pierre instead of making the cake for the festival. Father said that we needed to remember that you were an extremely busy lady, and we shouldn't expect much of your time once Shanty returns."

Indignation boiled inside Meredith. "Did he say that I wouldn't keep my promise? That I didn't mean it when I said I love you girls?"

"Nothing like that. He just said to enjoy you while you were with us."

"Oh, he did, did he?" The indignation erupted into a volcanic rush of fury. He had no right to make the children believe she would enter their lives, tell them she loved them, then fade from sight because they were an expense of time she might think wasted. How dare he encourage such lack of trust! How dare he not give her the opportunity to prove she would not abandon them as she had been abandoned! How dare he belittle the love that had blossomed in her heart for his children. *Motherless* children, at that!

"Please go and tell the captain I must speak to him."

Alex shook her head. "He won't come out as long as the girls are in the water. You'll have to go to him."

For just a moment, Meredith's resolve faltered. The lapping of the waves upon the shore defined the tide's increased pull, stirred by the storm's wake. She couldn't risk leaving the children unchaperoned. But a glance at Randy and Samantha easily maneuvering within the spirited surf encouraged her to act with a boldness she prayed would not leave her upon entering the water—a boldness that defied the fear so deeply instilled within her.

She set down the picnic basket she'd brought for later and made sure it was far enough away from the incoming waves that the food would not be soaked.

One step at a time, Meredith. Her teeth gritted back the tension engulfing her. A wave rushed over her feet. The chill of apprehension swept up her ankles, stiffening her legs and knees until she had to will them into moving, bending.

Take a deep breath. The water is not over the children's heads. Quade is there.

The realization that he would save her if she ran into trouble both relieved and irritated Meredith. She wanted to maintain the vexation she felt toward him, but it abated with every step deeper into the gulf.

"Miss Meredith, watch out!" Samantha yelled.

A giggle and then a slapping sound were her only warning. A surge of water splashed over Meredith's face, drenching her from head to waist.

Meredith sputtered, frantically brushing the water from her eyes in time to see Randy's second attempt to soak her. She blocked her face to keep from getting saturated. "Stop that, Randy! You'll make me fall." To Quade, she sputtered, "I n-need to speak to you immediately, but I'd prefer to do so ashore."

Randy's hands halted their attack, paddling to keep her afloat. "I was only playing." Hurt filled her tone.

"Keeping someone from seeing while in the water is dangerous and not considered play." Meredith's reprimand sounded harsh to her own ears, but she knew from days past that she must set boundaries for Randy or the child would test her very limits.

Quade swam up behind his daughter and lifted her onto his shoulders. "Come, Muffin. Miss Stanfield is right. Let's go rest a bit and see what's so important that she had to wade out here and interrupt our good time."

Meredith remembered every excruciating step back to shore. Everything inside her wanted to run as fast as she could toward the safety of the beach. Instead, she refused to let him witness how terror-ridden she found the effort.

"Ho, the beach!" A familiar voice hailed them from the promenade several yards downshore. A lantern swung back and forth, back and forth. "Captain, is that you and the blossoms?"

Quade jogged out of the surf, carrying Randy aloft as if she were a human headdress. "It is, Yori. And Miss Stanfield, as well." He almost stumbled on the basket of food. "We're to have a picnic, it seems."

"Care if Miss Shanty and I join you?"

"Shanty's back! Shanty's back!" Randy jostled up and down on her father's shoulders, her hands slipping down to cover his eyes.

"Watch it, Muffin. You'll break both our necks." Quade grabbed the palms locked over his face, separating them until both his and Randy's arms spread like eagles' wings. "By all means, join us."

To everyone's surprise, only one form approached. As the giant man drew nearer, Meredith saw that he carried Shanty in his arms. A splint encased the woman's leg.

"Howdy, my gally-girls! Don'tcha all look soaked and sassy." Shanty tapped on Yori's shoulder. He let her down gently, allowing her to find firm footing. "Why, I've only been gone a week, and you done went and grew up on me."

"Ooh, Miss Shanty, does it hurt?" Randy asked, running up to trace a finger of concern along the splint.

"Only when I walk, child." Shanty laughed at her own joke.

"Hand me one of those towels, will you?" Quade whispered to Meredith.

"Wh-what?" she stammered, suddenly realizing what he'd said, but not quickly enough to beat him at retrieving a towel from the basket.

He spread the linen on the ground. "Sit here, Shanty, and rest yourself. Tell us how it happened."

Yori and Quade helped lower her to the sand. All three girls waited patiently. After their father and Yori backed away, the children immediately took a seat next to the shrimp shop owner. Faces eager for every detail stared up at the mop-haired woman, waiting earnestly for her to speak.

"Well, you see, it was like this . . . me and Gizelda were walking the deck of the Flying Tecumseh, enjoying the blow of the storm that just passed, when suddenly a monster swell crashed over the bow and swept me over—"

"*Shanty*." The pitch of Quade's voice brooked no argument. "The truth."

Meredith discovered that her breath had caught in her throat, and quickly expelled it into the night.

"All right, all right. So I slipped on the floor where some fool missed the spittoon. It just ain't as exciting, Cap'n, to tell it that way. Folks wanna know a gal's had an adventure when she sallies off to N'Orleans."

Yori rummaged through the picnic basket and lifted a crock. "Now *this* smells adventurous. Big Yori's had nothing but his own cooking today. He'll give the owner of this bowl two bits or a kiss for a bite, whichever she prefers."

"Take the kiss, take the kiss," Randy chanted, eyeing Meredith. "I've seen him kiss Miss Winkle. She always looks real happy when he does."

Shanty deliberately held up the lantern. "Well, if the moon ain't conspicuousing them cheeks, this ought to. You ought to be ashamed of yourself, Yori Svengsen. Kissing in front of my gally-girls like that."

Sure enough, the Norwegian's cheeks were stained a healthy shade of crimson. "I had no idea they were around."

" 'Course he didn't," Randy defended. "We were spying on them."

"Randy!" Samantha and Alexandra complained simultaneously.

"Now we're in for it." Alex pinched the six-year-old's arm.

"Papa, she hurt me."

"I'll hurt you more if you—"

"Enough of that, girls." Quade pulled the two apart. "We'll discuss this *and* spying on Mr. Svengsen before we turn in."

"Which will it be, gally-girl?" Shanty coaxed. "The kiss or the two bits?" She winked. "Personally, I'd take the kiss, too. *I've* watched him with more than Miss Winkle, and Randy's right. They all walk away purty dad-gummed pleased."

Yori leaned to give Shanty a huge smack on her chubby cheek. "I am thinking, that goes for you too, old woman."

"Just 'cause my leg is gimpy, don't mean the rest of me—"

"The children," Quade reminded.

It was Shanty's turn to blush from cheek to double chin.

Meredith decided it was time to save Shanty from her rowdy self. "Well, actually, it's the *captain's* bowl, Mr. Svengsen. I only cooked the gumbo. The decision is up to him which he wants."

"In that case, come here, big fellow." Yori puckered and flung his arms open wide. "I am out of funds and was hoping the moonlit night would work in my favor, *ja*?"

Samantha giggled. Alexandra's eyes attempted to lift into her eyebrows, and Randy looked completely puzzled.

"Boys are supposed to kiss *girls*," the six-year-old announced to the shucker. "Ain't that so, Papa?"

"Most definitely, Miranda. And, by the way," Quade reached over and pressed a kiss upon Meredith's cheek, "I don't remember thanking you properly for fixing the gumbo, Miss Stanfield. It was above and beyond the agreement made."

Meredith's fingers pressed against the cheek his lips had brushed, unconsciously sliding to her mouth as if she could transfer his touch there. Thoughts escaped her as she fought to remember her earlier anger with him and to rouse the same indignation now. Everyone stared at her. Especially Shanty.

"And just what agreement was that?" Shanty's gaze shifted from Meredith to Quade, then back again to Meredith.

"I told him about the deal you and I made. He's allowed me to care for the girls until your return." Meredith attempted to calm the sensations rushing through her.

"Ye gally-girls feel comfortable with Miss Meredith?" Shanty stared at each child. Samantha and Randy readily agreed. Alexandra even consented without too much hesitance. "Good then. 'Cause ye're gonna have to count on her longer than I'd planned. Doc Bill said I ain't to be jump-bumping around on this here leg. All I gotta do to get ready for the festival ain't gonna leave me much juice to chase after ye young'uns."

Randy swung around to question the captain. "Does that mean Miss Meredith gets to stay with us, Papa?"

"It doesn't seem we have much choice, does it?"

Quade's intense regard enveloped Meredith. His words were rife with innuendo. One minute the man was kissing her, the next he acted as if she were the plague. "You do have an option, Captain. I can start the interviewing process in the morning, if Miss Andrews doesn't mind helping watch the girls while I'm actually conducting the interviews. In the interim, I can assist her in putting up her decorations. We can be of great help to one another."

"You'd do that?" Appreciation eased Shanty's features.

"Of course. Wouldn't you if I were the one injured?"

"Well, yes, but you're from Plantation—"

"Row? We're not so different, you and I, Shanty. I just happened to be fortunate enough to have a father who invested wisely. That's the only difference."

"Tell that to your sister." Yori thumped a spoon against his palm as if striking out at an injustice.

An emotion Meredith did not recognize echoed in the Norwegian's statement. There was something definitely afoot here. What had her sister done to instill such bitter feelings, and why did the watermen and women have such a low opinion of Angeline Stanfield's elder daughter? She must rectify the situation and question her selfish sibling at the first opportunity. "Is that agreeable to you, Captain?"

"Like I said—" He lightly tapped Shanty's splint. "—I have no other alternative. You've got to get back to doing what Stanfields do best, and I . . . well, I must keep my word to the committee."

Promises given. Promises kept. Is that what he was reminding her of now? She had pledged to keep the children until Shanty could replace her. But she hadn't expected Shanty to return incapable of seeing to their care. Meredith was torn between honoring her word or getting as far and fast away from Quade Cameron as possible.

He tested her willpower too greatly, making her yearn to break a promise she'd made long ago to a man who'd been swept away at sea—a vow that she would never care for another as deeply as she had cared for Phillip.

❖ *10* ❖

"CAN WE GO play now?" Randy squirmed in her chair for the sixth time in less than thirty minutes. Though a pleasant breeze blew through the shaded deck, the child had pleaded all morning to be set free.

At least Randy waited until the woman was out of earshot. The eighth governess walked away from Shanty's shack. Meredith was surprised that she felt both disappointed and relieved.

"Looky there at Dooley. Lovinia's gonna catch him for sure this time!" Randy craned her neck to watch the antics of other children darting in and out of the multitude of booths. Vendors, entertainers, and workers toiled diligently to prepare the wharf area for the coming festival. She clamped both hands over her mouth and closed her eyes.

"Eeeuuuww! Lovinia caught him. I ain't never gonna kiss *him* ever again."

Surprise registered on both sisters' faces as they stared at the youngest Cameron.

"You kissed Dooley Duckworth?" Alexandra's fists knotted upon her hips. "Papa will be furious."

Randy shrugged her shoulders. "Sure I did. He dared me to, so I did. If you tell Papa, I'm gonna tell him you—"

"Shhh!" Samantha held one finger to her lips. "There's still other ladies Miss Meredith wants to interview. She doesn't want them to hear us fussing. No one will want to take care of us."

"She's just wasting her time." Alexandra's eyes focused on the hustle and bustle that had occupied the seaport since long before dawn. Gone was the blossoming young lady ready to experience first love, the serious pacesetter compelled to lead, the initiator of most of the arguments. In her place was a child of eleven, ready to shed her boredom and be enraptured by fun. "Nobody wants three brats to look after anyway. *Nobody*."

Samantha became dutifully silent. Meredith saw hope in Sam's eyes but was uncertain whether she hoped to correct Alexandra's gloomy verdict or be set free from the interviewing.

"Don't seem fair making the young'uns waste any more of this dandy fine day," Shanty remarked, finishing the last stitch on the final pennant of the multicolored streamer she'd been devising all morning. "Ain't a one of them women choice enough to look after my gallygirls. Ye got these young'uns spoiled, Meredith Stanfield. Can't blame a solitary soul but yerself."

Though Shanty was correct in her estimation, Meredith felt compelled to continue the process until she found someone "choice enough" for the children. "Surely, we'll find one among these you'll like." Meredith stressed her conviction. "In fact, I believe the most likely prospect is next. Mrs. Sally Kirkland Price."

"But I want *you*, Miss Merry," Randy insisted, getting up from her chair to help Shanty struggle to her feet. Everyone else did the same.

"Me too, Miss Meredith." Sam's soul shone in her eyes. "*Nobody* is as good as you are with us."

Affection streamed through Meredith. The sincerity in both girl's voices brought her near to tears when Alex joined in.

"We're used to you now," the eleven-year-old granted. The shrimp shop owner gently gripped Randy's shoulder long enough to get her bearings, then proceeded to nail the streamer to the eastern corner of her shop.

"Here, let me do that for you." Meredith took the streamer from her friend. "I'll hold the nail while you hammer. There you go. Is that too high?"

"Lower that mast, Meredith. They'll just have to duck a mite if they're gonna buy from me."

Laughter brought tears to Meredith's eyes. She shed the tears without restraint, grateful for the excuse to cry without causing anyone worry. Her emotions had been off kilter all morning for reasons she couldn't name until now. She did not want anyone else caring for the girls. She loved watching them, teaching them, sharing their laughter and their view of the world. She would miss Randy's antics, Sam's sweet smiles and gentle kindnesses, Alexandra's bossiness. Why must she insist upon breaking her own heart by hiring someone to do what she'd come to treasure this past week?

Because you're afraid to be too near their father, her heart whispered.

"I'm not afraid of you, Quade Cameron," Meredith defended as she tied the streamer around the nail to make certain it was secured against any coming wind.

"What'd you say, gally-girl?" Shanty glanced up at her.

Flustered, Meredith realized she'd spoken the words aloud. "I s-said, I'm afraid if we don't tighten this down, Quade Cameron will complain about it being too loose."

"That isn't so, Miss Merry," Randy corrected. "You said you weren't afraid of—"

"Yes, dear, but I misstated what I meant and said it better the second time." She hastened to urge Randy back into her chair. "Now, let's prepare ourselves for the next interview."

An audible complaint resounded over the deck, but each child proved well-mannered enough to wipe the disappointment from her face. They greeted Mrs. Price with their best manners—credit due Captain Cameron.

"Good morning, Miss Stanfield." The slim, elderly

woman closed her parasol and took the seat opposite Meredith. She slid a bound stack of documents across the table for Meredith's inspection. "I have other credentials, but chose those I thought most appropriate to your needs."

Meredith scanned the papers.

Widow Price smiled at each of the girls and then at the shrimp shop owner. "Children . . . Miss Andrews. I trust you're all having a pleasant day?"

"We will be when we don't have to interview no more," Randy announced, then realized she'd said something rude. Her palm pressed her lips as if to make certain nothing else unpleasant exited.

The widow laughed and winked. "It is rather difficult to sit and watch wrinkled old faces and listen to boring talk when one is full of vim and vigor. You want to go and have some experiences of your own . . . don't you, little one?"

Meredith glanced at Randy and watched understanding dawn on the six-year-old's face.

"You mean, you don't mind if we go play?" Randy stood. "We don't have to stay here and let you look at us?"

Mrs. Price's gloved hands rested atop the tip of her parasol. "I've known your family for years, precious. Nothing Quade Cameron or his children might do would surprise me. I've raised four rascals of my own and survived the big conflict between the States. I believe I'm quite capable of dealing with three spirited and might I say lovely young ladies."

"You knew my mother?" Awe etched Samantha's features.

"Yes, dear. She was quite the beauty, as I recall. But age has its way with memory, I'm afraid."

Meredith studied Alex closely, wondering why she suddenly walked from the deck's shade and into the bright sun.

"She wasn't so pretty." Alex rubbed her arms as if

warding off a chill. "I was five when she : . . died. I remember."

A look of compassion passed between the adults. The child was hurting, still gripped in denial, often a part of grief. As survivors of the terrible war, all of them had witnessed this stage in too many of their friends and families.

"We all have times when we are and are not so beautiful. God welcomes us nevertheless." Mrs. Price's sympathetic gaze focused on Alex. "Would that we all were so loving as He."

"I guess I'll take her if she can cook." Randy gave Mrs. Price her stamp of approval.

"Me too." Samantha smiled shyly at the woman.

"Ain't many finer than Sally Kirkland Price." Shanty's mop of colorful hair bobbed in approval. "She can out-manner any lady on the coast and then some."

"And you, Alex?" Meredith's voice cracked, though she tried not to show the anxiety flooding her. Having Shanty's approval along with two of the three Cameron children was enough to forewarn her that she was about to achieve her morning's goal. Meredith's pulse thrummed in her ears. Her cheeks and mouth tightened. Bile worked its way up from the pit of her stomach to burn at the edge of her throat. Tears threatened to wet her eyes, though her mouth lost all moisture. She blinked back the sadness, trying hard to face the reality of her decision.

"If *you* won't be our governess," Alexandra turned her face from everyone and said over her shoulder, "then I guess she'll do."

Unanimous. Like a sail without wind, Meredith suddenly felt deflated. She'd accomplished what she had set out to do—to find the most qualified person available and to make certain that all three children agreed on her selection. So why didn't she feel more triumphant?

"Well," she exhaled with a deep sigh, "it looks like we've got that settled. I'll inform the captain of our choice and show him your credentials, Mrs. Price. Of course, it will be his ultimate decision whether or not to acquire your services.''

"Please call me Sally.''

"Thank you for your time, Sally. I'll let you know his decision as soon as possible.''

"No hurry, I hadn't planned to work until fall. Since I've completed my preparations for the festival, I have extra time on my hands. I'll be helping Miss Winkle with her booth until I hear from you. You can find me there if I'm not at home.''

"May we go now?'' Samantha grabbed Randy's hand. "I spotted Papa down at Yori's. He'll buy us a beignet and lemonade at Mrs. Paxton's, if we catch him before lunch.''

"Go on and play. Tell your father I'll join you in a couple of hours.'' Needing no further encouragement, the girls raced up the promenade to join in the activity. Though the powdered pastry sounded appetizing, Meredith doubted she could eat a bite. She needed time to regain control of her emotions and to see to Shanty's lunch.

"Don't you worry 'bout my lunch, Missy. Gizelda's coming by today and bringing me her special Romanian roast. In fact, she's gonna spend the afternoon with me, telling my fortune and conjuring me up husband number five.'' Shanty patted her splint. "I told her he better be a lumberjack, 'cause he's gonna hafta be strong to lift this old gal. Told her I want me a Yori with about twenty more years on him.''

"Yori is a wonderful man, isn't he?'' Meredith spied the Norwegian at his shucking house. Quade stood beside him, leaning down to listen intently to what Randy was saying. The captain's arm reached out and pulled Alexandra to him. She allowed him to hold her, finally encircling his waist with her arm. Meredith smiled. She respected a man who sensed when a child needed special attention.

"Yori's as good as they come, but in my way of thinking, gally-girl, there's one better.''

"Who?" Meredith swung around to question the shrimp shop owner.

Shanty looked her squarely in the eye. "The father of those children ye love and are gonna turn over to a total stranger. Ye are, aren't ye, gally-girl?"

Quade couldn't believe that Meredith had actually found a replacement so quickly. He should be happy about the hiring of Mrs. Price, but he couldn't help being more than disappointed that Meredith hadn't kept her word. She'd promised to watch the girls until Shanty could. Granted, she'd thought that would be only a week. But a person's word was her bond . . . no matter how long it must be kept.

He'd watched Meredith turn away the other ladies lined up for interviews and was surprised when she left soon after the fortune teller paid a visit. More unexpected was the fact that Meredith had not come straight to him to brag about the ease in which she'd secured her replacement. In fact, the hour was getting late and unless she returned for the children, he would be late to his meeting with Donald Paxton about the festival's security.

Where were the girls anyway? He'd gotten so busy discussing the schedule of races with One-Eyed Thomas that he had let the time get away from him. The three of them had wanted to meet the notorious Nelda Jo, a woman proclaimed as a spy by some, heralded as a hero by others. Her pigeons had flown messages between New Orleans and St. Louis during the war. Now, the birds would carry instructions from boat to boat as needed during the floating parade to ensure suitable distance and speed between each.

"Look there!" Yori pointed at a furious Elise Winkle marching down the boardwalk toward the open-air pastry booth. She bore down upon them like a warship, the sails of her feathered bonnet flapping askew, her voluptuous bosom bouncing jauntily.

One-Eyed Thomas squinted to see what had captured Yori's attention.

"The banker's daughter seems a bit ruffled, I am thinking." Yori set down his glass and scooted back his chair. "I've seen that look before, it is one of those I-am-going-to-yank-your-children-baldheaded-if-you-don't-make-them-behave expressions, *ja*?"

The sight of Meredith making her way toward him, with her sister in tow, distracted Quade. Then Yori's meaning sank in, and he focused on the banker's daughter. "Yes, seems my girls are up to something, doesn't it? I let them out of my sight a minute too long, didn't I?"

Thomas punched Quade playfully on the arm. "They *are* Camerons, after all."

"Yes, they are." Quade rocked back on his booted heels, but his smile disappeared instantly as Elise barged around Meredith and Savannah to make certain she caught Quade's attention first.

"Captain Cameron, I must speak with you this instant." The flustered woman came to an abrupt halt. "Your children owe me an apology, and *you* must reimburse me for the damage they've done."

Nolan Richards divided the crowd, making his way to stand beside the banker's daughter.

Quade and his two friends rose. "Just what have my darling daughters done to distress you so, Miss Winkle?"

"Captain, may I be of help?" Meredith stepped forward, making her presence known to Elise.

"It seems we've let our handfuls out of sight just long enough for them to create a bit of mischief, I'm afraid."

"A bit of mischief? A *bit* of mischief, you say?" Elise's face turned several shades of purple. "They've destroyed it. Completely and totally destroyed it!"

"Destroyed what?" Savannah placed a reassuring arm around Elise's shoulders as the woman began to weep. Nolan offered her a hankie.

"My booth! The ribbons and lace." Elise dabbed her eyes and handed the soiled linen back to him. "And they were so perfect. Then that *heathen* child—" She indicated the height of Quade's youngest daughter. "—pitched bread crumbs on the roof, and the other two joined her. The seagulls tore—''

Frosted silver-blue pools warned all that the banker's daughter had overstepped her bounds. A rush of pride and gratitude warmed Quade while Meredith's silent warning eliminated the need for him to defend his daughters' character.

''Those children should be watched,'' Elise sniffled, her chin rising defiantly at Meredith. ''And more closely.'' She could not meet Meredith's gaze for long and finally looked for support among the gathering crowd. Nolan offered Elise his handkerchief.

The trio of girls raced up the promenade, pushing through the crowd to reach their father. Randy slammed against Quade's leg and hugged him, leaning backward to look up with innocent eyes.

''Whatever she said I did, Papa, I didn't do it.''

''Well, actually, we did, Papa.'' Samantha edged close to Meredith and grabbed her hand for support. ''But it's not what you're thinking.''

''Alexandra Estelle.'' Quade watched his oldest daughter's expression as she halted in front of him. ''Is there any truth to what Miss Winkle claims? Did you girls deliberately cause the seagulls to tear up her booth by throwing them food?''

''Deliberately?'' Alex hedged. ''No. Nelda Jo said we could train a bird to do what we wanted. So, Randy pitched a bread crumb. It happened to land on Miss Winkle's booth. One seagull saw the crumb. Then you know how they act. If one sees another one eating, pretty soon there's dozens of them. It was an accident.''

''Accident, my one eye!'' One-Eyed Thomas teased.

Elise fanned herself elaborately. ''I expect full compensation.''

''Justly so,'' Nolan insisted, rousing others in the crowd to agree.

''I'll pay it,'' Meredith announced. ''The children were in my care. It should be my expense.''

''*I* pay for *my* children's mistakes,'' Quade reminded

her. His gaze locked on Meredith's, though his words were targeted at both her and Elise Winkle. "And as the girls informed me a while ago, you're no longer responsible for their care."

"Oh, but I am, Captain. You see, I've decided that a promise given is indeed a promise to be kept. I will continue to be the children's governess until Shanty is *fully* recovered."

A conspiratorial glance passed between the three children, causing Quade to stifle a chuckle. Their actions had definitely been no accident.

"What?" Savannah held tightly to Elise's arm. "You can't mean that, Meredith! What about Mother and I? We couldn't possibly run the house, the business, by ourselves. We don't—"

Yori was instantly at her side. "I can be of help to you, I am thinking. I love nothing more than a hardy challenge and the privilege to rescue such a beautiful lady, *ja*?"

"*Ja* . . . I mean, yes." Savannah blushed to her brunette roots. "Why, thank you, Mr. Svengsen."

"Yori?" Elise Winkle looked as if she'd been abandoned. Nolan Richards appeared to be insulted by her instant disregard of his presence.

"Just ask Miss Winkle." Yori beamed. "I've rescued *her* before."

Elise spun on her heels and marched away. Over her shoulder, she shouted that she would take the matter up with her father. Furthermore, the captain could expect a visit from the banker this evening.

Everyone chattered. Randy and Alexandra in their own defense. Samantha in an attempt to tell a true accounting of the actual offense. One-Eyed Thomas relating a tale of equal mischief about Quade when he was their age. Yori assuring Savannah that he barely knew the banker's daughter, and they were mere acquaintances. But it was Meredith's words Quade wanted to hear.

He moved closer to her. "You'll stay then?"

Their gazes intertwined. She nodded.

"What about Mrs. Price? The girls said she was perfect." He noticed that Meredith's breathing took on a hurried pace.

"Almost. She lacked one essential qualification."

"Which was?"

A becoming shade of coral colored the exposed skin of Meredith's neck and face. "Nowhere in her credentials did it say she knows how to keep a promise."

"And you do?" His own pulse raced to match the beat he saw throbbing in the hollow of her neck.

"I'd like to try." Her words were but a whisper as she added, "If you want me."

"Oh, I want you—" The rhythm of his heart settled into a steady, insistent cadence. "—and need you . . . for the girls, that is."

"Don't be taken in, Meredith," Nolan warned from a few feet away. "He and his brood are most likely running short of finances."

The man had no business eavesdropping on their conversation. It took every good manner Quade could rouse to keep his tone low and pleasant. "At least, Richards, I can honestly say I'm not running *from* anything. If I were Miss Stanfield, I believe I would make quite certain you could boast the same."

Tension layered the space that separated the two men until Meredith stepped between them. "Gentlemen, what you both need to understand is that most people consider me gentle natured and good humored. But make no mistake: that even temper is of my own choosing. I'm quite capable of knowing which of you is using me to his own end. Therefore . . ."

Quade witnessed the same squared set of shoulders, stubborn tilt of chin, and conviction glinting from her eyes that he'd experienced when she'd denied him the loan.

". . . do not underestimate me."

❖ *11* ❖

QUADE LAID DOWN his hammer and decided to rest a moment while he waited for Yori to stop showing off for the lady. Never relaxing completely, he grabbed the ever-growing list of activities planned for the festival. For the second time, he scanned the children's games to make sure he had covered every detail.

He had brooded over Meredith's words all afternoon, to the point that he sorely lacked concentration. He may have intentionally set out to know her better, but under no circumstances would he try to use her. God knew he didn't want to feel the passion that stirred inside him every time she drew near.

Get your mind on your work, Cameron. Quade gratefully retreated to the one oblivion that kept him from thinking and feeling. Frog jumping, sand castle building, and tug-of-war needed one type of location, whereas the knotting competition, sack races, and net throwing needed another. Best not forget the Maypole dancing and the siren songs or little Randy would protest loudly.

"This is all fine and good, but why isn't Alvina Bradshaw overseeing this aspect as she usually does?" he asked Yori while the Norwegian displayed his agility at knotting ropes.

Savannah twirled her parasol jauntily and counted off

the seconds for Yori. "Forty-eight, forty-nine, fifty. Just a minute, Captain, and he'll answer you. Sixty! Oooh, Yori, you're the fastest man on the coast! Imagine, fifty-seven knots in one minute. You'll win for certain!"

"Svengsen, can't that wait until later? We've got to get this bandstand finished before dark." Quade's patience had run out. "And I could use some help deciding what to do here. Alvina's backed out after all that fuss about it being a tradition for her to start the races."

Yori dropped the rope he'd been knotting and offered Savannah his arm. "You been on the wrong side of tomorrow ever since Meredith told you she would stay on. Why don't you yist admit you—" Yori paused, glanced at his visitor, then chose his words carefully. *"Ønoske* her?"

Savannah's hazel eyes widened. "You mean, he and Meredith are sweet on each other? He wants her?"

Surprise registered across Yori's face. "You know what I am speaking?"

"Ja, kjeereste, I am fluent in four languages."

"Every word I've said to you all afternoon?"

She nodded and twirled her parasol playfully.

"Yori Svengsen is in big trouble, I am thinking."

Grateful for Yori's blustering, Quade tried to get a handle on this new turn of events. If Savannah knew his attraction for Meredith, how many others would soon discover the same? And what did it matter if everyone speculated about the possibility?

It mattered if Meredith knew.

"Are you, Captain Cameron?" Savannah turned her attention unexpectedly upon Quade. "Interested in my sister for reasons other than taking care of your children?"

"Yes . . . no . . . I don't know." Quade didn't like the woman's tone. Was it an inconceivable consideration to think that Meredith was capable of . . . of what? Inspiring lust? Was that all he felt for her? No, the sensations that coursed through him at Meredith's merest glance were more. Respect? He had respected her long before she became his governess. Challenge? She'd certainly challenged him in more ways than simply changing her mind about a loan.

A mixture of all three seemed closer to the truth. Add to that something novel that had no clear definition. Why did he feel like a fish swimming in uncharted waters?

Yori cleared his throat, obviously thankful that the focus was now on Quade rather than himself. "Miss Stanfield would like to be the mistress of the children's ceremonies. That should resolve one of your dilemmas, I am thinking."

Quade shot him a don't-gloat-I-know-you're-loving-this look. Whatever else his friend implied, having Meredith Stanfield commandeer the children's games was an excellent idea. Hadn't she said earlier that they should never underestimate her? If she could handle his three hurricanes, she could certainly manage the games. Meredith's presence on the beach area, where most of the activities would take place, might also inspire her to face her fear of the gulf—a fear he vowed to help purge.

"That's a crackerjack idea. Meredith is the perfect choice."

Savannah elbowed Yori. "Tell him."

Yori looked slightly uncomfortable, although he attempted to hide the fact from Savannah. "Not Meredith," the shucker corrected, *"Savannah."*

Be tactful, Quade reminded himself, imagining the elder Stanfield sibling at the helm of several dozen children. "Uhh, I wasn't aware that you had any experience in dealing with Biloxi's youth, Miss Stanfield. This division of the festival can be daunting unless you are extremely skilled in diplomacy and subtlety. Not necessarily for the children, I'm afraid. But for the parents who usually watch the races. If their little Buford or Annabella doesn't win or happens to place lower than Mother and Father expect, you could find yourself in a very uncomfortable situation. Are you certain this wouldn't be taking on an undue burden?"

"You're wondering if I'm capable, aren't you, Captain Cameron?" She tilted the parasol to give him a full view of her face. "I assure you, I can be quite intimidating if the occasion calls for it."

For just a moment, Quade saw a resemblance to Meredith in the lift of her sister's chin, the spark of defiance in her eyes. Despite his opinion of the woman, he admired her grit. "Children can be rowdy, parents unrestrained."

"There are few Biloxians who haven't experienced the Stanfield kindness—"

Thanks to Meredith, Quade silently interjected, his admiration tarnishing.

"—and appreciate the value of helping to make my assigned duties a pleasant experience."

Meaning, everyone will be reminded which family is capable of donating money to future festivals and other social events. Though the idea didn't sit well with him, Savannah's standing in the community could serve to gain cooperation among the parents. None would complain to her for fear of offending one of Biloxi's better benefactors. "You have the role . . . under one condition." Pure impishness guided his next edict, justified by the need to offer the community a buffer should Savannah become too impertinent. "Yori has to help you."

"Now, yist a minute there." Yori backed away and almost dislodged Savannah's firm hold upon his arm. "Yori Svengsen cannot chase after *ungdoms*, I am thinking. I need to save my strength to climb the mast. Best you get someone else to—"

"But Yori . . ." Savannah moored her arm around his, refusing to let him drift. "You said you could convince Quade Cameron of anything."

"*Ja*, I did." Frowning at the grin slashing across Quade's mouth, Yori muttered, "But now I wish Yori was not such a big convincer, I am thinking."

"Guess she settled that."

Savannah smiled at Yori and patted his arm.

The wavering lift of his lips looked more like pain than pleasure. "Guess she did. You got yourself a mistress of ceremonies," his grumble lowered, "and a master of *bommerte*."

The gleam in Savannah's eyes showed that she knew what he'd said. She stood on her tiptoes to offer the Norwegian a kiss on his cheek. "I must go and tell Mother. She'll be so delighted. And Yori . . . you're no blunderer."

Deliberately, Yori turned his face so that her lips met a better mark, planting themselves fully upon his mouth. The parasol clattered against the promenade's wooden planks. One kid boot rose to help balance her, until Yori's arms encircled Savannah into a closer embrace. Startled gasps from passersby sparked a ripple of gossip through the people strolling the boardwalk. The area in front of the bandstand Quade and Yori had been crafting all afternoon became very crowded.

After a resounding kiss Yori released her, looking as dazed as she. "Thank *you*, Miss Savannah."

She backed away, nearly stumbling on her hem. "I-I've got to go now." She motioned behind her. "I must tell Mother . . . something important." Her gaze swept over the huge man, appreciation darkening the hazel of her eyes.

Yori winked.

She looked as if she might melt where she stood.

"I don't know *what* I have to tell her, mind you, but I *will* tell her. Come see me, Yori? *Senere*?"

Yori waved three fingers. "Later, Savannah-anna. I promise."

"Not too much later." She winked back, blowing him a kiss from the palm of her hand.

She headed toward her carriage, her skirts bouncing jauntily with the exaggerated sway of her hips.

"Yori, Yori, Yori," Quade admonished, shaking his head. "That's deep water you're treading. Savannah Stanfield is no wader. When that woman decides to fall in love, she'll dive in head first."

"Like her sister, I am thinking." Yori began to hammer the trellis they were erecting to keep curious hands clear of the musicians' stand.

"Perhaps not. There's something holding Meredith

back.'' Quade refused to admit the anchor restraining him. ''Another man perhaps.''

Quade wished he'd never used Meredith's acquaintance with Nolan Richards to put an end to the passionate embrace he and she had shared yesterday. The more Quade considered the carpetbagger and Meredith being anything other than business associates, the more he disliked the possibility.

He joined his friend, enjoying the steady *whack, whack, whack* of hammer against nail. The driving force focused the frustration and allowed him to rid himself of it physically.

Concentrating on his task, Yori didn't look up. ''There *was* another man.''

Quade's hammer stopped in midair. Then the key word connected in his mind, enabling him to continue the hammering. ''Was?''

''Phillip somebody, I am thinking. Can't remember his last name. Went to school with her in Boston. Worked for her father.''

At the time, Quade had been caught up in the war . . . surviving. Randy was newborn, Katherine distant. Still, he vaguely remembered the fellow. ''He was the man who drowned during the festival of '64, wasn't he? When lightning struck the steamboat docks and they collapsed?'' *Of course!* The moment he spoke the words, he realized the source of Meredith's fear.

Yori glanced up. ''*Ja*, I believe he was. You knew him?''

''No, just a guess.''*An unfortunate one, it seems.* Quade searched the crowd of people until he spotted Meredith and his children. They were helping to string paper lanterns between the food and vendor booths. Lindsay Littlefield, the teller at Winkle's bank, held the ladder while Meredith balanced atop its rungs. Nolan Richards stood beside him, pointing to where the next lantern should be placed. ''I don't suppose there's been anyone else in her life since? A beau, I mean?''

Wiping his brow with the back of his hand, Yori shook

his head. The Norwegian focused his attention in the direction Quade's gaze had taken. "No one she's serious about. But plenty are serious about her money. Especially Lindsay Littlefield and Nolan Richards, I am thinking."

"That pantaloon?" Quade studied the stocky man from tight-necked cravat to polished boot, easily dismissing him as a rival for anything. Richards was another matter entirely. "I didn't think Littlefield had enough grit to court someone like Meredith."

"He doesn't, but wealth is strong bait to a greedy worm. If you aren't going to do something about him trying to look up her dress, I am thinking I will!"

Quade matched Yori stride for stride. Why the devil wasn't Richards doing something about Littlefield's breach of honor?

"Look, Papa's here!" Samantha proclaimed from below, while Meredith attempted to hold Randy so she could string the next lantern on the corner of the candlemaker's booth.

In excitement, the six-year-old turned. Quade watched in horror as Meredith's hands slipped from Randy's waist. Then she misstepped. He raced forward. Randy screamed. Thundering bootsteps behind him confirmed that Yori had witnessed the danger too.

Meredith grabbed for the child. Her sole fought to regain footing. Instead of finding the rung, it crashed down on the tip of Littlefield's nose. He let go of the ladder and stepped backward, grabbing his face. Nolan attempted to move out of the way, but the clerk stepped on his toes. He sprawled backward. The ladder teetered and began to topple.

"Watch out!" Quade bellowed. The crowd parted as if he were Moses.

Alex's hands covered her mouth, her scream joining Samantha's. Meredith clutched desperately for Randy. One finger ... two ... ten ... snatched fistfuls of dress. The distance that separated Quade from his family passed in a haze of prayers. His gaze remained glued to the sight of his tiny daughter falling, propelling her and Meredith earthward.

"Look up, Littlefield!" Quade roared his alarm, but the baldheaded man's concern was for the blood spurting from his nose.

As they plummeted backward, Meredith's hands managed to lock around Randy.

Please, God, don't them be hurt, Quade prayed. *Let me reach them in time!*

❖ 12 ❖

"Ooff!" ALL THE air expelled from Meredith's lungs. Her back impacted against someone else's body, cushioning her fall. Still, she held on to Randy for fear the child would be hurt.

A tangle of bodies lay beneath her, yet she couldn't move, couldn't seem to catch her breath. The world spun before her eyes. She blinked and blinked again to see blue sky and a circle of faces above her.

"Can we do that again?" Randy squirmed to get up. "That was really fun, Miss Merry."

Meredith released her, finally gasping for air so the laughter welling inside her could exit. Deeper, more masculine chuckles echoed from beneath her.

A muffled "I hardly think so" roused the awareness of someone's face resting just beneath her thighs. Not only someone's face, but the face and lips of the man who stirred untold sensations within her even from a substantial distance and quite vividly in her dreams last night.

Laughter died in her throat. As if she'd sat on a hot coal, Meredith suddenly became all arms and legs. She attempted to regain a standing position. To her dismay, she found not one but four bodies beneath her . . . Quade Cameron, Yori Svengsen, Lindsay Littlefield, and Nolan Richards.

"Oh my goodness. I'm sorry, gentlemen. Do let me help you up." She offered a hand here, attempted to untangle a foot there, but didn't quite know where or how to extricate the men.

"Just make everyone back away, will you, Miss Stanfield?" Quade instructed her. "We need some room. The four of us will do the rest."

The crowd retreated without her asking, but maintained a tight circle of curiosity. One by one, the men began to peel themselves from the pile.

"I am thinking, if you don't get your lard butt off me, I will suffocate. And if I suffocate, then you will do the same. *Ja*?"

"Who are you calling lard butt?" demanded a voice that sounded as if it had been lodged in someone's sinus cavity.

Quade stood and offered a hand to the Northerner. Richards accepted the help. "That lick on your nose give you a bit too much gumption, Littlefield?"

"That's Yori Svengsen you're imputing," Richards warned, assisting the clerk to his feet.

Littlefield spun around to watch Yori stand, his head rising higher and higher as the Norwegian deliberately emphasized his imposing height.

Color drained from Littlefield's face. "Sorry, Mr. Svengsen. I didn't know that was you."

"*Sorry* does not translate well in any language, Littlefield." Yori took a step forward, causing the clerk to take three steps back. "If my little blossom has one petal bruised on her, skinning off forty pounds of *your* hide might be half enough to make amends, I am thinking."

"She's fine," Lindsay squealed. "Just look at her. Isn't a hair on her pretty little head out of—" Randy's riotous curls looked as if a strong wind had tangled them. "Well, anyone's hair would be slightly messy after a fall. But she's not the least bit hurt. Are you, dumpling?"

The child batted her lashes. "I don't feel real bad, Mr. Littlefield, but sometimes Papa gives me a stick of peppermint to make me feel much better. You know, the kind you keep in that jar near your teller window?''

The clerk's face turned green around the edges. ''Oh, yes, sweetums. Anything you say. You just come on by the bank and I'll see that you get a peppermint . . . no, make it three. One for you and each of your sweet sisters.''

''They didn't fall. I did.''

''And you are no more hurt than I am.'' Alex flicked Randy on the side of the head.

''Papa, she thumped me.'' Randy kicked at Alexandra.

''Girls. Why don't you start picking up the mess we've made while I have a discussion with Mr. Littlefield?'' Quade bent and retrieved the hat that had fallen off the clerk's bald head during the impact.

''Uh-oh, Papa's going to have one of his *discussions*.'' Samantha untangled the paper lanterns strewn about.

The warning set all three girls into a flurry of motion. Whatever *discussions* the captain had conducted previously must have had considerable impact upon the sisters, Meredith decided, if it was able to inspire such obedience.

''If your nose hadn't been so close to the hem of her skirt, you might have been paying more attention. You never, I repeat, never let loose of a ladder when a child's or a woman's safety is at stake.'' Quade pushed the hat into the stunned man's stomach. ''Especially *my* child and *my* . . .''

Woman? Meredith's body became alert with anticipation. Quade glanced at her, his expression unreadable, then returned his attention to Littlefield.

''. . . governess. Do I make myself understood?''

''But my nose. It may be broken.'' Littlefield grabbed the hat with one hand and pressed the back of his hand to his nose. Not receiving the sympathy he expected from the men, he looked at Meredith for support. Apology carved deep furrows in his brow. ''I'm truly regretful I failed to hold the ladder. It's just that everything happened so fast, and I let go without thinking. Please forgive me, Meredith. I shall make certain it won't happen again.''

''I'm sure you will, Lindsay. Fortunately, we're all safe

and none worse for the wear." Her gaze swept over Randy to confirm that the child was not harmed in any way. "Miranda seems just fine, thank goodness." Her hand dipped into the pocket of her skirt to retrieve a lace hankie, which she promptly offered him. "It's a good thing that this won't keep you from participating in the festivities. I'm looking forward to your analyzing our signatures."

The clerk sighed deeply. "I do hope you're correct, Miss Stanfield. I have a blazing headache and am not at all certain I shall be of appropriate mindset to discern anyone's demeanor." He dared a glance at Yori. "Although some—" He fought for a word choice. "—*Biloxians* expose their nature in other ways that don't require astute analysis. Pray the saints, I'll feel better by opening ceremony and will enlighten us to those in need of closer scrutiny." He bid her a brief good-bye.

"You going to let him get away with that, Svengsen?" someone in the crowd demanded.

"I wouldn't let no one talk to me like that," announced another.

"Did he just *forbanne* Yori Svengsen?" The insult thundered across the Norwegian's face. "He is not that *dum* or *modig*, I am thinking."

"You're right, Yori. He's neither stupid nor brave. Just full of too much pride for his own good." *As I am of naïveté*, Meredith decided. "Besides, he's already got a hurt nose. You would just waste a good punch."

"*Ja*, I would." Yori's hamlike fist smacked into the palm of his other hand, reminding all that fortune had smiled on Lindsay Littlefield this day. "I'll wait till the nose it gets better, *then* I'll show him 'closer scrutiny.' "

Though she laughed along with everyone else in the crowd, disappointment steadily seeped into Meredith, tainting her good humor. Lindsay's concern for his own welfare rather than for hers or Randy's seemed sad but true to his disposition. Few surprises there. However, Quade Cameron's rescue had been executed out of love for his child and a duty to guarantee a governess for his household.

She wanted the captain to *care* about her, not just need her. The fact that Meredith wished it to be a tribute of tenderness for her was the most astonishing revelation of the day.

Her body trembled with trepidation, not out of fear or need for protection but from a yearning to be held in Quade's embrace. To hear words of affection whispered from his lips. To see in the depths of his eyes that she mattered for reasons other than convenience. Right here in front of God and everybody, she wanted him—wanted him to want her.

Sanity reasoned with Meredith, calming the riot of sensations surging through her. She took several steps away from Quade, putting distance between her and the man whose very presence conjured wild images of the two of them entangled in passionate kisses—dangerous kisses that she knew would lead to something more if she dared let them.

Safety prevailed in being needed, not wanted. And God knew, she knew how to be needed. It was her one achievement in life. Her one strength. She offered every ounce of her soul to any cause, to anyone who needed her . . . for fear she was not offering enough. But to want Quade Cameron would only provoke risks—risks the past had taught her led directly to unalterable sorrow.

"You shouldn't let the man off so easy." Though his criticism was aimed at Meredith, Quade focused his attention on helping his children gather the streamer that had been torn from its moorings and the scattered lanterns everywhere. "Girls, this is why we don't add candles to the lanterns until the morning of the opening ceremonies. Otherwise, if they had been lit and had fallen, the promenade would have caught fire."

The captain would never know the devastating effect of his words upon Meredith. A fire on the promenade? A repeat of the disaster that had taken Phillip's life? A hand rose to cover her gasp.

Mistaking her sudden dismay for concern about his criticism of the clerk, Quade's tone softened. "I don't mean to upset you, Miss Stanfield. *Meredith*. But Littlefield doesn't deserve your forgiveness. He thought only of himself. What if the two of you had been hurt?"

"*I* broke her fall." Nolan reached to lift the bonnet that hung down Meredith's back and set it atop her crown.

Feeling ill at ease with Nolan's closeness, Meredith stopped him from lacing the bonnet under her chin. "Thank you, but I can do that myself."

The Northerner's fingers splayed open, palms out as if someone held him at gunpoint. "Suit yourself, Merry. But you needn't have worried about Littlefield one way or the other. I told you, whenever you need me, I'll be here."

Near, she revised his statement. *You're always nearby, Nolan*. The *why* of it seemed more than just the actions of a besotted beau. She would make a point of watching him, keeping him under "closer scrutiny," she amended, attempting to use Yori's humor to warm the sudden chill that assailed her.

"Seems to me *I* helped *you* up, Richards." Quade rose from his knees and braced his legs as if preparing for a challenge.

The two men began to circle one another like warring roosters, sizing each other up before launching the attack.

"Why is it that you stood less than a foot away from her, and both Yori and I were yards away, yet we managed to beat you to her? Seems to me a friend so bent on helping would have moved a lot faster."

"*Ja*, it seems."

"Stay out of this, Yori," Quade said. "This is my discussion."

Randy's first finger curled and wiggled, motioning the Norwegian to join her. When he hesitated, the six-year-old walked over and grabbed his hand, then led him back to where she had been working. "Papa don't like nobody bothering him when he's discussing. It's private."

"What are you insinuating, Cameron?" Nolan demanded.

"That for someone who has clearly set his cap for Meredith, you don't seem unduly concerned about her good health."

"And you do?"

"She's my governess."

"Is that all?"

"And if it isn't?"

"Gentlemen, this *discussion* has gone quite far enough," Meredith broke in.

The crowd moved closer. The air bristled with tension.

"Yori, do you have time to take the children back to their quarters?" Receiving a nod, she motioned them in the direction of the warehouse. "I would appreciate you staying with them until I can settle a few things here."

Yori hefted Randy up on his broad shoulders and took Samantha's and Alex's hands. "Best go with Big Yori, blossoms, I am thinking Hurricane Meredith is about to blow."

"To say the least." Meredith waited until Quade had secured the end of the streamer to the booth before turning to the crowd. "I should think that you all have better things to do than stand here and eavesdrop on business that is none of your concern."

"That's not the Meredith Stanfield I know," someone grumbled as the crowd dispersed.

"Ever since she took up with those Cameron sisters, she hasn't had time for anybody else," complained another.

Meredith wanted to shout at them all that she had a right to alter her life as she saw fit, but she could blame no one but herself for their disgruntlement. She'd spoiled them all, as surely as if they were the children she might never have. They'd come to expect from her what she readily gave—her effort, her money, but most important, her time. Anything and everything within her realm of control. Now that she'd chosen to take a bit of it back for herself, support and understanding were not offered . . . only reproach.

She wanted to reassure them, to reassure herself, that

all would be back to normal as soon as Shanty regained the use of her leg. Meredith deliberately smiled, attempting to set everyone at ease. "Go back to work, friends. I'm just a bit shaken from the fall, that's all. Hopefully, I'll be myself tomorrow."

But would she? Would she ever again be the person she'd been before Quade's kiss?

A touch at her elbow reminded Meredith that he stood in wait of her wrath.

"Is this the eye of the storm, or has Hurricane Meredith blown over?"

His light, teasing tone sent warm shivers down her neck. But she resisted the impulse to lean in closer and allow his lips to press against her earlobe. "This is the eye, rest assured, Captain."

"Would you prefer that we go somewhere private, or do you intend this to be a full frontal assault?" Nolan attempted to lighten the mood.

Meredith swung around, fists on hips. "I do not appreciate being made a fool of in front of my neighbors and friends. Nor do I want the children to be a party to what I have to say. Where do you suggest would be the most private place we could settle this matter?"

"How about the bathhouse near my quarters?" Quade suggested. "It's close and probably not in use at this time of day."

"Sounds perfect." Meredith tied her bonnet around her head and dusted the folds of her skirt.

"After you, Meredith." Nolan half bowed and waved her forward.

"Please do, Miss Stanfield." Quade allowed her to pass by him.

Meredith didn't care that eyes watched from various places along the promenade. Let them all look. She was tired of this tomfoolery, and the two men needed setting straight. On second thought, waiting until they were in the bathhouse alone might imply to prying eyes that she had something to hide. With an abrupt halt, Meredith faced them.

Following so closely behind, they almost ran over her. Quade's long-legged gait kept him one step closer than Richards. Meredith's hands splayed across the captain's chest to stop the momentum of his body. Feeling the warmth of his skin and the muscular expanse beneath the sun-heated material of his shirt, she condemned the breathlessness that resulted.

"I-I want you both to know that I intend never to marry. Not now. Not ever. My fiancé was killed several years ago, and I've dedicated my life to his memory. Surely, you both can respect love that is honor-bound to be once in a lifetime." The expression that crossed Quade's face puzzled Meredith, shaking the foundation of her anger. "And, please never argue over me as if I were some strumpet for the bartering."

Gaining courage from the captain's stony silence, she decided there was no time like the present to quell the dissension between them. "Also, I want you both to quit following me everywhere I go."

She craned her neck around Quade, but he didn't budge. "Nolan, trailing me like a moonstruck pup will not convince me to make up my mind about the bid any sooner. As I said, I'm not interested in courting anyone, so don't play those games with me. The contract will be given to the man who offers the best results for Biloxi."

"But you just imagined all that, Merry," Nolan protested. "As I told you before, I only wanted to make certain no harm came to you. After all, children can be quite a handful, especially the Cameron children. And you must admit, you haven't had all that much experience with them."

Quade turned, but Meredith sensed it was wiser to keep his attention on her rather than on the Northerner. She gripped his forearms, silently asking him to remain where he stood. "All children are demanding at one time or the other. When I can't handle them, the captain does. What I haven't quite determined is why he and his cohort, Yori, have chosen vantage points where they can spy on me also."

Her gaze met Quade's, her curiosity targeting on the man in question. "Is it because of the children? Probably. I can accept that, but there's no need to be sly about it. I'd expect you to make certain I'm doing my job. But if you think for one moment you need to watch me to see whether I'm going to give Nolan the bid, then you're wasting your effort. All of you. I happen to have three better things to occupy my time. They are Alexandra, Samantha, and Miranda Cameron. Do I make myself understood?"

"Perfectly." Nolan backed away.

"Not quite."

Quade's body offered a stone wall of resistance. Meredith allowed her hands to fall, but that only served to close the space between her breasts and his chest. Still, she refused to let him see how much his nearness disturbed her. "Not quite? What part do you not understand?"

"This."

Iron bands of rough velvet encircled her. The sun skyrocketed through Meredith in a blaze of blinding white heat as Quade's kiss melted her lips into a quivering mass of surrender.

❖ *13* ❖

THE WARMTH OF the tiny body cuddled against hers suddenly vanished, leaving remnants of comfort that caused Meredith to resist awakening fully. Was it already morning?

Quade's searing kiss had made sleep near impossible. Her thoughts ran rampant trying to decipher what it all could mean—this strange yearning to be in his arms, to experience the mind-bending thrill of his lips, to test the vow she'd given Phillip.

Her body pulsed all night with a torrent of energy and a craving unknown to her until Quade had lured them from some hidden depth within her. It was as if he had searched through the shell of her life and discovered its pearl. The beauty by which she should live. With all her will, she attempted to calm the currents stirring within her. Yet exhaustion alone had finally tamed the tempest of her emotions.

"Time to put stage two into action," Alexandra whispered from across the room.

"But we ain't through with stage one yet." Randy's voice squeaked as she attempted to find an equally tranquil tone. "Are we?"

"Shhh!" Alex and Samantha hissed in unison.

Resisting the urge to turn over and witness the scheme

in the making, Meredith deliberately feigned deep sleep. All the while she tuned her ear for details.

"We have to start stage two." Concern resounded in Samantha's declaration. "Stage one isn't working. They aren't getting along as well as we'd planned. Did you see how angry Miss Meredith was when she came in last night? Her cheeks were all red, and her eyes looked like they had smoke in them. Like maybe she was so furious she had caught fire."

"Is that how come she wouldn't speak to Papa no more?"

Meredith stiffened at Randy's question. Realizing she'd sucked in her breath, she exhaled it ever so slowly to keep the children from suspecting she listened. In her attempt to gather her wits after the kiss, she'd alarmed the girls. That was never her intention. She simply had no words to express the way she felt, and thought it best to keep silent until regaining her sensibilities. What Sam had mistaken for the aftermath of anger was blatant passion aroused by Quade.

"It must have been mutual," Alex said. "Father wouldn't talk to her either. Didn't you notice? He barely said anything to us the rest of the evening, even when he kissed us good night. And I heard him tell Meredith that she could send Yori after him if she needed him for anything."

"He slammed the door really hard. I remember." Randy bounced on the bed, jarring the headboard.

"Stop that. You'll wake her." Sam's reprimand softened into sadness. "Papa slept out on his boat again. I wish he wouldn't do that."

"He likes to be alone, and he always will be. I doubt anything we can do will ever change that." Alex's verdict rang with a disheartening pall.

"But you said we could." Two feet thudded against the floor as Randy's tone increased in volume. "You said we could have us a new mama if we acted really good and treated Miss Merry nice."

"We might have to go back to Miss Winkle's and see

if someone else will do. Miss Meredith and Father don't like each other much. Now stop jumping around, or you'll wake her up for sure.''

"I don't want nobody else." Randy stomped her foot deliberately. "I want Miss Merry for my mama."

Meredith could hardly breathe. The children wanted her as their mother! They had set out to find a mother at the finishing school and had chosen her instead. Tenderness coursed through Meredith. Her eyes stung with tears she dared not shed, for fear they might give away her eavesdropping. Yet she wanted to hug each child and tell them how much they meant to her.

"Don't give up," Samantha insisted. "Like you said, we haven't tried everything yet."

What did they have in mind? Meredith's curiosity made keeping her eyes closed difficult.

"We could show her some more about how good Papa is. Pick her some flowers. Cook her some breakfast. Do nice things for her and tell her Papa done 'em."

Meredith smiled, and she eased the covers up so no one might see should they walk around to her side of the bed.

"We tried that already. But Father keeps fouling things up." Exasperation echoed across the room. "He's such a—a—"

"Don't you say nothing bad about my Papa!" Randy warned.

Meredith's feet slid to the edge of the mattress, ready to launch herself into the midst of the fray threatening to commence.

"I wasn't, barnacle brain. He's just so used to having his own way that he forgets everybody doesn't do things the same. He's stubborn, that's what he is. Plain and simple set in his ways. She does things different than him, but she still gets it done. Father just didn't expect us to get along so well with Miss Meredith, when we haven't anybody else. Remember, she's the *first* governess we haven't run off."

"That's right, and we aren't going to let him chase her

away either.'' The usually undemonstrative Samantha took command. "I say we do this. . . .''

Suddenly the room reverberated with silence. The hair on the back of Meredith's neck stood on end as she felt someone's gaze focusing on her. Three pairs of feet padded across the floor, halted behind her, and waited.

"She looks asleep to me.''

A touch of someone's finger lightly brushed her shoulder, then instantly fled.

"That's it, barnacle brain. Shake her awake.''

"I just wanted to see if she was—''

"I think we better go downstairs before you both wake her and we *can't* talk about stage two.'' Again, the captain's middle child buffered her sisters' spat. "Time to get dressed and put Operation Everybody into action. Deal?''

"Deal.'' Alex and Randy's agreement echoed in unison.

Operation Everybody? Meredith could hear a slight slapping of palm against hand, three times, as if they were sealing a pact. It was all she could do to resist following them downstairs.

The little girl inside her wanted their plan to flourish, while the woman within hoped the secret might cast its net and snag the enigma that was Quade Cameron. The charlatan that she'd become chastised her unmercifully for disregarding the promise she'd made to Phillip.

"Good day to ye, lass.'' One-Eyed Thomas tipped his seaman's cap at Meredith as she walked among the entertainers who had assembled to practice their varied talents.

"Good afternoon, Thomas.'' Meredith shaded her eyes from the sun. "Have you seen the girls? They've been with Yori most of the morning. I thought I'd check on him and give him a break. But they don't seem to be in any of the usual places.''

"Aye, that I have, lass. They're all doon at the steamboat docks causing that Norwegian a bit of a stir, they are." He fell in step beside her, his peg leg beating a steady rhythm against the planked boardwalk. "Have a mind to join ye, I do. Ain't seen that Viking so flustered in all my years of knowing him. It does me old heart good to know there's a match for everyone. Even a strapping fellow like him."

Apprehension spurred her stride. What were the girls up to, and how did poor Yori figure in Operation Everybody?

"Save a leg there, lass! I'm half the runner ye are." Thomas huffed and puffed as he fought to catch up with her.

"Sorry, Thomas. It's just that those three can be very innovative when they tire of being with someone. Crawfish in shoes, snapping turtles in unmentionable places, and the like." She allowed the yarn-spinner to link his arm with hers, offering balance so they could make better headway.

"Viragos of the first order, me dearly departed Malovera would say. Spirited and full of sass."

Thomas waved to a man dressed as a court jester, tossing objects into the air. Mayhaws, the delicious fruit found only on river bottoms, flashed from the juggler's hand at incredible speed, while the nuts of a pea shuffler shifted so swiftly Meredith could not determine where he had hidden the pea. A troubadour strolled along the promenade, dressed in medieval clothing, strumming a lyre and serenading the hive of workers.

Excitement filled the air. Even her concern over the children's antics could not altogether dampen the anticipation of opening day. "It looks like everything is going well, doesn't it?" she commented. "The booths are set up. The decorations on the floats are almost completed. There are so many singers, musicians, and acrobats, there's something for everybody to enjoy. Everyone should be pleased."

"That's true, lass. But there's one among us who is not so happy."

Meredith knew the friendship between One-Eyed Thomas and the captain was close. "You mean Captain Cameron, don't you?"

"Aye, that I do."

"I'm sure there is a lot of gossip going around." With the kiss Quade had given her yesterday in front of everyone on the wharf, how could there not be? "But there really is nothing between us."

"Nothing, ye say? I think *ye* believe that well enough."

Indignation rose within her. "And you don't?"

"I believe that the captain is more distracted than I've seen him in years. That he's troubled by the way the girls look up to ye and learn from ye."

"He should be glad of that. If not me, it would be some other governess or teacher."

"Aye, but it's more than that, lass. Ye show him he has not been all that he thought he was to his children. Ye're satisfying needs and teaching them to grow in ways only a woman can. That's a hard oar to row for a man like Quade Cameron. For a man who has vowed never to need another woman in his life."

"He must have loved his Katherine greatly to mourn her so."

"Aye, he did, lass. But I sometimes wonder if his Kate truly realized how much."

The man known as Biloxi's town gossip became strangely quiet, talking no further of Quade's wife and the sad circumstances that had parted them.

"I'm sorry he's so unhappy." She thought of her own loss. "But at least he has three wonderful daughters to bring him a measure of joy and fill his time."

"He needs more, Miss Stanfield. He yearns for more than to be needed."

One-Eyed Thomas's words startled her. Could she and Quade Cameron have suffered the same fate? Did he work constantly to prove himself in some way? Isn't that why she volunteered? By giving away her time, she kept herself too busy to look closely at her life . . . afraid she would see how empty it had become. Hadn't that emptiness set her on this very path? Emptiness that urged her to take the role as governess to his children? Emptiness that challenged her to change the sameness of her days?

Perhaps Quade Cameron needed her as desperately as his daughters did. Perhaps she could teach him to live again, and in the teaching, she might learn how to go on. Meredith's steps became brisker.

"We should have taken a carriage." Thomas pointed to the shoreline ahead of them where the promenade appeared worn and less stable.

"It's a beautiful afternoon. The walk will do us good." Then Meredith realized to whom she spoke. "Unless *you're* not up to it, Thomas."

"Me? I can amble with the best of ye!" He deliberately set a pace to force her to keep up. His wooden leg suddenly sank from view, a plank loosening beneath his weight. But the man quickly regained his balance. "Shiver me timbers, as they say . . . literally."

They laughed and became more aware of their footing. She watched for missing slats to make certain her hem didn't tangle in the occasional board that had warped.

"The docks certainly need repair," she admitted.

"Aye, that they do, and the captain's the man to mend them."

"Now, Thomas, I promised I would give my decision at the festival and everyone knows that. Please don't try to persuade me to—"

The shrill whistle of a steamboat out in the lee startled them. A paddle wheeler steamed into the harbor. Its calliope sent out a jaunty tune to the children waving from the shore.

"Look there, isn't that the girls?" Meredith smiled at the uncustomary exuberance Alexandra showed as she waved to the people on the steamboat. Could Lazaro López be on that boat? No, she doubted even Alexandra's hawk eyes could spot the man that far away.

Her own eyes peered more closely at the scene before her. Yori and several of his fellow shuckers stood in a line, their hands holding out their aprons as if they were voluminous ball gowns. Randy had taken a position in front of the men, with her hem wadded in each hand. The child slipped one leg behind the other, curtsying.

"Well, would ye look at that!" A loud guffaw erupted from Thomas.

Meredith's giggle followed. The sight of mountainous Yori Svengsen and his burly crew attempting to curtsy for little Randy filled her with instant joy. The novice contestants, whose sea legs boasted no superior, resembled newborn colts.

So *that* was Operation Everybody! The girls intended to get everyone to work with them on winning the Little Princess title. A sense of relief and joy coursed through Meredith, for she had suspected something a bit more devious.

Yori looked up, spotted Meredith and Thomas's approach, then hurriedly instructed the men to take off their aprons. Each man shed his work garment quicker than Randy could protest. The Norwegian pointed behind her, and the child turned to see what had instigated the mutiny.

"Uncle One-Eye, Uncle One-Eye, you're here! We thought you'd never come."

Meredith glanced at Thomas. "They were expecting you?"

Thomas winked. "They were expecting *us*, lass."

"Suddenly, I feel like I've been led on a *Merry* chase."

"That's a good one, lass. Sort of like the half-blind leading the unwilling to see?"

"Thomas, what are you up to?"

The yarn-spinner's chest seemed to billow in full sail. "A good deed, lass. Hasn't a man the right to do a good deed?"

"Indeed he does," Meredith countered, spotting a table covered with Spanish lace. Sitting all by itself at the end of the pier, the table offered two chairs and an already-lit hurricane lamp. Place settings of china and crystal goblets indicated that a meal for two was to be shared. In the middle of the table, someone had taken a great deal of effort to secure a lace parasol to offer shade from the sun.

Suddenly Operation Everybody no longer seemed easily explained. "What's this?"

"Oh, that!" Thomas motioned her forward. "I'll let the children tell you. My task was to get you here . . . er . . . I mean, I was supposed to help you find them."

"You've never been a good liar, Thomas. It's too late in life to start trying now."

"Hi, Miss Merry." Randy ran up to her and grabbed her hand, helping to rush her along. "Me and Sam and Alex thought you might be real hungry or something. So we made you a special dinner. You are hungry, aren't you, Miss Merry? It's real, real, *real* good food. We had Miss Opal make it."

Meredith approached the table. The platter of food had been covered, evidently to preserve its warmth. "There are only two settings. Aren't you all going to join me?"

"Nope. We already ate." Randy rocked back on her heels, looking extremely proud of herself.

"You've already eaten." Meredith corrected the child's grammar.

"That's what I said," Randy repeated. "We already ate."

Noticing Yori and his men waving to someone upshore, Meredith turned to see who had drawn their attention. Quade Cameron escorted her sister in this direction. What were the two of them doing together? Had this meal been planned for other purposes and the children plotted to alter the captain's choice of guests?

"I think we should be going, children." Meredith suddenly didn't know what to do with her hands. Her hair was a mess. She had taken the morning to rearrange the captain's quarters slightly to give the place some variety. When she'd realized how much time had gone by, she'd gone searching for Yori to see if he was tired of the girls' company.

Savannah, on the other hand, resembled a model from a Paris fashion salon. Every hair was in place. The gown she wore accentuated every becoming curve of her figure.

Her sister couldn't have looked lovelier gracing the captain's arm.

Jealousy spewed its green wrath in low-breaking waves. Meredith reeled under its force and had to sit in order not to fall. The moment her bottom touched the chair, she realized that her sister might presume she had come to intrude. Meredith jolted to her feet.

"Yori, sweetling. Here he is. Just as you instructed." Savannah unlinked her arm from the captain's and instantly wrapped it around Yori's forearm. "It took a great deal of persuading, but as you can see I have accomplished the impossible. I have taken Quade Cameron from his work long enough to make him stop and eat."

"What is the meaning of this?" Quade halted a few yards from Yori. His gaze swept over the Norwegian and his men, the children, Thomas, and finally Meredith. "I don't have time for games."

Samantha walked to her father and gently reached for his hand. He accepted hers and allowed himself to be led forward. "It's not a game, Papa. We thought you and Miss Meredith might be hungry, that's all. You both work, work, work. And I know neither one of you ate breakfast this morning. We decided to have Miss Opal cook you something special." She guided him into the chair opposite Meredith's. "We just wanted it to be a surprise, so we asked Yori and Thomas and Miss Savannah to help us get you both here."

"You definitely did that." Quade's tone was more growl than compliment.

Anxious faces stared at the two of them to see if the gift would be accepted. Meredith slowly sat in her chair, realizing that she'd actually been envious of her sister. Green-eyed, hackle-raising jealous. She unfolded the lace napkin and spread it over her lap. "They've gone to a lot of trouble."

"And had quite a bit of help, it seems."

"Lift up the lid, Papa," Randy encouraged. "We had Miss Opal cook you some lobster and crab and oysters. But eat the oysters first. They're supposed to be afro . . .

afro . . . something-or-others, but we had to get them out of this ocean. It would take too long to sail to Africa for 'em.''

''They're *aphrodisiacs*, not from Africa.'' Alex stared at her sister in disgust. ''Don't you know *anything*?''

''Where the high seas have *you* learned what that means, General?'' Quade glanced one by one at the adults present, but each vehemently shook their heads. None could keep a straight face.

''Miss Shanty said it's food that contains a love potion,'' Samantha defended them all, her tone sincere with apology. ''We didn't know it was anything bad, Papa.''

''I suggest the easiest way to get through this situation is to thank everyone and just enjoy the meal.'' Meredith bit back her grin.

''You're right, I suppose.'' Quade's stern expression eased. Immediately four arms launched themselves into his chest.

''You two are definitely a handful.'' Quade hugged Samantha and Randy.

''Alex helped too. She's the one who said we should have it out here on the steamboat docks so Miss Merry could see how much you need to fix them.''

''Girls, Miss Stanfield will decide who is the right man to repair them. I won't have any of you trying to persuade her otherwise.''

''But Papa, you said you wanted to get to know her better so you could change her mind about the loan.''

''That was because I didn't know her.'' Quade shared a long, estimating stare with Meredith. ''Now that I do, I have no doubt she will do whatever is best for Biloxi. Now, unless you want to climb up here in my lap, you'd best let me eat this delicious-looking meal and get back to work. Otherwise, we won't have a festival for one of you little princesses to reign over.''

Randy and Samantha backed away, their faces shining with their accomplishment.

''Miss Savannah and I will take them for a swim and then a nap, Captain.'' The Norwegian waved the girls in and gathered them around him. "Enjoy your dinner, and we will see you later this evening. Shanty's having a fish fry tonight and has invited you and Meredith to come along. Opal said she'd watch the girls for you so Meredith can have the evening out. And Thomas promised to help Opal if she'd cook him some of her clam chowder. Coming, Thomas?"

"Be right there, me bucko." Thomas hobbled toward the table. "Ye know, Captain, I was thinkin' we could—"

"*Now*, One-Eye!" Savannah insisted. "If you don't want Yori to chop a new groove in that peg leg of yours."

"A *kvinne* after my own heart, I am thinking. Oh, I forget. She knows what Big Yori is saying." Yori's eyes widened in mock trepidation at the girls.

"What did he say?" Randy asked.

"Who cares?" Alex declared.

"Yori wouldn't say anything he didn't mean," Samantha assured them all, her defense a testament to the man's good nature.

"Let's hope that's true." Meredith's sister flashed a smile at the crowd. "Because he's said a lot the last two days." She flicked open her parasol and headed back toward town.

The girls and Thomas followed. Yori did the same. Yards away, he turned around, hands splayed on his chest. Then he opened them, palms up to the sky. His brows arched in a silent question, as if to say, "I don't know what the devil I said. It could have been anything."

Meredith's laughter joined Quade's. She allowed herself to enjoy the deep, resonant quality of his mirth. Finally, she wiped tears from her eyes, glad that she could express these feelings and mean them wholeheartedly. "It seems Yori and Savannah are courting."

"Officially, for a couple of days now. Unofficially, I think he's hankered for her for a long time."

"Oh, I hadn't noticed."

"She's been speaking his language," Quade quipped, "ever since she discovered Yori was being freer with his feelings than he might have been otherwise.''

Meredith eyed the feast. "Well, they should have stayed and joined us, don't you think? There's enough here to fill a steamboat. Where shall we start?"

His gaze slid seductively to the half shells of oysters. "The chefs did indicate their preference. How about a dozen or two, Miss Stanfield?"

The man was a flirt! Meredith played hard to please. "I'll take the crab. It appeals to me at the moment."

"*Touché.*" Not easily dissuaded, the captain waved away her attempt to choose a portion. "Allow me."

He selected a crab, cracked open one leg, then carefully slid the white meat from its shell.

She watched his dexterity, marveling that such strong hands could handle something so delicate. Instead of setting the meat on her plate, he dipped it into the tiny bowl of melted butter served alongside. A premonition of his next move made her throat dry in response. Quade held the tempting tidbit to her lips.

"Try this. It's messy but has a certain appeal."

The emerald fire of his eyes seduced Meredith. As if it had a will of its own, her tongue darted out to lick a bead of butter that threatened to drip from his fingers. The rough texture of his skin against the sensitive tip of her tongue proved her undoing. Before she could stop herself, her mouth had encompassed his fingertips, satisfying the urge to suckle every delicious drop.

"Savor it, Meredith." Quade's voice seemed huskier than before. "Whet your appetite, but always insist upon your share of the *pièce de résistance.*"

He was not speaking of food, and they both knew it. She jerked away abruptly, trying to blink back the haze of seduction Quade had created. She could not look at him, certain she would lose control of the slim hold she had upon her senses at the moment. Her fingers toyed with her wine goblet. "How easily we fall into their trap," she whispered.

A brow quirked over one of his eyes. "Then *you* had nothing to do with this matchmaking scheme?"

"No, and you?"

"No inkling whatsoever." Quade reached across the table and stopped her fingers from rubbing the droplets on the glass. "But what if I had? Would you have come?"

At his merest touch, he stirred a hunger within her that no food would appease. "I can't love you, Quade."

"That's not what I asked." His fingers rubbed hers, caressing the length of them in long, slow strokes.

"I don't want to care about you." Reason almost forced her hand away, but her body refused to obey. A deeply seeded need demanded that it remain.

"But you do."

"No . . . yes . . . I don't know." His aplomb spurred her to ignore the warmth kindling her desire.

"Am I so common that you can't consider the possibility?"

"No, Quade. It's nothing like that." She didn't know what to do with her hands now. Though empty and in her lap, they were still afire with his touch. Her lips flavored with the taste of him. "There are things you don't understand. Circumstances I could never explain to you. Vows I've made that must last forever."

Bitter laughter rang out over the harbor. "Then we have no problem." His eyes focused on hers. "I don't believe in forever."

"Well, you should." She stood, finding comfort in the sincerity of her beliefs. "And I do. That's one of the reasons you must never kiss me again. Good afternoon, Captain."

❖ 14 ❖

"Did you and Papa have a nice lunch?"

Startled, Meredith looked up from the papers she had been studying while the children rested. Stanfield Enterprises had done amazingly well this last quarter. Her father had invested wisely for the future, bless his soul. Glad to let debits and credits flee from her thoughts, Meredith concentrated on finding out what had brought Samantha downstairs. "You didn't nap long, Sam. Just not sleepy?"

Sam sat on the edge of the davenport, then smiled when Meredith opened her arm to allow the child to snuggle in next to her.

"No, I couldn't sleep. Did you? Have a nice lunch, I mean?" Eagerness lit the sapphire of Sam's eyes.

Should she spoil the child's efforts and tell the truth, or lie? Meredith opted for the truth but tried to soften it. "You girls went to a lot of effort. And your father and I appreciate it, but I suppose we both weren't very hungry."

Disappointment made Sam frown. "Why don't you and Papa like each other, Miss Meredith?"

Meredith stared at the concerned freckled face. "We like each other. It's just that we've both suffered great tragedy in our lives and aren't prepared to change. Liking each other more than just as employer and employee, or even as friends, requires alterations neither of us is willing to make at the moment.''

"That sounds like you might want to in the future. Haven't you told us girls that we should always be prepared for the unexpected?''

Meredith fingered the end of Sam's braid, admiring the thick silken mass. "Yes, but I meant that a lady must be prepared for a change of events at any given moment. Particularly if she finds herself in unusual circumstances or situations she hasn't counted upon.''

"Well, see there. You're in an unusual circumstance. You don't normally watch three children, and this is definitely a situation you didn't count on.''

Setting her paperwork aside, Meredith faced Samantha. She tapped the tip of the child's freckled nose with her finger and smiled. "What made you so smart?''

Unable to meet Meredith's gaze, Samantha glanced down and worried the pocket of her trousers. "I have to be smart because I'm not pretty.''

"Who told you that?'' Meredith knuckled the small chin, gently lifting it so Sam would be forced to look up. Studying the nine-year-old's face, she imagined the beauty waiting to flourish.

"Miss Winkle used me as an example in her class. Alex told me so. Miss Winkle said that I'm too gangly and thin, that my skin is freckled and my hair is two colors. She said no boy would ever look twice at me.'' Tears pooled in her eyes. "And she's right, Miss Merry. Russell Kirk called me 'Bird-Legs' yesterday. I *have* to be smart because I won't ever be pretty.''

"That . . .'' Meredith struggled to control her anger, ". . . *woman* doesn't have the sense God gave a shrimp. If she would quit staring in her own mirror long enough to take a real look at you, she'd see that you're going to be one of the most beautiful women Biloxi ever spawned.''

Sam giggled as Meredith gently wiped the child's eyes with her kerchief.

"You make me sound like a salmon, Miss Meredith.''

She tried to smile despite the misgiving that filled her tone. "You don't think I'll always be this way?"

"You look like a nine-year-old should, Sammy. But if you want a glimpse of what you promise to be in a few years, I'll show you. Run upstairs and wash your face. Unbraid your hair and brush it until it's really shiny. Let me know when you're finished, then I'll come up and we'll show Miss Winkle that she's a blindsided flounder."

Samantha threw her arms around Meredith's neck and hugged her fiercely. "I love you, Miss Merry. I don't care if Papa does or not, I do."

"And I love you too, Sammy, and always will."

"I'll hurry."

"Take your time, sweet. I'm going to clean up the kitchen a bit for Opal and Thomas."

Remembering that she had loaned the girl her kerchief, Meredith did the most unladylike thing—she allowed her hand to wipe away the tears brimming in her own eyes. If Mother could see her now, she would surely complain that the captain and his children had tarnished her good breeding. Good breeding be damned! She sniffled. Those three little words Sam had offered meant more to her than all the social status in the world. Three precious words that had the power to bubble pure joy to the surface.

Her elation evaporated as quickly as it had emerged, followed by a feeling of being watched. The fine hairs on the back of her neck rose. Meredith swung around to see Quade Cameron step from the shadows near the door. "You were spying on us?"

Quade tossed his seaman's cap on the nearby secretary where he kept his ledgers. "I was trying to be quiet so as not to wake any of you if you were sleeping. Apparently, I was mistaken."

"Alex and Randy are still napping. Samantha's upstairs cha—"

"Yes, I heard."

He looked tired, in need of sleep himself. Bunking on a boat and working day and night had taken its toll on the man. "Can I get you something to eat, Captain?" A hand shot up to straighten the chignon at the base of her neck. "You didn't have breakfast or lunch. You must be starving."

Quade waved away her concern and took a seat in one of the cushioned chairs opposite the davenport. "It's so late now, I'll just wait and eat at the fish fry."

"I don't mind at all, Captain. It won't take me—"

"Please sit down, Meredith. We need to talk about other things before this . . . any of this . . . goes further."

Meredith seated herself on the davenport. "Before what goes further?"

"Your telling my children that you love them and will forever and forever." Sarcasm emphasized his last three words.

"Ahh." Anger stirred inside her. "I forgot. You're a man who doesn't believe in forever, so you want your children to share those beliefs."

"I prefer that they know the realities of life, Miss Stanfield."

"Such cynicism. Indeed, a fine trait to pass on to one's children."

Quade leaned forward, his eyes intent. "I *won't* permit you to promise them something you can't possibly guarantee. There is nothing permanent in this life, and they need to learn it now."

Meredith rose. "Perhaps forever is a state of mind or a duty assigned by the edicts of society, Captain." A sense of relief overwhelmed her. She'd been expected to mourn Phillip forever. Expected to honor him until her own death. But hadn't she been dead inside *before* he was swept away, and all these years since? Numb from pretending their love had been mutual? "Let the children enjoy now for what it is. My *love* for what it is. Maybe enjoying now can be a springboard to forever."

He reached out to her, then seemed to think better of it and let his hand return to his side. "I've sailed that sea before and came up shipwrecked, Meredith."

"I can't believe you would allow the loss of fortune over the years to make you so caustic."

His gaze focused on the windows, staring out into the bay. "Fortunes are made and lost. But love . . . ah . . . real love comes only once in a lifetime."

She walked over to the window and pressed a hand of compassion upon his arm. "You and Katherine must have truly loved one another. How I envy you."

"Don't." He turned, gripping her shoulders. "Open your eyes, Meredith. Appearances can be deceiving. Don't ever allow yourself to be blinded by what you believe instead of seeing the reality of what you have."

Meredith searched his face. Had his and Katherine's relationship been something other than idyllic? Perhaps they both harbored secrets.

Quade let her go and turned away. Grabbing his cap again, he placed it atop his head. "I've got to leave. I promised Wisdom that I'd take him out to check over the fireworks, so I'll send Yori and Savannah to escort you to the fish fry." He exhaled a heavy sigh. "I'll do my best to meet you there later."

"Before you go, Captain, there's something I would like to discuss with you. It's about Samantha."

"I've given you full rein on the girls, Miss Stanfield. Your judgment is sound. Feel free to use it where she or the others are concerned."

"No, Captain. Samantha needs *your* attention in this particular matter."

"Is it something that can't wait until after the festival?" Concern battled exasperation in his tone. "As you can see, I really am stretching my time to its limit."

Her fists curled against her hips. "Then put something else off and take time for this. You have more responsibility to those children than just being a provider."

His palms raised in surrender. "All right. You have my full attention for two minutes. Then I have to go or Wisdom will ride my stern the rest of the evening. He's already boiling because of that bird-feeding incident. What's happening with Sam?"

Meredith began to pace. "If she comes down while

you're still here, I want you to brag on how truly beautiful she is. Really pour on the charm.''

"Easily done. She is beautiful." A smile curved the corner of his lips. "You think I have charm?"

Men! Eyeing the stairs, Meredith crept closer to him. "This is no time to boost your ego. Sam needs to be told time and time again how pretty she is. Reaffirm her opinion of herself."

"Has something happened to lower it?"

"Someone was extremely cruel to her. Said some things that would have hurt anyone's feelings, much less a sensitive soul like hers. Sam happens to believe she's ugly and will never be beautiful."

Exhaustion faded from Quade's features, replaced by parental outrage. "Who hurt my little girl's feelings?"

"That's not what's important now. Mending Samantha's self-confidence is what you should focus on."

"Let me talk to her. I want to know just exactly what was said."

Meredith held up her hand as if to push him away, backing toward the stairs all the while. "No, that will just make matters worse. Go on and meet Mr. Winkle so you can get the meeting over with and catch up with us at the fish fry. But when we get home . . . I mean, *back* tonight, be sure to mention how lovely she's becoming."

"You're sure you don't want me to handle this?"

"Manhandling her was not what I had in mind and won't solve anything."

"You're becoming a better parent than I am, Miss Stanfield."

Remembering what One-Eyed Thomas had said, she tried to reassure Quade. "Not a better father, though, Captain. You have the market on that."

"I thought I did, until you showed me I have a long way to go. I don't know whether to thank you or keep you as far away from them as possible."

"The old what-they-don't-know-can't-hurt-them belief?"

"Something like that."

"Captain, if you would only slow down your working and live a little, you'd discover that those darling daughters of yours know far more than you'd ever suspect. Now, off with you and your considerable tasks. I happen to have one of my own this evening before I can enjoy the fish fry."

"Oh?" Curiosity arched his brows.

What started out as a giggle spurred Meredith into a fit of laughter. He looked at her as if she'd lost her mind. What she had lost was what her mother would surely deem her social sensibilities. "You see, Captain, I intend to ensure that a certain guilty party receives her just desserts."

❖ 15 ❖

Taking inventory of the pyrotechnics hadn't taken as long as Quade had expected. Wisdom Winkle agreed that the festival committee had procured enough to stage a dazzling display on the opening and closing nights. Quade made sure all were well guarded from the hooligans who slithered out of every bayou to pillage and spoil coastal celebrations.

The fish fry was probably well underway by now. Perhaps he ought to go home and free Thomas and Opal to join the others. As he hiked toward the warehouse, Quade decided he was being unfair to Yori and Savannah. The two would feel obligated to entertain Meredith because she was without an escort. They deserved to enjoy the beautiful moonlit night as other courting couples should. Walking on the beach hand in hand. A stolen kiss. Whispered yearnings.

Good manners won out, or so he believed. Quade convinced himself that he must join her, not only to give his friends back their courting time but to find out the identity of the person Meredith planned to retaliate against for insulting Sam.

Meredith had been right this morning. His responsibilities for the festival had taken him away from his little ladies more than he planned. Although Quade appreciated the trust and felt an obligation to the community, he relied on Shanty, their former governess, and now Meredith to see to his daughters' needs. From now till the festival's opening, he would make a point of spending at least the evenings with his children. If time or duty didn't allow, then he'd ask for more help.

Once the decision was set in his mind, Quade hurried toward his quarters, eager to check on the children. Best make certain they hadn't overwhelmed their caretakers for the evening. A one-eyed sailor and a near-blind cook were hardly a match for three observant scamps.

His chuckle filled the night air as he smiled at Randy's precociousness, Sam's peacemaking, and Alex's guardianship. Different as summer, fall, and winter, yet each one his pride and joy. And, as Meredith had shown him on every occasion . . . they were the singular good that sprang from his disastrous past.

Images of Meredith waiting for him, expecting him to arrive, spurred his steps into an eagerness to join the fish fry. Voices called to Quade on the evening breeze. *Forget the past. Enjoy the night. Discover the woman.*

When he arrived home, he knocked to announce his presence before opening the door to let himself in. "Hello, everybody still sane and all in one piece?"

"*Buenas noches, Capitán.* They are all in bed." Opal Ortega pressed a finger against her lips. "Thomas put them all to sleep with his storytelling. Ouch!" The plump woman stubbed her toe on the coat rack standing next to the secretary. "It has taken much time to learn where the furniture has been placed now."

"I forgot to have Miss Stanfield tell you about the switch. Forgive me, Opal." Impressed with Meredith's arrangement, the thought never occurred to him that the change might upset Opal. With poor eyesight, she probably maneuvered through his quarters out of sheer memory alone. "Would you like for me to move everything back the way it was?"

"No, *Capitán.* The *señorita*, she has a fine eye for detail. The place, it feels more . . . how do you say . . .

homey now. I am an old woman.'' She patted the gray chignon at the back of her head and glanced at the peg-legged man resting on the davenport. ''I need new challenges.''

''Did they kill him?'' Quade teased, noting the slow rise and fall of the sailor's chest.

Opal blushed and laughed softly. ''No, but he told me if I ever accept his proposal that we will now only have one *muchacho,* not a dozen.''

''And will you ever agree to marry him, Opal?'' Quade eyed the woman and marveled that love had a way of shining from a person's soul no matter how damaged the eyes.

''*Sí, Capitán.*'' She giggled like a young girl. ''When he agrees to the dozen again.''

Quade hugged her. ''He will, Opal. Tomorrow, when he's recovered from tonight. I find that to be true every morning when I wake up. About the time I believe I can't handle another solitary shenanigan, they do something so angelic that my heart is glad all over again that they're mine. Then, like you, I wish I had a dozen more.''

''Speaking of morning, *Señor*, it is my wish that you go upstairs and look at the *niña*. Do not wait until morning or it might be too late.''

Alarm filled Quade. After all Meredith had told him, had his daughter's evening been spent in tears? Sam was such a sensitive soul. He should have stayed. He should have assured her of her coming beauty. He should have listened to Meredith and taken time out for his daughter. Rushing toward the staircase, he took the steps three at a time.

''Shhh!'' Opal reprimanded. ''Your eagerness will wake them.''

Quade forced himself to slow his advance. When he reached the landing, he tiptoed across the room, surprised to see Alex and Randy sleeping in the same bed, rather than his two older daughters. Creeping past them, he shifted toward the other bed, immediately halting upon the sight of his middle daughter.

The child lay on top of the covers, dressed in a gown as blue as the color of her eyes. White-gold waves cascaded over her shoulders, brushed to a fine sheen. A band of shells held the thick tresses back from her forehead, looking very much like a tiara. In her tiny hand, she held a stick with a star-shaped object at its end. A starfish! Or a scepter? Indeed, Samantha looked like a fairy princess.

Afraid that she might turn in her sleep and harm herself, Quade tried to ease the stick gently from his daughter's grasp. Her fingers flexed and gripped, refusing to release their prize. Sapphire eyes blinked open.

"Hi, Papa. Did you have a hard day?"

"Evening, sweetheart. Not so hard. How about you?" His gaze swept over her. "You look so beautiful tonight. You must have had a really special day."

Joy radiated over the child, setting her aglow with his compliment. "Do you really think I'm beautiful, Papa?"

"More than beautiful, Sammy. You're positively captivating."

She sighed deeply, her eyes hooded with sleep. "Thank you, Papa. You are too."

Quade bent, pressed a kiss upon her forehead and took the makeshift scepter. "Now you go back to sleep, sweet. I'll just put this right over here so you don't hurt yourself with it during the night. I don't suppose I can get you to change out of that dress and into something more comfortable, can I?"

"I want to wear it just a little while longer. It's making me have such nice dreams. You don't mind, do you, Papa?"

He unlaced her shoes, pulled them off, and set them beneath the bed. "Wear it for as long as you like, baby. And sweet dreams."

"Sweet dreams to you too, Papa."

Quade tiptoed over and carefully tucked in each child. He pressed a kiss on Randy's cherubic cheek and Alex's forehead, then headed downstairs. At the bottom of the stairway, he paused and looked upward, caught in an emotion that made it difficult to stem tears of parental pride.

But he remembered he was not alone. Though overly sentimental at the moment, he shifted to bid Opal good night until his return.

The housekeeper handed him a basket and whispered, "Have you ever seen anything so . . . how do you say . . . *precious* in all your days?"

"She's going to be quite an enchantress, much sooner than I'm ready for, I'm afraid."

"*Señorita* Stanfield helped the child find pride in herself. I have never seen Samantha so happy. You must offer my gratitude should I not see her later."

"I will, Opal. In fact, I'm headed there now to thank her myself." He jiggled the basket. "What's this?"

Opal gently nudged him toward the door. "Something to help you to thank the *señorita* properly. A special drink I made for later. A little orange and lemon peel, cinnamon and cloves, some cognac, and dark, roasted coffee."

"Your *café brûlot*?"

"*Sí*. To enjoy on such a moonlit night."

Quade lifted her hand and brushed a kiss lightly across her knuckles. "Thank you, Opal. Now go back and enjoy the rest of your evening with Thomas."

She smiled. "I am afraid good Thomas relished it too much." Opal pointed to the jug sitting within arm's reach of the sailor. "My *brûlot* relaxed him so much, he closed the other eye."

"So *that's* what's in that jug. I've been wondering." Quade grinned and headed for the door. "We'll try not to be too late."

The woman shook her head. "Do not worry about the time. I will curl up beside Thomas. He will not mind, and the girls . . . they will not wake until morning."

Anticipation filled Quade as he left his quarters and hurried down the promenade toward Shanty's. A gentle breeze rustled the leaves of the trees but not enough to cause undue concern about a chill dampening the festivities. As far as he could see, the moon lit the night, reminding him of the seaport's beauty and inducing its calming effect upon worries of the day. Each step seemed more tranquil, urging his thoughts onto pleasant prospects.

Strains of music captured his attention first, then laughter. Hands clapped in time to a jaunty rhythm. The pungent aroma of roasting fish filled the air, making his mouth water. Quade's stomach rumbled dissatisfaction while a sharp ache for food gripped his tastebuds.

"Look there, it's Captain Cameron!" a loud voice boomed.

A volley of voices welcomed him; hands waved to him to join the party. Quade peered at each face, surprised by some of the pairings of couples that had occurred among the fun-seekers, not so amazed by others.

"Over here, Quade."

Yori's voice cut through the darkness urging Quade to focus on a huge bonfire flaming several yards away from Shanty's shack and the promenade. Down on the beach, the blaze outlined some of the participants.

"What are you doing over there?" Quade quickly crossed the distance.

"Roasting a sweet potato. Want one?" Yori offered him a stick, impaled with a variety of vegetables and fish, dripping with succulent juices and scented with smoke. "Here, I have already eaten five of these. I will not be able to chase Savannah if she decides to resist my charm, I am thinking."

"Don't worry about that, Big Yori," Savannah cooed, rising from a blanket on the sand that she had been sharing with Meredith. She gently tugged at Yori's arm. "The night is still young. Now you and I will take that stroll we've been wanting. We'll walk off some of that sweet potato, just in case."

"*Ja*, we will." Yori had eyes only for Savannah, but before they progressed too much farther down the beach, he turned and cupped his hands over his mouth. "Have Gizelda read the captain's future, Meredith. See if it's the same as yours."

There wasn't a tactful bone in the man's body, Quade decided. "May I?" He looked askance at Meredith before sitting down beside her on the blanket.

"Please do." She glanced up at him and scooted over in case he needed more room.

"Will you hold this for me until I get settled?" He handed her Opal's basket and sat down, crossing his legs.

When she set the basket to one side, he noticed that part of her hair had been pulled back from her temples and tied with a saffron-colored ribbon to match the off-the-shoulder dress she wore. The rest of its auburn mass hung almost to her waist. When she faced him, his breath caught at the sight of her beauty, the moonlight adding luster to her alabaster skin, coloring her silver-blue eyes with twilight.

Perspiration beaded at his brow and above his upper lip. His palms grew moist, and his shirt clung tighter to his skin. Quade wondered if they sat too close to the fire. When his hands began to shake, he decided his reactions were easily explained. He'd simply waited too long to eat.

"Are you all right, Captain? You're looking at me rather strangely."

Then he knew with all certainty what engulfed him. He felt like a schoolboy again, sitting in the presence of the first girl he'd ever imagined himself in love with! Quade focused on taking a potato off the stick, glad that it was too warm. He could blame his trembling hands on its heat. He shook them vigorously. "Almost burned myself. Guess I'm hungrier than I thought."

"Is there something in the basket you can nibble on until that's cooled?" She opened the lid and lifted two cups and a jug. "What's this?"

"It's Opal's special coffee."

"I'd love some. How about you?"

"Please." He waited until she had taken everything from the basket, then angled the stick inside it, propping the lid so the speared vegetables wouldn't slide. "There, that ought to hold it steady until the food cools."

Quade watched as she poured the coffee, then accepted the mug she handed him. After she poured one for herself, he held his mug to hers. "I'd like to offer a toast."

"To whom?"

"To the woman I owe an apology—Miss Meredith Stanfield."

"For what?" She looked genuinely baffled—which endeared her to him. If he angered her, she did not dwell on their arguments. She spoke her mind, and that was the end of their disagreement. Despite her station in life, there was nothing pretentious about Meredith Stanfield.

"I came down pretty hard on you this afternoon about the girls and about that *forever* business." He looked at her over the brim of his cup. "You're right. I've allowed circumstances in my life to make me distrustful. But you've given me no reason to feel that way about you or your word. You've always been honest with me." He chuckled, remembering that disastrous trip to her office. "Even when I wasn't expecting it."

"I haven't made my mind up completely about the docks, Captain." Meredith stared at the rim of her mug. "As I told you—"

"Let's not broach that subject tonight. I know what you've said, and you know where I stand. Tonight, I simply want to apologize about the argument and let you know how very much I appreciate all you're doing for my daughters. You've taken on their care and are doing the job quite wonderfully. I can't thank you enough."

"In that case," she clicked her mug with his, "I accept the toast and the apology. Only if you accept mine in return. You see, I tend to be too helpful and forget that people like the opportunity to resolve their own problems. It's a curse."

Quade reached out and gently squeezed her hand. "Don't ever stop being you, Meredith. There's something quite charming about having someone care enough to set you into the current when you're glaringly off course." He stood and offered to help her up. "Would you care to walk with me for a while?"

She started to set down her mug.

"No, take it with you. I want to sip mine."

"What about your food?"

"I'll just grab a bite for now and eat more later." He

helped her stand. A test of the vegetables' heat assured
him that they could be eaten without setting his tongue
afire. He slid off a potato and a piece of fish and ate
them slowly, savoring their succulent flavor. "Where's
Shanty?"

He glanced toward her shack, where it seemed every
lantern in the house glowed. "Why are we roasting instead of frying the fish?"

"She's with Gizelda. Everyone decided Shanty didn't
need to wear herself out cooking for the lot of us, so we
built a bonfire instead. The Gypsy offered to read fortunes, and you know how interested Shanty is in the tarot.
She demanded to sit in on the card reading so she could
learn how it's done. No one seems to mind because
Shanty keeps Gizelda from going overboard with her
doomsday predictions."

"How about you? Have you had yours read yet?"
Quade took one more bite, then returned the stick to its
mooring. He grabbed the jug and filled their mugs again.

"That's enough for me, thanks. If I guess correctly,
Opal's put something special in that coffee."

"Cognac."

"Oh, so that's why I feel a bit dizzy."

"Here, anchor yourself to me. We'll rock the boat together."

She linked her arm through his, and they set off down
the beach for a leisurely stroll.

"You never did answer me about the fortune telling.
Did you have your cards read?"

"I will later. There were so many who wanted them
read, Gizelda had us draw numbers."

Footprints on the beach revealed where other couples
had gone.

Quade wanted to sink his toes into the sand. "Want to
take off your shoes?"

"That's a great idea."

She asked him to hold her mug, but he gave her his
coffee instead. "Allow me."

Quade bent and lifted the edge of her hem high enough

to find the laces at the top of her kid boots, but her wealth of petticoats kept getting in the way.

"I feel a bit like Cinderella." Her voice was only a whisper of wind.

"And I feel like her frustrated prince. Next time I have a chance, I'm going to order the royal shoemakers to design something a lot easier to slip off the foot. If it weren't for these confounded pettico—"

"You can tuck them into my sash. Like I did that night I went wading."

Challenge permeated her tone, urging Quade to glance up. Every breathtaking curve rose above him, initiating a boldness to accept her dare. "That's a delightful idea."

He reached between her ankles and grabbed the back of her hem to bring it forward. Raising the volumes of petticoats unbalanced her.

"The coffee! Watch out!"

He ducked. The mugs flew skyward. Quade waited for the sting of hot coffee down his back, but moments ticked by and it never came. Both were too stunned to speak.

"I think I'll change my profession in midstream. A cobbler's life must be mighty interesting at—" His words halted as he realized that she rested fully against him, her face lit with laughter and joy, her eyes full of welcome. His response was instinctive. "God help me, Meredith, for I can't help myself."

He pulled her to the sand and pressed his length against hers, kissing her with all the hunger of a man long denied sustenance. Latent yearnings swept logic from his thoughts, leaving in its wake a compelling need.

He waited for her to object, to pull away, but she didn't. Instead, Meredith's fingers delved into his hair; her lips moved hungrily against his own.

Desire blazed through him like a gust of blistering summer wind, setting his soul afire and bringing his blood to full boil. Years of wondering if he might ever know true passion faded. All that he'd ever dreamed it should be, of how its touch would incite sensations beyond his comprehension, became sudden reality in his arms. Quade knew, with all certainty, he tasted the ambrosia of life—heaven created by two hearts destined to love.

Breathless moans of desire mingled in his mouth. Her moist, demanding, hot tongue parried to rouse the depths of Quade's need. His world careened with wanting. Needing. Cherishing.

But sanity was a jealous mistress, demanding him to regain some semblance of control. It called upon his honor to remember Meredith as a woman who had suffered a past equal in sadness to his own—to recall that he'd offered her cognac-laced coffee and taken advantage of the shadows, pressing against her in wanton abandon.

Whispered echoes of caution reminded Quade that he'd once believed in love and given his heart freely to another, only to have it wounded by treachery. Though he knew Meredith far better than he had thought possible, dare he trust another so readily with what was left of his heart?

Like the tide flowing out to sea, Quade's passion ebbed. He shouldn't . . . no, he *wouldn't* make love to Meredith now. Not until he knew for certain that she could speak the same promise she'd offered to his children. He'd dreamed of true love for too long, hoarded away that fragile belief as if it were treasure hidden layers deep within his heart.

Voices approaching from farther down the beach gave Quade a reason to end the kiss abruptly. He nearly jolted to his feet. "Hurry, I don't want anyone seeing you like this."

She seemed dazed for a moment. "Y-yes, of course."

He offered to help her stand. "Dust yourself off while I grab the mugs."

"Quade?"

The breathless quality of his name upon her lips sent a shiver through him as she reached out and touched him. "Yes?"

"I'm not sorry you kissed me. I hope you aren't either."

He couldn't lie, no matter what sanity reasoned. "I'll never be sorry for that, Meredith."

She brushed the sand from her dress as best she could and attempted to straighten her hair. "Do I look all right?"

A swift appraisal from head to damned kid boot was not all that reassuring. "You look kissed."

"I should. I was . . . and quite well, I might say."

Despite all the qualms he should have been experiencing, triumph catapulted inside him, showering him with happiness unlike any he'd ever known.

"Fancy meeting the two of you out here. We wondered where you'd gotten off to." Lindsay Littlefield's whine raked across Quade's nerves as if someone had deliberately scraped a shell against the promenade.

"We thought you'd gone wandering on your own, dear." False concern filled Elise Winkle's voice. "After all, you've been alone most of the evening."

Quade noted that not only the clerk but also Nolan Richards escorted the banker's daughter.

"Some of us prefer waiting to share our . . . *time* . . . with others." Meredith intentionally added innuendo to her words and laced her arm through Quade's. "I hope the three of you are enjoying yourselves."

"Quite." Nolan's reply was brusque.

The insinuation breezed over Lindsay's head like a stone skipping over water. "That we are! I had no idea Mr. Richards was so interested in my studies. Why just a few minutes ago, he asked if I could—"

"Isn't it about our turn with Gizelda?" Nolan interrupted, urging his company away from Quade and Meredith. "We'll miss our opportunity, and you know you wanted to see how well your studies matched the tarot reading."

Elise's teeth chattered visibly. "I am a bit chilled, Lindsay. I believe I'll accept that glass of wine you offered earlier."

"Well, yes, of course." Lindsay nodded. "Good evening to you, Meredith. I do hope you'll let me call upon you soon."

"I'm quite busy with the children most of the time. But perhaps at a later date."

When the trio turned to walk downshore, Meredith abruptly covered her mouth to muffle a laugh. "Oh my goodness," she blurted. "I should tell . . . no . . . no." She began to hiccup, she was laughing so hard. "This is far too deserving. She shouldn't have slandered Sam. Just deserts, that's what it is."

"Tell who what?" Quade peered closer at the strollers who had obviously set Meredith into her frenzied amusement.

Elise Winkle's hem was caught in the waistband of her pantaloons, showing her backside to all the world. No wonder the woman claimed a chill! Quade glared at Meredith suspiciously, remembering her vow to get even. The banker's daughter was the culprit who had insulted Samantha. "You didn't?"

Meredith shook her head but giggled all the more. She raised a palm to ward off his doubt. "Honestly, I'm not to blame. I'd planned to put crawfish in her wine, but the opportunity hasn't yet presented itself. The woman is an embarrassment waiting to happen. I should have known I didn't need to retaliate. She'll do herself in time. I'd say when she returns to the bonfire, *someone* will enlighten her."

"You have a mischievous streak about you, Meredith Stanfield." For just a moment she reminded him of a wood nymph—part sprite, part temptress. The combination wove an appealing tapestry of attraction. "I'll have to remember that."

Quade motioned toward the tallest of the trio. "I wonder why Nolan Richards would take up with a pantaloon like Littlefield?"

"Lindsay's certainly a pest, but he *is* a likable pest, most of the time," Meredith defended.

Though he'd been taught better manners, Quade thought the banker's daughter needed the lesson she was about to learn. He chuckled, feeling a bit sorry for her, yet not enough to want to alter the outcome.

Instead, he focused his attention on her two companions. Richards's wildly gesturing hands and Littlefield's slumped shoulders and turtlelike neckline didn't suggest two friends enjoying a seaside chat. "Richards doesn't strike me as the sort to spend time with likable people. He wants something out of the relationship. What does Lindsay own or have access to that a man like Richards wants?"

"He's a teller in the bank. He knows the records of most everyone's accounts here in Biloxi. But that's it. Nolan may be trying to determine who among us would be better benefactors to his cause should I not bankroll his bid, but Lindsay couldn't possibly get his hands on the actual money. Wisdom Winkle is too shrewd for that."

She tugged on his arm, urging Quade to turn around. "I'm afraid I don't have much time. I pulled the number after Lindsay's, so I'm next with the fortune-teller. Are we going to concern ourselves with his new friendship or will you finish that walk you promised me?"

"Walk," Quade decided as his gaze swept over her. He thought Meredith the most beautiful and sassy woman he'd ever taken strolling. "As long as we leave our shoes on."

His boisterous laughter joined hers. While their stroll took them farther and farther away from the fish fry, Quade's suspicion grew. Richards had something devious up his sleeve, and it wasn't a tarot card.

"Quade, please leave it alone, will you?"

Meredith's plea brought them to a standstill.

"Leave what alone?"

"Whatever you're brooding over. You're with me now. Can't you just enjoy yourself? Being with me? Not having to act as chairman of the festival this particular moment? Nor captain of your fleet or even father or friend, but just plain Quade Cameron—man?"

She was right. His mind was far away from appreciating her company. He didn't feel comfortable with simply relishing the walk along the shoreline. It had been so long since he had allowed himself a moment's reprieve from anything that didn't stem from work.

"I'm afraid I've forgotten how, Meredith."

"Then slow down and rediscover yourself. Find out who you really are, instead of always wondering if everyone else is doing his job or what people might be conspiring. It may surprise you to learn how fine a man you've become."

The night cast such a mesmerizing spell, Meredith almost convinced him he could forget, almost made him believe that he could forgive himself for the past. Almost made him see a glimmer of forever. But she'd said the exact words to startle him back into the reality of why he would never offer his heart to another—why he poured himself into his work so he didn't have to feel or be anything but a taskmaster.

"A man's core is his foundation. It doesn't matter what he's become, if what he's *been* hurts those he loves."

"What is it you've done that's so terrible you can't be pardoned?"

"Run back to the safety of Plantation Row and your untormented life," he demanded, evading her question and the reasons he refused to answer her.

He kissed her, almost brutally this time. He released her with a shove. "Devote yourself to someone who can return your love as equally as you offer it. For I cannot."

❖ 16 ❖

"*THAT'S WHAT IT says for sure.*" *Shanty's head bent over the table, brushing back her mop-colored hair with one hand.*

Meredith attempted to focus on enjoying the carriage ride she'd given the girls to reward them for their diligence this morning. They had practiced their gracefulness up and down the steps of Stanfield House's grand staircase until each could descend without having to watch where they stepped. Deciding they needed to learn the etiquette used during carriage rides as well, Meredith had chosen a reward that would serve two purposes. But visions of last night's fortune-telling kept rushing back to haunt her. Reluctantly, she gave in and closed her eyes.

She watched Shanty study the last of the ten tarot cards before looking to the Gypsy for confirmation.

"Danger precedes you. Trust another who has tread its edge many times." *Gizelda's cryptic tone matched the eeriness of the walls, which were decorated with all manner of shawls and scarfs.* *"Have faith in what has gone before. For this is the final test, and Destiny will smile upon the deliverer."*

Though Meredith scoffed at the warning, a strange tightness in her throat made it difficult to swallow. Flames from lit candles placed in intervals around the makeshift

*parlor flickered simultaneously, then caught, sending
trails of smoke to entwine. Suddenly, the sound of the gulf
lapping at the shore seemed more prominent, as if the
promenade no longer divided land from sea. The pungent
smell of the Sound on a rain-washed eve blended with the
scented wood shavings Gizelda burned during her fortune-telling.*

*The Gypsy rose abruptly, jingling golden hoops that
dangled from her ears and others that covered her wrists
and forearms. "Do not scoff at the Wisdom of the Ages,
Miss Stanfield. It is your guardian and loves you well."*

*The woman's black, almond-shaped eyes added an age-
less beauty to her exotic features. Meredith wondered just
how old the "Wisdom of the Ages" might be, but she
doubted anyone would ever know. Gizelda always
changed the subject if questioned. A striped kerchief covered the thick raven tresses that cascaded well past the
Gypsy's waist. Her white off-the-shoulder blouse was
stark against dark olive skin. As she moved around the
table, the multicolored layers of her skirt tinkled with bells
sewn at the hem of each flounce.*

*Meredith fought the impulse to leave. She stood. "I
g-guess I'd better get back to the girls and relieve Thomas
and Opal." She motioned to the opening in the curtain of
shawls. "I'm sure there are a dozen others waiting for a
reading."*

*Gizelda reached out and took Meredith's hand, her
gaze demanding Meredith's attention. "Beware the sea,
Miss Stanfield. What you will give her, she takes."*

*Meredith snatched her hand away as if she'd been
burned by fire. The woman couldn't possibly know the
stark terror the sea evoked within her.*

"Miss Merry, are you all right?"

A tiny finger gently touched Meredith's hand, concern
filling Sam's voice. Her eyes flashed open. "Y-yes, Sam.
I'm just a bit preoccupied at the moment."

"Papa was too this morning." Sadness sobered the

nine-year-old's expression. "Did you argue with him last night?"

Meredith fingered one of the white-gold curls dangling past Sam's shoulders. The child had made a special effort to style her hair as instructed yesterday, and had chosen a dress of bougainvillea purple to wear rather than the overalls. All she had needed was a bit of encouragement.

"No, Sammy. We had quite a lovely night, in fact." Meredith's gaze swept over Sam with approval. "I'm just being foolish. I let something frighten me that shouldn't have."

Finally, the child's words sank in. "The captain left before breakfast, and I didn't get to see him," Meredith said. "You told me he acted strangely this morning. How so?"

Puzzlement grooved the tiny brow. "He said something about Gypsy nonsense. Miss Gizelda told him to beware of the sea and said something about danger and a whole lot of other things." Her eyes rounded in curiosity. "You don't think any of that's true, do you, Miss Merry?"

If the Gypsy and Shanty gave the same prediction to him—and probably to everyone else, for that matter—how could it possibly be anything to fear? Relieved, Meredith laughed, feeling the heat of embarrassment rush over her. How gullible she'd been!

"No, sweet. Miss Gizelda makes her living feeding on people's hopes and fears about the unknown. Having so many fortunes to tell at the fish fry last night, I'm sure your father and I got fortune number seven or eight." *With my luck, it was thirteen.* Meredith winked at Sam. "Just so we all didn't exhaust her mind."

Comforted, Sammy exhaled a huge sigh. "Good, 'cause I don't want anything happening to Papa."

Alex scooted up from the seat behind Meredith and Sam to make certain she was heard. "It wouldn't take a card reader to decide what would happen to us if it did."

The bitterness in Alex's tone drew Meredith's concern, making her turn around and stare at Quade's oldest child. "What *would* happen to you children? Has the captain assigned you a ward in the event of his . . .'' She forced away the image that swept over her like a wave crashing against the shore. "If for some reason he couldn't continue raising you?"

The thought of them living in another city filled her with dread, yet she'd never heard anyone mention Quade's siblings. His father had remarried, if she remembered correctly, and Quade was a result of the second marriage. "Do you have aunts and uncles?"

"Aunt Victoria would want to raise Randy and Sam for sure." Alex squeezed her little sister's cheek.

"Stop that!" Randy swatted at her.

"She thinks Randy's just *adooooorable,* and Sam's quiet so she's not much trouble. She thinks I'm too bossy."

Samantha frowned at her squabbling siblings. "Uncle Matt's touring with a Shakespearean company, so it would be hard for him to take care of us. And Uncle Cole is on an Amazon expedition." Her hand splayed against her neck. "I'm not sure I want to live anywhere near headhunters."

Exotic scenarios raced in Meredith's mind as she listened to the *clip-clop* of the horse's hooves.

Alex quit pestering Randy. Her finger traced the back of the seat that divided the four passengers. "Don't worry, Miss Meredith. There are plenty of aunts and uncles to divide us among. You wouldn't have to be our governess forever."

"Divide you?" Meredith whispered the unthinkable. That would be like dividing land, sea, and air. The three children were so much a part of each other's existence, one couldn't function without the others. "Isn't one of them capable of raising all three of you?"

"Aunt Jean Marie would," announced Randy as she bounced on her seat as if it were made from a springboard.

"It would be our luck, we'd get stuck with Aunt Jean." Alex grabbed the blanket that the coachman had draped over her and Randy's lap to ward off the breeze's chill.

"Hey! Give me that back!" Miranda fussed.

"Just a minute and I will." Alex wrapped it around her

shoulders, then raised her right hand above her head dramatically. Her toe pointed in opposition to the theatrical pose. "Look at me, I'm Lady Godiva."

"Quit making fun of Aunt Jean. She just likes to be different, that's all." Sam frowned at her sister, then offered Meredith an explanation. "Our Aunt Jean Marie sort of does things *her* way."

"Strange things. Silliness no one else would think of," Alex grumbled. "She'd probably dress us like ladies-in-waiting or barge bearers. She has a fondness for Cleopatra and calls the creek at her ranch The Nile."

Meredith chortled.

"Don't laugh. Last year when she visited from Texas, she had us all write President Grant a letter about the stinky cigaros he smokes. She hates smokers. She said if we didn't watch out, pretty soon a huge fog of smoke would cover the entire country and we wouldn't see one single amber wave of grain. Ever since Father taught us all how to write, at least once a year she makes us write someone who's upset her about something."

Aunt Jean sounded fun. Meredith would have to meet this "virago of the first order," as One-Eyed Thomas would call her. But it was obvious from the child's readiness to condemn that no choice would be the right choice for Alexandra.

"She has us write good letters, too," Samantha defended. "They all aren't all ba—"

The carriage swayed.

"Looks like I'm about to lose a wheel," the driver announced over his shoulder. "But not to worry, missus. I'll get you delivered."

"Shouldn't you stop?" Meredith insisted, wondering if the man was taking an undue chance. "We can walk from here."

"It'll just be a little bumpier than usual, and we've only a little ways to go." He sounded adamant and concerned that he might lose a fare.

"But sir, it's really not that far, and I'm willing to pay for our ride just the same."

"I deliver what I'm paid for." The man refused to stop.

Exasperated that his insistence on fulfilling his commission might cause them harm, Meredith's pulse sped. *Get the children's minds on something else.* She forced herself to smile and hoped the alarm racing through her did not register on her face. "Tell me more about your Aunt Jean."

"That would take us all day," Alex announced. "And I don't want to live with anyone who's going to make me wake up guessing who I'm supposed to be that day."

"I'm going to be a sea princess!" Randy exclaimed, shaking her hips back and forth. "And I'm going to make everybody dance."

The carriage teetered.

"Stop the coach!" Meredith demanded, knowing that Randy's small weight could not have produced such an effect. "This minute, sir, or I'll report you to the law!"

The driver complied, reining so abruptly that the wheels did not have sufficient time to halt their rotation. The back upended, hurling Alex and Randy into the front seat. A ripping sound rent the air. Wood splintered. The horse screamed its terror. The man hurtled out of the driver's box. Arms and legs tangled. Meredith desperately clutched for smaller flesh than her own . . . touching . . . grasping nothing.

"What happened to the four of you?" Quade crossed the floor to the children's bed. Meredith was propped against the headboard with a book in her bandaged hand. The elder two of his daughters lay on either side of her, and Randy was curled in her lap.

Randy's left eye looked as if someone had taken charcoal and drawn a half moon beneath it. She smiled at her father, and for a moment, he had to remind himself that she had been missing her front teeth *before* whatever had happened today.

Samantha's foot, covered with white gauze, rested on a pillow. Alex appeared unscratched. On closer inspection, he realized that the tip of her tongue rested between her lips for a purpose. The bloodstained kerchief in her hand hinted at the reason she had not answered his question.

"A long story." Meredith closed the book. She winced and attempted to shake the pain away from her hand. "We had one lesson too many today."

If they hadn't been such a pitiful sight, Quade might have been angered. But each one of them looked miserable. "You *are* teaching my children *refinement*, aren't you, Miss Stanfield? *Genteel* etiquette?"

"Don't be angry with Miss Merry, Papa." Samantha attempted to sit but was unable, because she couldn't scoot herself up with her foot. "We were taking a carriage ride and the wheel broke. We flipped, and all of us got tangled up . . . kind of."

Quade bent on his knees next to her. "Are you okay, Sammy?" His gaze swept over her as he made certain she hadn't sustained worse injuries. He glanced at Meredith. "Did you call in the doctor?"

Silver-blue eyes assured him. "Mother did. We were taken to Stanfield House after the accident. Pomender brought him within minutes. We've all been checked thoroughly. I decided it was best we be taken home . . . I mean . . . here. I thought the children would prefer being in familiar surroundings."

She nodded at Sam's foot. "It's not broken, just sprained. And Randy only suffered a bruised eye. Alex, I'm afraid, will have difficulty in talking for a few days. She bit her tongue. And me"——Meredith waved her hand— "It's going to be sore for a while, but not much cause for alarm."

"Is too, Papa." Randy tried to look under the covers. "Miss Merry's legs are real bruised."

"They're fine." Meredith gently pressed her hands against the covers to silently ask the child to leave them down.

"Can you walk?" His concern averted from his daughter to the woman who had obviously suffered the worst brunt of the accident.

"Yes, I'll just be sore for a few days."

"That's two spills you've taken, Miss Stanfield. I hope the old saying about threes is just that . . . an old saying." He noticed the pallor around her lips, the pain in her eyes. "Shall I hire Mrs. Price and allow you to return home?"

Color drained from her face. She glanced away. "That's unnecessary, Captain. But of course, it's your decision. I assumed since all of us are a bit worse for the wear, we could practice our lessons here and recuperate . . . together."

Three small pairs of eyes stared at him, pleading. Meredith's gaze joined theirs, waiting . . . entreating.

"Are you sure you feel up to this?" He relented. They would all mend faster if at ease. Perhaps mentioning Mrs. Price was not a good idea after all. "They might heal quicker than you. These four walls can get mighty crowded when you're cooped up with young ones who would rather be outside. I know. I nursed them through the chicken pox."

"Opal will be here every other day, and you in the evenings," Meredith encouraged. "Mother and Winifred will stop by, I'm sure. And the way Savannah's spending time with Yori, she'll be in the area if things become desperate. We'll get along just fine, won't we, girls?"

Two of them offered an enthusiastic "Yes." Alex's was more of a muffled "Yeth . . . *oww!*"

Now was not the time to tell Meredith that he wouldn't be able to promise her his evenings. She would know soon enough. He rose and turned away, giving himself time to conceal his deception. "Then it's settled, I suppose. How about I prepare you all some hot soup for supper?"

"Col . . ."

It sounded as if Alex were strangling. Quade swung around.

"It's too hard to say the *d*, Papa." Randy stuck out her tongue and held the tip of it. "Thee? It feelth 'ike thith."

Quade placed a kiss on top of his oldest daughter's head. "I understand, General. Nothing hot for you."

She nodded.

"I'll return in a minute." He headed for the stairs and glanced back, endeared by the sight of his shipwrecked scamps. A need to safeguard them from themselves, no doubt, came over him. "Don't sail without me, hear?"

Samantha laughed, taking up his banter. "We're docked for a while, Papa."

Meredith joined in, closing one eye to imitate their good friend. "Anchored by injuries, we are, me bucko."

"En*gulf*-t, tho to thpeak." Alex erupted into a fit of giggles.

Randy looked at all of them as if they had lost their senses and unknowingly made it a unanimous pun. "I don't see what's so funny."

"Sea!" Quade, Meredith, Alex, and Sam shouted it at the same time.

Alex laughed so hard she started crying. Meredith couldn't quit giggling. Sam tried to explain to her little sister, but Randy couldn't quite understand. Meredith finally just pulled them all closer and offered a group hug.

Not wanting to be left out, Quade included himself in the cuddling. Joy and peace, unrivaled by any he'd ever known, suffused Quade with such a sense of belonging that it nearly jarred his bent knee off the mattress.

Meredith mouthed silent words.

Surprised, Quade questioned silently, "What?"

"We need to talk about the accident when we're alone."

He could barely detect her whisper, but nodded his understanding.

The tiny head that separated him from touching Meredith's lips took voice. "Ooh, Papa, doesn't that feel so goood. Let's do it again."

His gaze locked with Meredith's. This did feel good, and he certainly wouldn't mind repeating the hug. "I'd love to do it all night, Princess, but I've got to feed you ladies and keep your strength up." A grin lifted his lips as the governess's cheeks stained a dusky rose. "The contest is only days away. Gotta have you at your best, don't I?"

Samantha pulled away abruptly, her hands rising to cup her cheeks. "My goodness, the contest. I won't be able to walk right, and Randy's got a black eye!"

"I wan be aba to tak." Disgust darted across Alex's face.

"What we gonna do, Papa?" Randy wailed.

"We can't look like this." Sam scowled at her foot. "I've got to practice my balance." She pointed to Randy's eye and nearly poked it again. "Oops, sorry. We've got to find something to cover that up." A glance at her older sister carved her features with despair. "What can we do about her tongue? She won't talk right for days! We can't stay inside. We've got to get help!"

A mutiny was in the making. Quade raised both palms to ward off their discouragement. "I'll think of something. Maybe Shanty can help—nooo, she's got a broken leg, that won't do. Perhaps Gizelda . . . oh yes, that's smart, Cameron. Send a doomsayer to cheer them up."

Meredith tittered. "You're quite charming when you're confused, Captain."

"You stay out of this." Quade shot her a teasing grin, loving the way her eyes lit with amusement. "Or, I'll send Yori over to nurse you. Or worse—" His tone grew villainous. "I'll dispatch Savannah to your rescue."

"Please, no. Anything but that, Captain." Meredith swung her head back and forth as if she were being flogged. "Keelhaul me, make me walk the plank, send me to Davy Jones's locker, but don't let her lash me with that complaining tongue."

Alex's gaze slanted toward Meredith. "Leave tongueth out of thith, will you?"

"I'll be back before you can say sea shells sink in the seashore on the summer solstice," Quade promised, aware that Meredith was being deliberately silly for the girls' sake. Was there something sinister about the carriage accident? "Just leave it to me."

❖ *17* ❖

Believing that Quade had left something behind, Meredith was surprised that he bothered to knock. She opened the door to discover Savannah and Yori instead of the captain.

"Where's he going?" Savannah thumbed backward at Quade's retreating figure.

" 'Off to make final arrangements' is all I'm ever told." Meredith waved them in from the evening sun. She sounded like a nagging wife, and they weren't even married.

Quade carried a bag of tools, looking to all the world as if he were, indeed, off on another mission for the committee, but Meredith had begun to believe he was deliberately avoiding her and the children.

Nothing she'd done during the last three days of recuperation brought to mind a reason for him to avoid her, but the man sat only long enough to eat a few bites of a meal before leaving to do the next "task."

"Dedication to his work is one thing, but surely even the committee doesn't expect a man to give up his whole life to the project?"

Yori took a seat on the davenport. "Quade Cameron is a driven man. He works because he wants to, I am thinking. It is good to provide well for his children, *ja*?"

Meredith stared after Quade, unwilling to close the door yet. Though his stride was purposeful, his shoulders were not quite as straight as yesterday, the swing of his arms certainly less carefree.

Besides the preparations for the festival, he had investigated the carriage accident and discovered that the driver could not be found. Though she believed the man was afraid to show his face because he had not followed her instruction to stop the first time, Quade was not so easily convinced. He had launched an investigation into the man's whereabouts, convincing Meredith that the captain thought the incident no accident.

Quade was beginning to show signs of exhaustion. Someone had to stop the man, or he would suffer ill health.

"Enough about the captain." Savannah sat next to Yori. "How about you, Meredith? Are you feeling much better?"

Meredith hated to admit it, but Quade was right. She needed a break from the warehouse. The walls were closing in on her. The call of the outdoors lured her. The captain returned so late each night that she fell asleep without forcing herself to challenge the surf. And she simply hadn't felt it would be right to leave the girls alone. Alex had cried in her sleep the last two nights, yet when Meredith woke her, the child merely shrugged and implied that a nightmare had caused the tears.

Tomorrow might prove a good day to test Samantha's foot and let them all venture out, but tonight Meredith needed a moment's solitude. "You know, Savannah, it would feel wonderful if I could just get away for a while. Perhaps to walk and let the wind blow on my face a bit. Would you mind?"

Yori shook his head. "Savannah, she was thinking that you would need that very thing. So we came to watch the blossoms. You go have your walk, *ja*?"

Touched by her sister's thoughtfulness, Meredith smiled. The Norwegian had caused many changes within Savannah since beginning his courtship of her. She looked forward to a long engagement between the two. "Thank you both. I think I'll go see how Shanty is. Now I understand how frustrated she must be, cooped up in that shack."

"Take your time."

The scent of magnolias on the evening breeze drifted through Meredith's senses like an exotic perfume. She inhaled the fragrance deeply, sauntering down the promenade at a leisurely pace. Night sounds filled her with an awareness that the twilight promised a particular magic. Yet she couldn't define what alerted her to the spell weaving itself around her.

Perhaps she suffered from cabin fever, and her pores simply cried out in jubilation of badly needed air. Katydids droned in the sweet gum trees. The deep, throaty *barrruupp-barrruupp* of bullfrogs calling to their mates provided bass notes for the buzzing tenors. Waves undulated against the shore, adding a pulse to the night rhythm. Meredith filled herself with its cadence, letting time and troubles ebb with the tide.

Though she needed the solitude, Meredith never felt more alone than she did now. This was an eve to impart secrets shared only by two.

"Guess Shanty will have to do," she said after a while, wondering where Quade might be working at this hour. Full darkness encompassed the wharf now. Only an occasional lantern lit the path before her.

Waving to a seaman who was netting late, she made her way past several of the better homes that fronted the promenade. The Campbells' house glowed from every window, full of merriment and music the whole summer long. For the hundredth time, Meredith imagined herself being escorted to the various planned galas on Quade Cameron's arm. She would be the envy of every eligible belle in Biloxi.

What foolishness! The captain was as married to his work as she was afraid of the gulf. When would he find time to attend any of the parti—? Meredith peered more closely into the Campbells' open windows. Was that

Quade? In formal black frock coat and cravat? Surely, she was mistaken!

Like a child deciding whether to pilfer the cookie jar, Meredith weighed the outcome of what she intended. If she was very careful, she could open the iron gate and it wouldn't squeak. Then if she tiptoed through the maze of shrubbery and didn't happen to stumble upon any lovers tempting the moonlight, she might be able to reach that bay window and take a closer look.

The gate opened with only a slight squeal. No matter how well one oiled the hinges, the salt air wreaked havoc on the wrought iron. Stealthily, she crept from bush to flowered bush, watching her steps closely for ground cover that might crack or rustle.

At the fourth bush out, her nose twitched. Her eyes watered. An incredible urge to sneeze overtook her. She tried to block the coming explosion with the back of her hand. Even a furious rub did no good to halt its imminent blow. Meredith's head felt as if someone had filled it with tons of sand and black pepper.

"*Achoo!*" Relief dampened the back of her hand. "Yuucckk!"

"God bless you," offered a masculine voice.

"Thank you," she replied and accepted the handkerchief being handed around the bush she'd chosen as her latest shield.

"You're welcome."

The deep, rough, velvety voice jarred her into realizing that she'd been discovered. Meredith waved the kerchief like a flag of truce. "I . . . uhh . . . I can explain this. It's not at all what it seems."

With startling awareness, she focused on the towering form that now stood next to the bush, arms folded. No matter how casual his stance, Quade's broad shoulders and narrow hips threatened her as surely as if they were weapons at his disposal. His black frock coat and stark white cravat fashioned a sleek, dark deity poised to lure her into his lair.

The bold, open manner in which he stared made looking away impossible. Rooted in place, Meredith stared back, unable to blink. Though he stood in the shadows, every nuance of his face had carved itself in her memory—memory spurred by countless dreams she'd experienced under his roof, endless fantasies she'd envisioned while in his presence, perpetual passion evoked by his kiss.

She caught herself returning his appraisal with as much intensity, only to watch his well-shaped lips curl to a wickedly disarming smile that sent tingles down to the tips of her toes.

The furrows on either side of his mouth lent a playfulness to his savage handsomeness, mesmerizing her. Finally, their gazes met. She was suddenly swimming in the darkest emerald pools she had ever seen, and it no longer mattered if she drowned.

A gust of wind carried with it the fragrance of honeysuckle. She hardly noticed. He stepped closer, his shoulders blocking out the world beyond them. Her heart plunged to her stomach. Did he intend to kiss her again?

An odd yearning swept through Meredith as the warmth of his skin emanated through his clothes, scenting her with his very essence. A rush of heat ignited every pulse point in her body, urging her to lean into him as a moth drawn to its fiery doom.

His finger gently tapped the tip of her nose and traced a tantalizing trail to her lower lip. "Be careful, Mermaid. You might catch what you're fishing for."

A threat? "And what do you think I'm after?"

He shrugged. "I know why *I'm* here. Why are you?"

"I took a stroll and thought I'd stop by the Campbells'. It seems such a lovely party."

"It is. So, why didn't you come inside instead of playing bush tag out here?" He gently touched her cheek. "Your face is going to be swollen in the morning, I'm afraid."

Honeysuckle. She'd been hiding behind honeysuckle bushes, for goodness' sake! She would look like several well-ripened strawberries tomorrow. Lumpy strawberries at that! Petulance lifted her chin. "I was not playing bush tag. Frankly, I was trying to find out why you're here and dressed like that."

"Ready to head home?" He motioned toward the gate.

"Don't ignore my question and, yes, I'm ready to go if you are."

"You look a bit cold."

There was no way she would tell him the shiver resulted from his nearness. "A little. Honeysuckle and I don't get along well. I'll look awful tomorrow. It's a good thing *I'm* not running for Sea Princess."

"Here, take this." Quade shed his frock coat and wrapped it around her shoulders. "That should warm you."

It surely did. Quade's heat lingered in the silken lining, cocooning her as if he held her in his arms. Meredith's nostrils flared while she breathed in all the scents that were Quade Cameron—sea . . . man . . . temptation. "Why aren't you out finding your children a new mother, Quade?"

"For the same reason you aren't looking for a new fiancé, I suppose. Who knows all the reasons we choose not to change?"

"Then you have a choice?" She was surprised to find herself willing to talk. "I'm not so sure I do."

"Tell me about Phillip. What was he like?"

"Dark hair. Shorter than you. Very wise—he liked me, you know."

They laughed.

"Tell me more." Quade took her hand in his and fell into step beside her as if they were a matched team.

"He promised to show me Atlantis on our honeymoon, but my wedding day never took place."

"The sunken city? That would put a damper on any honeymoon, I am thinking." Quade imitated their Norwegian friend.

She gently jabbed him with her elbow, then pointed to the east. "Phillip was an archaeologist of sorts. He loved to guess where ancient ruins were located. He told me about a map that pinpointed the exact location of Atlantis, just off the coast of Florida to the southeast.'' Meredith raised her face to the moon. ''He said if you sailed those waters exactly at midnight on the summer solstice, the moonlight would illuminate the golden columns and make them look as if they were lit by thousands of stars.''

''I've seen seaweed that's been stirred up leave a luminous trail in a ship's wake,'' Quade admitted. ''I suppose anything's possible.''

''Except bringing him back.''

Silence ensued, and she was grateful. He was stirring up old memories as surely as the ship had disturbed the seaweed.

''Do you miss him . . . even after this long?''

''Sometimes.'' *Not as much as I should*, but she would never tell anyone that. ''In a small way, you remind me of him.''

''Because I'm always gone?'' Quade tried to laugh off the comparison.

''Partially. But I think it's more because you work yourself constantly to prove something. He did that . . . until it killed him.''

''Well, aren't you the cheerful one this evening? Been taking lessons from Gizelda and Shanty?''

Meredith laughed. ''You're right. We should be talking about other things . . . like what were you doing at the Campbells'? I seem to hear an echo, don't you?''

''All right. You did ask . . . *three times*. I guess you deserve an answer.''

When he hesitated, her foot tapped impatiently. ''I'm waiting.''

''I . . . uh . . . was helping serve her guests. I needed the extra money, they needed an extra servant. So I filled in.''

She halted and faced him. ''But, Captain, that's work done by—by—''

''Commoners?'' Disapproval widened his stance, and he started to walk off. ''I had no idea you were such a snob, Miss Stanfield.''

''I'm not!'' She caught up with him, though it took her

several yards to do so because of his longer stride. "You simply have a hundred more talents than just filling the drinks of Biloxi's finest."

"But you've forgotten, Meredith." When he came near the warehouse, he quieted his tone. Sound reverberated over the water. "Biloxi's elite are the very reason I must take this extra employment, if I intend to raise the money needed to compete for the bid. I have to earn the balance of what you would not loan me."

With palms splayed, he warded off her defense. "I'm not complaining, mind you. Now that I've had a chance to reconsider, I'm glad that I must rely on my wits and brawn to achieve the result I'm after. It reaffirms that a man gets out of life what he's willing to put into it . . . with the sweat of his brow."

"But you're not spending time with the girls, as it is."

"I'd rather they not know about this job. Samantha will fret herself silly worrying about my health. The General is so angry with me most of the time, it would just stoke that fire more. Randy . . . well, Miranda might not fuss, but I'm used to assuming the worst and working up. That way, everything turns out better than I expect."

Meredith's plans had backfired. She'd thought by denying him the loan she would keep him at home with the children. Instead, he worked night and day to gather the money on his own, without her help. The man's pride was as bountiful as the sea. Perhaps she'd judged him too harshly. Maybe she shouldn't have judged him at all.

"Thanks for walking me back."

"My pleasure, Meredith."

God help her, she didn't want this moment to end. "Was it, Quade?"

He swore under his breath before catching her chin in his fingers. His mouth demanded hers with such a fierceness that she had to encircle his neck with her arms for fear of losing her strength to stand. Finally, he pulled away and pressed featherlike kisses over her cheek, to the lobe of one ear.

"Did you kiss Phillip like this?"

She looked into his eyes. "He never made me feel this way."

"And how *do* you feel, Meredith?"

"As if I belong in your arms and nowhere else. Yet I'm confused and angry too. Please let me go, Quade. Stop making me want you. I swore I would love Phillip forever, don't you understand? When you hold me, I can't remember that vow."

Quade's kiss was wet, warm, achingly sweet. Her resistance melted away under the rush of excitement churning inside her.

"Kiss me, Meredith," he whispered against her lips. "Kiss *me* and forget. Make *me* forget."

His words lured, intrigued, hypnotized. Seduction cast its spell upon her until she was willing to throw caution to the night wind and follow him into the gulf itself if it meant staying in his embrace.

His long fingers buried themselves in the auburn curls that cascaded to her waist. He nuzzled the underside of her chin, and his tongue traced tantalizing circles over the curve of her neck. Feverish sounds rushed breathlessly from her throat as if the growing need inside her had taken voice.

Her fingers caressed, admiring the hard slope of his shoulders. His shirt was hot, moist against her palms. With a will of their own, her hands buried themselves in the thick blond hair sliding gently through her knuckles. This felt so right . . . so wonderful.

Meredith welcomed his kiss, opening her mouth to return the tormenting sensations. Her knees turned to water as he sent her swimming in desire. She forgot what she was doing, where she was, and who she was doing it with.

His hands were everywhere, in her hair, on her back, pressing her hips into his. The buttons down the front of her shirtwaist gave way easily to the pressure of his fingers. She could no more deny him than she could stop breathing. His hand slid beneath her chemise, covering the high, hard tip of one breast that strained to appease his touch.

"*Quade* . . ." Her breath mingled with the heat of his mouth. Triumph volleyed through her as he groaned deep within his throat.

Suddenly, he spun her around, thrusting her behind him. "Cover yourself."

His demand was but a croak, yet his tone tolerated no defiance.

"So there you are, Meredith!"

Nolan Richards's greeting was thrown like a bucket of winter water upon her senses. Rapidly, she refastened the buttons, willing her fingers to stop trembling with the desire Quade evoked. She turned, ready to give the man a lecture on intruding at an inopportune moment. But the grim line of his mouth and frosty glare warned that the paper he held in his hand was of dire importance. She had not been quick enough to hide all that had transpired.

He thrust the missive toward her. "This is for you." The man eyed Quade. "I thought you'd be overjoyed. Now, I'm not so certain."

Meredith snatched the paper and began to read. Her heart felt as if it sank to the pit of her stomach. "Oh my God!"

"What does it say?"

Quade's question faded as if he had spoken it from a great distance, yet he moved closer as the promenade seemed to sway beneath her.

She glanced up at the captain and whispered in disbelief, "Phillip is alive."

❖ *18* ❖

THE CIRCLE OF solemn faces staring at Meredith made thinking difficult. She fidgeted, knowing that all those who sat in the warehouse parlor awaited her reaction, her decision . . . to do what? If only she knew.

"How can he be alive?" Savannah poured everyone a refill of coffee before seating herself next to Yori. "People saw him swept under."

Meredith's hands trembled so badly that she was unable to keep the paper from rustling when she held it up. "I kept every letter he ever wrote. This is definitely Phillip's handwriting."

She stared at Nolan who had taken a chair opposite her own. "I don't understand why he hasn't contacted me before now. All those years of grieving, believing . . ."

Pushing himself away from the window where he'd been staring out at the water, Quade purposefully moved alongside Meredith. "What I want to know is, why did he send the letter to the bank rather than to Stanfield House? Everyone on the coast knows the Stanfields reside in their family home."

Suspicion layered the room, emphasizing the animosity between Quade and Nolan.

"Perhaps he thought she'd remarried or was vacationing in Europe?" Nolan shrugged. "Who's to say? All I know is that I happened to be at the bank when it arrived. Littlefield was so excited about seeing the sender's name that he didn't want to wait to finish his duties to bring it to you. I told him I would be happy to deliver it myself.'' Disapproval narrowed his eyes. ''Unfortunately, that took much longer than I'd anticipated. You were away from your duties and occupied with other matters.''

''Those other matters are none of your concern, Richards.'' Quade reminded the Northerner that Southern honor demanded that a gentleman not discuss a lady's private affairs.

Nolan rose from the chair and pointed directly at the captain. ''You know, Cameron, I'm getting tired of always having to point out to Meredith just how much you're playing her for a fool. She doesn't even realize it.''

The Norwegian stood, towering over the group. ''You don't slander a man in his own home, either. I am thinking I will invite you outside to discuss this matter.''

The finger lost its target, curling into a ready fist. ''Wouldn't you know he'd have to depend on his friends to bail him out of a scrape? Just like he depended on Meredith's grief and raw emotions to coerce her into granting him the bid. Is that what you were doing, Cameron? Wooing her so you would gain favor? What are you going to do when her fiancé returns?''

Before Meredith could think, Quade had the man by the collar. His fist twisted the taunter's cravat until Nolan's face turned various shades. The captain's eyes met the Northerner's dead on, sending a chill of apprehension through Meredith. If ever she'd seen a look that promised no quarter, this was it. ''Quade, please . . .''

''Please what?'' His question exited as a snarl. ''Please remember that I have daughters upstairs that I refuse to allow to be awakened by this man's stupidity? Please remember that this split-tongued blackguard is insinuating you've done something improper?'' He tightened the noose. ''Or should I simply forget that, though I'm not as wealthy as this carpetbagger, I'm still a civilized man who controls his brutality because he chooses to?''

"I'm j-just the messenger, C-Cameron," Nolan sputtered, gasping for breath. "Phillip's your threat."

"Quade, let him go! This is no way to resolve . . ." She gripped his fist, applying gentle pressure. "Please."

The granite-carved knuckles beneath her palm lost their rigidness, turning to gently grip her hand. With the silent pressure, he vowed that he would fight for her. That he wasn't willing to let *her* go so easily.

"Get out of my house, Richards, and never set foot across its threshold again. If you come near me or mine—" His gaze encompassed Meredith in that company. "—I'll not let respect for my children and their governess keep me from rearranging your smirk next time."

"Good night, ladies." Nolan straightened his collar and grabbed his hat. "Miss Stanfield, I trust the letter was met with enthusiasm. According to what I've heard, Phillip was beloved among the people of Biloxi. I'm sure everyone in town supports you in your coming happiness." He hurried past Quade.

When the door slammed, Quade started after the man. "Don't, Quade. He's just angry." Meredith glanced toward her friends for help. "I couldn't bear it if they fought over . . . over . . ."

"Stop him, Yori." Savannah instructed the Norwegian as if she had the right to boss him. "Go after the hothead."

Yori looked doubtful, but willingly obeyed. "He is under full sail, I am thinking. I cannot promise the captain won't scuttle the scalawag."

Meredith cupped her eyes with her hands, unable to stop the flow of tears. "God help me, for the first time in my life, I have no idea what to do." A sense of helplessness washed through her. "How am I supposed to feel?"

Two hands gently pulled her palms away from her face. Savannah stared at Meredith, her hazel eyes full of sincerity.

"I know I've not been much comfort in the past, Merry, but I'd like to try now . . . if you'd let me."

"I think I'd like that very much." Years of indifference between the pair fell away like sand shaken from their hems. They hugged one another.

"I'm afraid I've relied on too much of my own opinion to ask yours on anything." Meredith backed away to brush a hand across her eyes.

Savannah laughed and handed her a hanky from the pocket of her skirt. "And I've been spoiled because I always knew I could count on you to get things done. Yori and the captain have certainly swept in and changed our lives these past few days, haven't they?"

"Yes. And you . . ." Meredith stared at the light in her sister's eyes, the expression on her face when she said the Norwegian's name. "You are most definitely in love."

Savannah swung around as if she were a little girl testing the buoyancy of her flounces. "*Ja.* Completely and wholeheartedly in love with Big Yori Svengsen." Her gaze finally focused on Meredith. "And you, Merry? Do you love the captain?"

"Love?" She started to touch the nape of her neck, then realized it had become a habit when she evaded the truth. "I think I am. I want to be. But I can't, Savannah. I *can't.* You know the promise I made Phillip. I pledged to love him forever. Till death do us part."

"But death *did* part you. You've been faithful to his memory until now."

"But don't you see? I wasn't. Not really." Understanding what her words implied and needing to calm her sister's startled expression, Meredith explained, "No, nothing like that, Savannah. I found myself wanting Quade's arms around me, his kisses on my lips. If Phillip and I truly loved one another, is that possible? To love two men?"

"I think the answer lies in here." Savannah pointed toward Meredith's heart. "And I believe the question is not whether you can love two men, but whether or not you ever loved Phillip in the first place. Forgive yourself, Merry. After all, you are just as human as the rest of us."

"I'm afraid to trust my heart," Meredith admitted. "I

did so once before, and I haven't yet recovered from the pain of that betrayal.''

Savannah seated herself on the davenport. ''Do you believe Nolan? Do you actually believe the captain is toying with your affections only to gain his own means?''

Meredith paced. ''I don't want to believe it, and yet . . .''

''I wouldn't presume to tell you how to feel . . .'' Savannah's hands rubbed up and down her arms as if she were caressing herself. ''But I can tell you there is no greater love than the one who sees past what everyone else spurns and is willing to examine a person's true heart. Trust the captain. Trust how he makes you feel. Believe in him when there doesn't seem to be any reason to.''

''When did you get so sentimental?'' Meredith marveled at the woman she was only now beginning to perceive.

''When love gave me Yori.'' Tears of happiness shimmered in Savannah's eyes. ''And it's not being sentimental. It's finding wisdom.''

Meredith's temples drummed. ''Wish me some of that wisdom, will you? I have to decide whether or not I'm going to honor my betrothal to Phillip. He's returning in two weeks.''

''Does the letter say *why* he's stayed away for all these years?''

Meredith reviewed the missive again. ''It seems he hit his head and lost his memory until recently.''

''How convenient.''

Phillip might one day be her husband, so Meredith reluctantly defended him. ''I've heard of such things. *Amnesia* is the official term.''

''*Scheming* is how I define it. And I ought to know.'' Savannah blushed. Suddenly, her shoulders straightened. Her face lit with anticipation. ''They're back.''

''How do you know?'' Meredith looked on with amazement as the door opened and the two men entered.

''The sound of his footsteps on the promenade. He walks a certain way.''

Envy wove through Meredith as she realized how attuned her sister was to the man she loved.

"Just remember one thing." Savannah stepped forward so neither man could hear the last of their discussion. "Memory or not, Phillip sent a letter. Quade Cameron is man enough to walk back in here to confront this situation in person." His familiar form shadowed the light beaming through the door. "Ask yourself, who cares the most?"

❖ 19 ❖

ALL MORNING, THE girls' moods matched the sagging clouds that had swept ashore during the night. Meredith tried her best to fight off the gloom, but the children's squabbles and the captain's early departure dampened her efforts. Everyone seemed ready to argue.

"Are you going to leave us now?" Sam glanced up from her uneaten lunch and stared at Meredith. "We heard some of what happened last night."

Alex's head bowed over her plate. "I heard it all."

Meredith studied each girl, understanding now why they had been such scamps all morning and balked when she said that she would be leaving them with Shanty and Savannah this afternoon. "What makes you think I'd go simply because of what was said last night? I told you, I just have some business to conduct this afternoon and can't take you with me. I'll be back later this evening. Perhaps then the weather will be better, and we can find something to do to help your father."

"You'll leave us 'cause your man's coming back." Randy laid down her spoon, refusing to eat another bite. "You won't want to marry our papa. And we need a mama real much."

"Not just any mother." Samantha rose from her chair and limped over to stand by Meredith. "We want *you*. I-I don't remember my mother, but I think she must have been just like you, Miss Merry. Please don't go away."

"Don't beg." Alex's head jerked up. She hurled her fork across the room and glared at Meredith with malice. "Don't expect *me* to beg her to stay."

"I'm gonna tell Papa on you." Randy pointed a finger at Alex. "You know it's not polite to—"

"I'll handle this, Randy." Meredith suddenly understood Quade's objection to her promises to the girls. Sam, and particularly Alex, were deeply wounded by their mother's absence. Since Katherine was no longer around to love them, then he believed *she* could not vow the same. Meredith decided she would discuss this with him and ask how she might help them overcome their grief.

"Children, I could never take your mother's place, no matter if your father and I ever ... married. But I do not offer my affections lightly. I told you I'd love you forever, and I mean that most sincerely. Please believe me that no matter where I live, here with you or at Stanfield House, I will always, always consider you my very best friends. You can be with me anytime you wish and your father allows."

Samantha threw her arms around Meredith and hugged her. Randy rushed out of her chair and launched herself into Meredith's lap. Meredith looked askance at Alexandra, but the eleven-year-old wouldn't budge. Before Meredith could think, words escaped her. "Someday, Alex, you're going to have to forgive your mother for dying."

Alex thrust her chair backward and bolted to her feet. "How could you possibly know how I feel about my mother?" Tears spilled over her cheeks as rage flushed her face and sharpened her accusation. "Don't go around giving advice if you don't know the whole story."

The child fled the kitchen.

"Alex, wait! I'm sorry. You're right. I didn't—"

The sound of the front door slamming jarred Meredith to her feet, almost causing her to drop Randy.

"Go after her, Miss Merry." Samantha limped ahead

of Meredith. "She's been crying all night, thinking you were going to leave us, too."

"Grab Randy's hand, and you girls go straight to Shanty's. Take a parasol, in case it starts raining. Tell Savannah I'll be there just as soon as I find Alex."

"Yes, ma'am."

"Find my big sister, will you, Miss Merry?" Randy pleaded. "She's real, real sad right now. She's not so smart when she's crying, and she might get hurt."

"I'll find her, Pumpkin. Don't you worry. I won't stop looking until I do."

"So, there you are. I've been searching *everywhere* for you." Meredith's gaze swept the long stretch of beach. She'd never wandered this far from the promenade before. It was an isolated spot, tranquil, a good place to recover one's emotions. That is, unless the brooding clouds decided to drop their burden.

For just a moment, Meredith remembered the festival and all the decorations that would be ruined if the weather worsened. Disappointment filled her . . . for the town's sake and for the children. If the festival failed, so would the Little Princess contest.

"I'm surprised you found me. Father's never even searched this far before." Alex threw a pebble into the surf and watched it skip across the surface. "I doubt anybody has. This is *my* place."

"May I sit beside you?"

"Suit yourself."

Meredith joined her, duplicating the child's cross-legged position. The wind whipped at her hair, blowing it into her eyes. She brushed it back. "Then you've run away before? This isn't your first time?"

Mint-green eyes stared at her. "In case you haven't noticed, I don't get along well with my father all the time. Of course, I've run away before."

Meredith's fingers traced a pattern in the sand. "Seems to me that if I were deeply hurt by someone abandoning me, running away would be the last thing I would do."

"W-what do you mean?" Alex's face quickly masked the surprise that had darted across her features.

"Well, you obviously are very hurt by your mother's death and feel that she's abandoned you in some way. By running away, aren't you abandoning the person you're angry with? Why don't you stand and tell them exactly how you feel and why you feel it? Isn't that what you wished could happen? That your mother could come back, and you could scream at her about the unfairness of it all? Let go of that scream that's been buried inside you."

"Leave me alone!" Alex bolted to her feet and raced down the beach.

Meredith ran after her, refusing to let her elude her feelings again. She caught the child, gripping her gently. Ignoring the child's twisting and turning to liberate herself, Meredith demanded, "Stop, Alex. Be still. Don't push me away."

She loosened her grasp enough to show that she would not force the child to stay unless she wanted to. "Just let me hold you, General. You don't have to be so tough. I won't tell anyone you cried. I promise. Go ahead. Let it all go."

A wail shattered the air. The child's arms flung around Meredith's waist. Scream after soul-wrenching scream erupted from deep inside the girl, raising the hair on the back of Meredith's neck. She hugged Alex closer, trying to soak all of Alex's suffering into her own body.

But this agony had been Meredith's companion for six years now. She'd believed Phillip dead, berated herself for arguing with him before he left, rebuked herself countless times for not being with him in that fateful moment, condemned herself for living on. How much greater the pain must be for one whose love was certain for the departed! Despair honored no generation.

Meredith absorbed Alex's pain and shouted her anger at the sky. "Let it all go, General," she challenged them both. "Nothing we . . . *you* could have done would have changed the outcome. You're not to blame. It's all right to go on living."

*　　*　　*

"But we must talk," Meredith demanded.

Quade balanced on the yardarm, perched high above her head. "I really don't have time for this, Meredith."

The Union standard whipped and popped, fluttering in the increased breeze. Colorful banners were strung from every sail. It looked as if the boats had sprouted wings.

"Tomorrow evening the festival starts. I'm trying to get done before nightfall, but it doesn't look like the weather is going to cooperate with me. And I can't wait for it to blow over tonight, because the Paxtons are having a gathering at their house. I'm serving for them."

Meredith held her hand over her eyes to watch him paint the mast. "Won't you come down, Captain? We really need to talk. Not only about last night, but I need to tell you about Alex."

He laid the paintbrush across the bucket dangling from a nail hammered into the yardarm, then shinnied down the mast with the ease of a monkey. Upon landing, he waved her to one of the seats on the boat's bow.

The boat undulated with the tide, causing nausea to rise in her stomach. "Could we go ashore, Captain? I'm not quite up to this yet."

Shallow boats to be used in the flotilla had been moored at the end of each wharf that extended out from the promenade. Each was linked by planks that connected boat to boat. During the parade, the planks would be removed, and only colorful streamers and ropes would connect them. For the child's sake, Meredith had left the security of land to seek him out two boats away.

Quade took her hand and helped her onto the first plank. "Don't look down. I've got you."

A wave rolled in, rocking each boat. Her fingers clutched at his fearfully. "Quade?"

His breath warmed her neck as his face rested inches behind her, his body blocking a fall backward. A band of iron encompassed her waist. "Take easy steps. It's just the wind stirring up the tide. Nothing to worry about."

Tentatively, she moved forward. One step. Two.

"That's the way, Merry. See? You can do it. There's nothing to be afraid of."

"Not if I'm with you." Meredith realized she'd said the thought aloud. Her cheeks tightened with embarrassment.

"I'm glad you trust me."

She did. Above all things, she trusted Quade Cameron. The recognition made her steps bolder. Meredith easily reached the first boat. When she touched the deck, she turned and smiled at him. "Thank you."

"You did well." Admiration filled his eyes.

"You're a wonderful teacher."

"Easily taught when the student is willing."

What else are you willing to do? his eyes seemed to question. "One more," she murmured.

"One more what?" he asked and moved closer.

Kiss? her heart encouraged, but reason commanded her voice. "Boat to cross."

"Then by all means." Again, he offered her a hand up.

Traversing this boat was as easy as the last. When Meredith's feet touched the wharf, she was surprised to discover that the relief she had expected to feel was unnecessary.

Something about being in the protection of Quade's arms had taken away a good deal of the sea's terror. She wanted to give credit where it was due. "You've helped me overcome some of my fear. Thank you, Captain."

He immediately released his hold upon her waist. "I assumed you'd recovered because your fiancé is no longer its victim."

An ocean of silence divided them now.

"Do you still love him?"

Not "*did* you," but "*do* you." Meredith felt she was under full attack. She faced him. "I don't know what I feel at the moment. This is all too new to comprehend."

He motioned them toward the bench next to Yori's shucking house, where he often fished off the end of the wharf. Quade gently gripped her elbow, guiding her forward.

"Surely a woman who believes in forever didn't give up hope her lover might return? Particularly if a body was never found?"

Why was he expressing such anger? The Camerons, both young and old, were a brooding lot. "Think about what you're saying, Quade," she countered. "Several people saw him swept away. How could I not believe him dead? This has nothing to do with believing in forever. It was a quirk of fate . . . a cruel, unjust whim of destiny. What made you so distrustful?"

He didn't answer. Instead, he guided her onto the bench then took a seat beside her, staring out at the decorated boats. Finally, he triangled his fingers, resting his brow upon his fingertips. "Because I was once blinded by believing that love *could* last forever."

Too many questions about his and Katherine's marriage posed themselves in Meredith's mind. Thomas had hinted of discord between the captain and his wife. Could Alex's sense of abandonment derive from more than grief?

The sense of release she'd shared with Alex earlier urged Meredith to convince him to let go of the past . . . no matter how difficult that might prove. "Tell me about Katherine."

Misery stared back at her as a low hiss slithered through Quade's clenched teeth. His fingers no longer formed the triangle. "She was everything to me. The reason I rose in the morning. The thrill of hurrying home every night."

Though Meredith wanted to know, she found it difficult to hear the loss in his tone . . . the old longing that had not been completely buried with his wife. "You must have loved her very much."

"Apparently, not enough." His laugh was bitter. "At least not enough to keep her from running straight into the arms of another man."

Meredith's heart clenched with the pain of betrayal he must have felt. At least she had not suffered the same with Phillip. Her fiancé had abandoned her emotionally long before his death. "I thought she was killed in a steamboat accident. I had no idea—"

"No one does. I made certain of that." His gaze searched her face. "I've never told anyone of her infidelity before."

A horrible thought consumed Meredith, reminding her of the brutality he had displayed last night with Nolan. But she quickly dismissed the thought.

Quade stared out into the gulf, trying to see the past. "I wanted to give her everything, but the war kept taking it all away as fast as I could earn it. She was accustomed to having more than she needed, not just surviving. I was too busy making ends meet, assuring that we didn't lose Belle Raven, to realize when she must have begun her love affair with the soldier."

Compassion filled Meredith, urging her to reach out and touch him. Quade stared into her eyes for a long while before continuing. His hand pressed over hers, tracing circles over its surface. Banners of desire streamed up her arm, sending heat to the nether regions of her body.

"He was a moneyed Northerner stationed at the fort on Ship Island. I came home one evening to find Sam and Alex out in the gazebo watching the baby—a newborn, mind you—while she and her lover were upstairs in the master bedroom."

His fingers stopped caressing as pain-laced fury filled his voice. "Can you imagine? She didn't have the decency to see that the children were properly chaperoned during her tryst. Satisfying her lover was more important than making certain our children were tended."

One hand curled into a fist, and he struck his other palm. "I was glad when she told me she was leaving with him that very morning. Glad that she was out of my life." His voice broke. "But I didn't hate her so much that I wanted her dead."

Quade searched Meredith's face for understanding, for lack of blame. "I never hated her at all. I loved her. I believed she loved me."

"I think I understand something now." Meredith took his hands in hers, silently asking him to uncurl his fists. Quade surrendered to her gentle persuasion. "You work so hard to prove yourself worthy, don't you, Quade? You believe you didn't give her enough, and *that's* why she left.''

"Perhaps. But what I didn't give her was more than possessions. Apparently, I didn't give her the passion she needed. My love for her wasn't enough to hold her.''

"Love isn't like the keel of a boat, Quade, always keeping everything aright. Sometimes it rocks the boat rather than keeping it afloat.'' Meredith spoke with sad certainty. "Don't blame yourself. Be glad you found out about her affair before she died. That she freed you. Otherwise, you would have spent the rest of your life dedicating yourself to a false memory. Like I did.''

The reality of her relationship with Phillip hurt too deeply to continue talking about it. Meredith forced herself to remember that she was the consoler, not the one to be consoled. "Did you demand that she leave the children, or was it her choice?''

He stared at her in confusion. "I would have never separated mother from child, if that's what she wanted. But she didn't want them . . . at least for a while, she said. Kate wanted to go north and establish herself with his family—to seek an end to our marriage and begin a new one with her lover. Then she intended to send for the girls.''

"Would you have let them go?'' The answer was important to Meredith—important to understand all that had transpired this afternoon.

"No . . . if she'd loved them truly, she would have never been willing to give them up . . . even for a little time.''

"That's why you were so angry when I told the girls that I would love them forever. You doubted that someone who wasn't their flesh and blood would do what their own mother couldn't.''

"That's right. I'll do anything in my power to save my children from someone's mistaken affections, just as I would deny Katherine's betrayal if you ever told anyone about it. I don't want them harmed by scandal. I don't want them living the gossipy life that thrives on Plantation Row.''

''Mistaken affections?'' Meredith removed her hands from his. ''Is that what you think I feel for your children?'' *For you?* ''I would never betray their hearts or your confidence. But in your effort to keep them from learning the truth, you've also kept them from knowing their true heritage.'' Understanding continued to dawn. ''Is that why you closed Belle Raven? Everyone in Biloxi believes you moved out of it to live in the warehouse quarters because you mourn Katherine. That you can't walk the same halls she lived in. Are you afraid the scandal might come to light if you live there?''

''I'll open it again when the girls are ready to marry and make it a happy place once more.''

''And when will that be, Captain? When *you* believe the time is right?'' Exasperated, Meredith stood and began to pace. ''Can't you see what is happening in front of you? Alex is growing up now. She should have a choice about the kind of station in life she wants. The girls deserve to experience both of your worlds—the docks *and* Plantation Row. To learn what it is that makes you the kind of man you are. You're not just Quade Cameron, sea captain; you're also Quade Cameron, Southern gentleman. Let them know you completely, Captain. Quit hiding from them and the truth.''

''This is none of your busi—''

''I'm making it my business. I care about those girls. Whether you like it or not, I've come to care about you.'' She halted in front of him and met his gaze. ''If you refuse to believe in forever, then believe in *now* and the dreams of those darling girls. They all crave the title of Little Princess like it's a goal almost beyond their reach. Yet it's in your power to offer them the same kind of status, the same kind of special happiness, on a daily basis. Quit being so selfish by trying to give them everything *you* think they need. Give them back their choice.''

The wind whipped furiously at the hem of her dress, but it didn't matter. Let it blow! She was too caught up in emotion to worry about whether a storm might destroy the festival.

The advice she offered him suddenly sank in. Hadn't she helped others to the point that she deprived herself of her own choices? Hadn't she denied her feelings for Quade and mourned Phillip as a widow might have simply because it was expected of her? Hadn't she refused Quade's loan because she felt he should deal with his children in *her* way? "I owe you an apology, Quade."

He stood and reached for her hands, staring into her eyes. "No, you don't. What you've said has made more sense to me than anything I've heard in a very long time, Meredith."

"I'm glad." She licked her lips, aware that her attention was drawn to the sensual way his mouth moved as he spoke. "But I meant concerning the bid. I should have never turned down your request. I'm going to tell the committee that I'm awarding you the money and the bid. But I want you to know why I gave you such resistance.

"When I believed Phillip dead, I couldn't bear to see your daughters suffer the way I had. Phillip kept himself busy doing tasks for the wharf men and women. I didn't resent his dedication at first, because the people he helped were my friends too."

She turned and stared out into the gulf. "But then he was always gone. There was always one more task he must complete before he could spend time with me. I was a girl of sixteen, Quade. I was in love with being in love, I suppose. At that age, a girl wants to be courted . . . cherished. She dreams of moonlight strolls, endless dances, stolen kisses in the garden. Not years and years of grieving . . . and denial."

Meredith closed her eyes, remembering the kiss she and Quade had shared in the Campbells' garden. The warmth of his hands suddenly caressed the back of her neck, sending a shiver of wanting through her.

"A man truly in love wants no less, Merry."

"I need to believe that, Quade, but I knew . . . long before he was swept away that Phillip and I would never have that all-consuming passion we're told comes to the lucky few. I had accepted my fate and thought I must simply wait for it to happen between us one day.''

He gently urged her to turn around, then lifted her chin with one knuckle. ''You never lost faith, did you, *querida*?''

She bit her lip. ''I did in Phillip, but never ever in hoping that true love might find me as long as I was willing to believe in it. And if that meant forever, then so be it.''

Quade loomed over her, his eyes glittering with an expression she couldn't quite read. ''He's to return in a few weeks now. Your faith served you well.''

''He's not the one, Quade. I know that now, but I haven't stopped believing love might still find me.''

His warm breath fanned her face, and his essence enveloped her, intoxicated her. She inhaled deeply, feeling her head reel with her emotions, her desire, her fear. There was no turning back no matter what his own feelings. He pulled her close.

''I want you, Meredith. I want your warmth, your strong spirit, your kind soul. I want the light inside you to purge the darkness within me.''

Meredith's heart pounded in her ears. ''I can't give you just a part of me, Quade,'' she whispered. ''What I offer is forever.''

''Then teach me how to believe in eternity.''

The gentle kiss explained what his words would not. He pulled away, his eyes searching deep into hers for resistance. She could only surrender to his passion as surely as the wind whipped the trees and the waves crashed against the shore.

''Where?'' he asked with husky urgency.

Stirred by the special madness found in his arms, she whispered, ''I know a place.''

❖ 20 ❖

Meredith stared transfixed at the shelter of magnolia trees and bougainvillea vines that hid the isolated area of the beach where she had found Alex this afternoon. For a moment, she wondered if she should have selected somewhere else to go, but the haven was the perfect place to rendezvous with Quade.

Too many eyes watched from the promenade and took note of wherever she and the captain went together. His plan made sense. Slipping past the girls and Shanty would be difficult. She could stroll along the beach past Shanty's shack, alone, as if she were enjoying the sand and surf. He would follow a few minutes later, taking the long way around behind the shops along the promenade.

Meredith worried that the delay might change her mind about meeting him, but she discovered that the waiting made her want him even more. The passion he'd stirred within her whispered through her bloodstream like a caressing wind.

She pushed aside lush tropical vines and stepped into the haven. Despite the overcast day, she felt the heated softness of the sand underfoot. The fragrance of magnolias and salt air made her inhale deeply.

Meredith's mind reeled, partly from the heady combinations of scents, but more from her mounting anticipation and desire. She strolled to the water's edge and stared out into the great expanse, finding it ironic that she chose such a place to offer her heart.

Wishing now that she'd thought more of their comfort and less of the aching need driving her to distraction, Meredith berated herself for not at least stopping to get a blanket. No one would have questioned her for taking one along on the walk. Many beachcombers carried a quilt to sit on and enjoy a particular view.

Should I undress? she wondered, feeling suddenly awkward and uncertain.

Air stirred behind her, and she could almost hear his heartbeat. The back of her neck tingled, as if a warm wind blew its breath across her shoulders. Seagulls stopped their raucous calls and sailed on the wind, leaving only the soft cry of a dove to fill the inlet.

He stood only a few yards away, watching. She sensed it without turning. Her fingers trembled. Her breath caught in her throat.

Tell me what to do, she asked him silently. *I know only what I feel.* But he did not move closer, leaving her to take the initiative. Slowly she turned to face him, trusting the sensations he aroused within her, wanting him as she'd never wanted anything else in her life. Needing to belong to him.

One by one, she unfastened the buttons of her dress. She let the dress slide from her shoulders and down to the sand. A shiver swept over her skin, but she was not cold. The heat of his gaze warmed her.

Her chemise hid nothing from his sight, stirring a surprising boldness within her. If he wanted to keep a distance, then let him see what she was only too willing to offer. A gift she'd made to no man before him and would make to no other.

Meredith tugged on the tiny ribbons holding the fine lace closed. It parted like a whisper over her breasts, freeing them. Cool air rushed over her, making each nipple peak. She laughed with the pure wantonness of it, letting the chemise fall to the sand as well. When she pulled the string on her pantaloons, they slid like soft down around her ankles.

He stood at the edge of the trees, a golden silhouette against the approaching twilight. Still, he did not move.

Unable to read his eyes, Meredith stood there, waiting for him to step toward her—to say something. The stillness lingered. For an awful moment, she began to doubt his passion for her after all. Had he changed his mind? Was her wanting of him greater than his own of her?

Her chin lifted stubbornly and her shoulders squared. She refused to cover herself. Let him see clearly that she was unlike Katherine. She offered him all that she was and would not hold back her life, her self, to his scrutiny.

"I am here, if you want me," she stated softly.

As he sauntered toward her, Quade shed the frock coat he wore. "We should have brought a blanket, but my coat will do."

The fierce desire that had possessed her since the first moment he'd rescued her from the surf now shook her. It seemed an eternity until he stopped before her, when in reality it was mere seconds. Meredith forced herself to meet his gaze, aware that her skin felt as if a thousand suns burned beneath its layers and set her blood afire in her veins.

"You are the most beautiful woman I have ever seen." Awe filled his husky whisper as he gently removed the pins from her hair and let the auburn curls cascade through his fingers.

"I'm told Katherine was more lovely than most." Though considerate, she did not want him to reassure her. "You need not appease me."

"I would not tell you anything but the truth, Merry." He reached out and stroked her cheek lightly with his thumb. "You're the perfection I thought impossible to find. God. You don't know how badly I've wanted you since the moment I saw you sitting behind that desk."

"At the office?" She searched his face for teasing, but found only solemn sincerity.

"The way you looked at me. Like you wanted to protect me. And you did. You wanted to protect me from myself. Yours was a face full of caring, Meredith. And a heart full of forever.''

With exquisite tenderness, his mouth brushed over hers. Her breath caught, her lips opening in invitation. The kiss became more demanding as he pulled her into his embrace, branding her with his desire.

"Merry," he whispered. "I've waited for you, wanted you all this time. . . .''

Warm fingers trailed down her back, cupped the swells of her buttocks, and drew her closer. His tongue tasted her deeply, its hot tip taunting her to meet its every thrust. Her arms raised up over his shoulders, wanting to absorb his body into her own so desperately that a moan of frustration escaped her.

He buried his hands in her hair, his fingers caressing her temples. "I want you," he whispered against her lips. "I need you."

His passion came unreined, invading Meredith's senses until it took her breath and robbed her of an ability to stand. She swayed against him, returning the intense embrace with as much fire and need as was given. His body quaked beneath her touch as a husky groan mingled with her own moan of desire.

Like a blind man who had suddenly been given sight, he worshipped her first with his eyes, then allowed his hands to move over her ever so slowly, caressing. Fingertips trailed a heated path along the curve of one cheekbone, down the slope of her nose, and past her throat. The warmth lingered at the rise and fall of her breasts. He cupped their taut fullness gently in his palms, brushing his thumbs over the sensitive, straining peaks.

This was what she wanted. This and a thousand other pleasures in his arms. "Your touch feels so wonderful," she whispered, unable to find the words to express the exquisite torture.

Slowly, his body slid down hers until his hot breath warmed the valley between her breasts. Anticipation filled her as she waited, straining forward to satisfy the aching need for them to be taken into his mouth. His shoulders trembled with tension as he balanced, restraining his power over her.

His hands played over her back, rubbing, caressing, tempting her with the circular motions she wanted from his tongue. Hungrily he drew her to him, covered one nipple with his mouth completely. She cried out his name as he lavished the peak again and again, tantalizing her until she lost all awareness of her surroundings. There was nothing except the two of them on the stretch of secluded beach.

She almost wept aloud, sensing some tremendous wind of change about to rush over her. Yet she raced headlong into it, knowing there was nothing to fear if Quade led her there.

Suddenly, his body was pressing hers into the sand. He moved lower, slowly. His hands blazed a heated trail that his mouth followed. His teeth nipped, his lips kissed, kindling a burning need in their wake. His hand fanned over the flat plain of her belly, caressing.

As he kissed her there, she thought she heard him murmur, "One day, it will be rounded with my child."

The thought of Quade's baby inside her brought tears to Meredith's eyes. She wanted that more than life itself, wanted him to fill her completely.

Fingers kneaded the curve of her hip, brushed the center of her thighs. Her muscles tensed. She reached for him, uncertain of what he intended. Sliding her hands into his golden hair, she realized the action only served to guide him more closely to his destination. His fingers stroked her, sending wave after sensual wave echoing through her. The powerful line of his shoulders flexed as he wrapped his arms around the backs of her thighs and raised her body slightly up to him.

As his lips nuzzled the soft auburn curls, her fingers let go. He stopped and looked up at her, desire burning hungrily in the smoked emerald of his eyes.

"I want to kiss every part of you."

The rough huskiness of his voice pebbled beads of excitement along the surface of her skin. Unwilling to deny him, she smiled and nodded her consent.

Her blood was on fire. Her skin aflame. An all-consuming hotness drove her beyond desire to a desperation of senses that threatened to shatter her. She threw her head back, letting her auburn hair spill around her.

Suddenly his touch stopped, leaving her pulse throbbing in every wet, warmed place his lips had caressed. His body slid up the length of her, making her aware that his own skin was on fire with passion.

Pleasure curled his mouth. "Do you still want me, *querida?*" he whispered. "As much as I want you?"

"Yes," she responded hoarsely, urgently, knowing that if he stopped now, she would surely die from this madness. "I want to touch you the way you touched me."

She reached and fumbled with the buttons of his shirt. When the effort took too long, she tore them open to expose the muscular cords of his chest to her touch.

A deep chuckle rumbled from him. "We have as long as you wish, Merry."

Her hands dropped to his waistband to free the barrier of buttons holding back the hard press of his manhood. Finally, the buttons gave way. She shoved back the offending garment, releasing his aroused virility into her hands.

He raised her hand to his chest, thrilling when she curled her fingers into his tawny hair. Her slim shoulders rose above two glorious globes of alabaster flesh, then tapered to a narrow waist. He was awash with the heat of her body, the clean female fragrance of her that made him quiver with anticipation.

Her fingernails trailed downward. "I want to touch all of you."

Quade's breath caught and a sheen of perspiration glistened wherever her hands cast their spell of enchantment upon him. She paid homage to his body as he had done to her. His hips slid back and forth in rhythm to her erotic touch.

With extreme effort, Quade gently moved backward.

"God, Meredith. You've got to stop or I'll not be able to finish this . . . and there's so much more I want us to share."

Quade's knee gently pried her legs apart, instinctively opening her to a deeper touch and compelling her to wrap them around him. His hands slid beneath her buttocks, helping her lift her hips to welcome him more fully.

"This may hurt," he murmured against her lips. "But I will never hurt you again, *querida*."

Nothing could ache as much as the need to have him inside her. To feel him moving within.

"Kiss me, Merry. Let me kiss away any pain."

She granted his request, crying out in surprise when he thrust deeply inside, stretching her, filling her.

"Forever," he whispered into the curve of her neck. "You're mine forever."

A cadence began, as if their bodies tuned themselves to a dance intended for only them. Soft sighs rippled from them like eddies sweeping out into the night. They ceased to be individuals, becoming one heart, one body, one long, glorious moment of forever. Like the ocean's current, the power of their passion flowed over them, hastening them toward unfathomable ecstasy.

Her gaze locked with his as his body made her oblivious to all but his deep thrusts. She writhed, frantic for a release that would not take him from her but would forever bind him to her.

"Promise me forever, Merry." His hips moved and ground against her. "Forever."

"Yes," she wept. "I promise!"

She arched against him once again and started to shatter, felt him tense and tremble in the same moment. A cry of joy and exultation tore from her as he called out her name and spent the hot torrent of passion inside her.

Searing her with his kiss, Quade finally laid his head against her shoulder and murmured, "Forever mine."

He smiled, awed at her beauty. Meredith still slept, yet her body glowed luminescent in the moonlight. He reached out to touch her, tracing his fingers over the smooth planes of her face, through the flame of hair that tumbled past her shoulders. He smoothed the swell of her bottom lip, drawn by its lushness and the memory of her kiss.

Her lips curled at his tenderness. Something inside him awakened, and he acknowledged the emotion with gladness. The depth of longing he felt for this woman was amazing. He had not known he loved her until now. Respected her, yes. Wanted her, undoubtedly. But loved her?

The reality of it all sank deeply inside. Now he understood. Years of anger and the pain of betrayal fled his soul. If Katherine had loved her soldier even half as much as he felt for Meredith, then Quade could understand what had driven her to give up all. To want to be by her lover's side. At long last, Quade forgave Katherine, because love . . . true love . . . had taught him how to truly forgive.

With forgiveness came a certainty. Meredith Stanfield had given her word to marry Phillip. She had nothing to compare tonight to. Quade couldn't hold her to a promise of forever and must now love Meredith enough to let her choose.

❖ 21 ❖

MEREDITH WOKE AND stretched, feeling the sand shift through her toes. Then she remembered. . . .

All the glorious sensations of being in his arms made her body blush. Never, in her entire realm of fantasies, had she imagined the reality of making love with Quade.

Realizing that he no longer occupied the space beside her, she propped herself up on her elbows and searched the beach for sight of him. He stood in the surf, dressed in his trousers now, letting the waves wash over his powerful calves where they had been left bare.

She thought of grabbing her chemise, but the desire to be by his side was too great to wait for propriety. Meredith ran to the water's edge and discovered that no fear gripped her now, for she knew Quade would be there. He would always be there. Forever, they both had vowed. Together.

As if she had touched him, he turned and waded toward her. She opened her arms and ran into his embrace. Burying her face in his neck, Meredith kissed it as Quade lifted her and she locked her legs around his waist. Her lips indulged themselves in tasting the lobe of his ear, the strong curve of his jaw, his cheek, and finally his lips.

When at last her world quit spinning, she gently pulled away and shouted, "I feel so wonderful!" Laughing with the pure pleasure of loving and being loved, she stared into the emerald of his eyes and allowed her heart to speak. "*You* are so wonderful."

A smile curved his lips. "Did you sleep well?"

Embarrassment tightened her cheeks. "Better than I have in ages. But not as well as I plan to from now on. Forever is a glorious word, Captain. Simply glorious."

His shoulders tensed. His eyes closed as if he were shutting something away. His hold upon her relaxed. Meredith unlatched her legs from around him and stood, feeling the cool sweep of water rushing over her ankles. "Did I say something wrong?"

"We've got to get back."

She felt bare, as if something had stripped her of the gift of happiness he'd presented her. She shuddered, chilled by his silence.

"What's happened, Quade?" An undertow of sadness pulled at her. Had his words been spoken in a moment of heated passion? Did forever mean so little to him after all?

"Nothing's happened," he evaded, leading her ashore. Quade bent to gather the clothes they'd shed. "We've just got to return before we're missed. Shanty will send out a search party, thinking you've gotten yourself lost, and I'm supposed to be at the Paxtons'."

He moved with such precision that she wanted to scream. Couldn't he set himself free for just one night? Meredith's hand halted his from picking up her chemise. "Look at me, Quade."

Their gazes met. He looked tortured. Driven.

"Even now, after what we've just shared, must you work?" She didn't want to draw the comparison, but perhaps his silence had pushed Katherine away too. "Is that why your wife left? Your work was more important than helping her understand?"

He flung away Meredith's touch. "You wouldn't understand, even if I try to explain it. My work is all I will ever have." Quade began to dress.

She did the same, but refused to let him brood. "Why

don't you let me determine what I can and cannot understand? I have an intelligent head on my shoulders and can argue a good point when the need arises."

"How can I explain to you something *I* can't comprehend myself? But I do. And because I do, I should regret every moment we've spent together tonight."

He grabbed her roughly, pulling her into the granite-hard wall of his chest. His kiss seared her, imprinting his claim upon her soul. When finally he tore his lips from her mouth, he pushed her away.

"But I don't, don't you see?" He raked his fingers through the golden hair at his temples, deep furrows grooving his brow. "I don't regret a single moment of loving you. But . . . ."

"But what?" Meredith reached out to him, feeling as if he'd slapped her when he backed away from her touch. Something compelled him to withdraw from her. Something indefinable. If it were real, if she could see it, Meredith would battle that force with all the fierce rage stirring inside her.

"Phillip is returning. You promised to marry him."

Relief coursed through Meredith. So that's what this was . . . the fear that she might want Phillip? "I love *you*, Quade. I couldn't possibly marry him now."

He raised his palms to ward off her approach. "No, Meredith. It's not that easy. You have nothing to compare tonight to. I do. I know what I want and who I want. But you don't know what you'll feel when you see him again."

"You're wrong." Meredith's chin lifted defiantly. "I could never love any man the way I love you, Quade Cameron. And Phillip's return will never change that."

He handed her the remainder of her garments. "I'm counting on that, Merry. But until he does, and you know without doubt that you no longer feel any measure of affection for him, then I must keep my distance."

Meredith stared at her clothes as if they were remnants of the rapture he so easily tossed away. She watched him complete his dressing and reluctantly did the same. Each

garment seemed a piece of armor she fastened to cloak
the sadness filling her heart—each button a closure of that
gift of herself she would give to no other. When she had
finished, she dusted off his frock coat and held it open
for him.

He hesitated, then slipped his arms into it, allowing her
to nestle it over his shoulders. She lifted his hair out of
the collar and ran her fingers through its thick mass. Her
body trembled with wanting, but she forced her words to
be brusque. "What if Phillip never comes back? Will you
always deny my right to love you?"

He faced her, gently taking her hand and lifting it to
press a kiss along her fingertips. Quade's eyes glittered
with hope. "Believe me, *querida*. If Phillip doesn't show
up, I'll spend every day of my life making you glad you
honored me with your love."

"Then I promise you one thing." Her hand lingered in
his. "I am going to spend every moment of the day when
I'm not tending the children discovering how Phillip suddenly came back from the dead and why."

"If that wind keeps up, it'll kill the celebration for
sure." Quade teetered, nearly pushed into the warehouse
by the force of the gale. "I hope everything's battened
down tight or half the decorations are going to be floating
on top of the gulf."

Meredith took his hat and coat and hung them on the
rack next to the desk. She reached out instinctively to dust
him off, then realized he'd made it clear they were not to
touch each other again. Her fingertips tingled from the
need, but she let her hand fall to her side.

"I know, Merry, but we may have no choice." He
glanced upstairs, his brows arching in question. "Too late
to go up and tuck them in?"

She shook her head. "No . . . I was reading to them,
and Randy asked for a glass of water. I was just headed
back up."

"Then I'll go with you. But first . . ." He walked over
to the large mahogany highboy that took up a good deal

of one wall. Opening the bottom drawer, he pulled out a patchwork quilt and pillow, then strolled over to the davenport and spread them out. "Hope you don't mind, the water's too turbulent to use the skiff. I'm going to have to sleep here tonight."

"That won't be comfortable." Her gaze swept over him to test his height, but found herself remembering other things. Desire ignited in her bloodstream. "Why not sleep in your bed? I share Randy's. I don't use yours."

"Opal will be here in the morning. I'd rather she not know we slept under the same roof. You're the first governess who's stayed overnight while I'm in town. It might start talk. I'll have the blanket put away and be gone long before she gets here."

Meredith couldn't help herself, a hunger for him making her bold. "Don't you think it's a bit late to be worried about my reputation?"

"Only you and I know that . . . and no one will ever hear such from me."

I love you, Quade Cameron, her heart took voice. *And everything you do and say declares you love me too. Why are you being so damned honorable?* Phillip could be everything she remembered, but it would not let her love Quade any less.

"Best go on up." She sighed, feeling an exhaustion that had nothing to do with the day's activities and everything to do with waiting for the time to come when she might truly belong to him. "They've had a long day. We all have, I'm afraid."

"Is that you, Papa?" Randy stood at the top of the stairs and rubbed her eyes with both fists.

"It's me, Muffin. What are you doing out of bed? Those sleepy little eyes need to close if they're going to look bright and shiny for the festival tomorrow."

"Miss Merry was going to get me a drink."

"I have it, sweet. I'll carry it for you until we're off the stairs."

"Up you go." Quade lifted the child into his arms and

she bear-hugged him, pressing her tiny cheek against his shoulders.

"Papa, you smell so nice." Randy rubbed her nose in his shirt. "Kind of like Miss Merry."

Meredith blushed. When she returned and changed into her nightwrapper, she had lifted the clothes they'd laid upon the sand and was immediately engulfed by the scent of him that lingered.

"There you go, Muffin." He lay the child gently on the sheets and pulled back the blankets. "Now crawl inside and close those eyes so the sandman can work his magic."

"The sandman?" Meredith had never heard this story before. "Who's he?"

"He is the king of all the beaches in the whole wide world," Randy informed, looking pleased that she knew something that someone as smart as Meredith didn't. "He sprinkles magic sand in our eyes so we won't be afraid and can sleep when Mama and Papa sleep in their rooms."

"That's just something Father told you so you wouldn't be such a scaredy-baby," a sleep-filled voice admonished. "The sandman is about as real as Santa Claus."

"Is too!" Randy bolted upright. "Ain't he . . ." She glanced at Meredith. "I mean, isn't he, Papa? The sandman and Santa Claus are real. Same as you and me."

Meredith's brow arched. This was going to have to be handled delicately. How could she help him? Thoughts raced to assist.

"Well, Muffin, it's like this . . ."

"No, Captain. Let me explain." Meredith reached out and nudged him aside. She sat on the edge of the bed she shared with Miranda. "There really was a man named Nicholas Klaus. He and his wife lived centuries ago, about the fifteenth, I believe. In a little German village. Because they had no children of their own, every year on the eve of Christ's birth Mr. and Mrs. Klaus would deliver toys he'd carved for . . ."

By the time she finished the tale, both Alex and Samantha were listening intently. Quade smiled at her, gratitude shining from his eyes.

"But what about the sandman?" Randy asked, breaking the spell of relief the adults had exchanged.

Quade chuckled, looking as if he'd fallen into a hole, and there was only one way out. "Lesson number nine hundred fifty two, Meredith. This child has the memory of Methuselah. She never forgets."

Meredith stood. "Well, that answer's just going to have to wait until another day, then. But I promise, I'll read up on the real story of the sandman and let you know what I find out."

"Good luck," Quade muttered.

Her eyes narrowed playfully as if to warn, *Do you want me to get you out of this or would you prefer to satisfy her curiosity on your own?*

"By all means." He pretended to cough. "Excuse me."

Meredith accepted his clever apology. "Your father has a thousand things to do tomorrow, and you've got to get some sleep or else you won't feel your best for the festival tomorrow afternoon."

"If there *is* a festival."

"What do you mean *if* there is one?" Alex demanded, sliding from the bed to stand.

Samantha flung back the covers and raced to her father's side. "Why wouldn't there be, Papa? We've all worked so hard. Isn't everything ready?"

"Yes, all we have to do is finish painting a certain mast in the morning—" His glance at Meredith made her aware of why that particular job had not been completed. "—and I wouldn't want to be the man who draws that mast to climb in the race. Everything else is ready. But it's the weather, girls. The wind's blowing so hard, the waves will rock the floats too much. You wouldn't be able to keep firm footing, and a good many of you would become seasick."

"Not us, Papa," Samantha reminded him. "You taught us how to not get sick if the water gets rough, remember?"

The children became a gaggle of questions and demands.

Meredith wrapped an arm around Samantha, wanting to comfort the disappointment she heard in the child's voice. All three were not worried about the string of decorated boats that would form a sailing parade across the bay, but instead were concerned about whether or not the Little Princess contest would be canceled as well.

Unfortunately, in times past, if part of the festival was suspended, the entire celebration was called off. Superstition had carved a strong foothold in Biloxians' minds, and they did not tempt fate by ignoring the season's warning. If the wind blustered so heavily that they had to be concerned about opening night, the threat of a hurricane might end the celebration completely. Instead of celebrating, they needed time to board up their shops and make their way to higher ground.

"I suppose we could see if the committee would agree to put the festival off one day," Quade conceded.

"But could you actually persuade everyone to do so?" Meredith was glad he felt the same way she did about the superstition. It was nothing more than chance if the wind buffeted the seaport the remainder of the week. "I hardly think it's possible to get them all in agreement."

Alex's fists shot to her hips. "You just don't care if they don't have the contest. What does it matter to you? You get to be a princess every day in that big old house of yours. You're mean and selfish and . . . and . . . just like Miss Winkle!"

"You didn't mean any such thing." Samantha slipped from Meredith's arms and went to stand by her older sister.

"Apologize to Miss Stanfield, Alexandra." Quade stood, his face a mask of parental irritation. "Or you won't go tomorrow whether the contest does or doesn't occur."

Alex crawled into bed and turned over so neither adult could see her face. "I apologize."

"Good night, Papa." Samantha kissed her father's

cheek, hesitated, then pressed a quick peck upon Meredith's.

"*I'm* not mad at Merry, Papa. I'm just mad at that ol' wind." Randy lay on her pillow and folded her arms across her chest, frowning.

"They're not blaming Miss Meredith for this, Muffin," he said in a tone loud enough for all to hear while he tucked in his youngest. "They're just disappointed because they think they're not going to get to be a princess. But I know just the thing to resolve that." He glanced up at Meredith. "By Bluebeard, just the thing! We'll have a princess ceremony of our own . . . at Belle Raven!"

✦ 22 ✦

"Is EVERYBODY READY to go?" Quade bounded up the stairs, then thought better of it, coming to an abrupt halt midway up. "Is it safe to come up?"

"Yes, Captain." Meredith moved to the edge of the landing and motioned him forward. "All is in order."

His eyes told her what his lips did not. The silver-blue off-the-shoulder gown that had been her father's last gift fit Meredith as though it had been tailored for only her. His bold gaze swept up her, lingering at the provocative décolletage that defined the voluptuousness of her figure. Approval darkened his eyes to jade.

"What a beautiful morning, I must say."

His compliment pleased her, making it worth the trouble of sending for the dress. Perhaps if she continually strove to entice him, seduce him, like waves washing against the shores of his determination, she might convince Quade that she wanted him and not Phillip.

But this was not her day to spend with Quade. It belonged to his daughters.

When he reached the landing, she announced in her most formal voice, "May I present Princess Alexandra, Princess Samantha, and Princess Miranda Cameron."

"Princess *Randy*," the youngest insisted, rocking back on the heels of her jade slippers.

All three of his daughters stood in a row, bedecked in long flowing dresses the color of their eyes. Jade for Randy. Sapphire for Sam. Blue-green to catch all the shades of Alexandra's. Matching ribbons held their hair back from their brows and entwined in various points amid the fashionable curls atop their heads.

"We thought you'd forgotten, Papa. Did it take that long to paint the mast?" Suddenly, Samantha smiled, her freckled face radiant as she spotted what he had taken from behind his back and now held in his hand. "Oh, Papa, how beautiful! Wherever did you find them?"

"Someone said they were just growing baby spiders in her attic." He winked at Meredith and handed her the three tiaras.

"Savannah?" Appreciation for her sister's thoughtfulness broadened Meredith's smile.

He nodded. "Will you do me the honor, Merry? I'm afraid I'll mess up their hair."

"Here, I can do mine!" Randy grabbed hers and stuck it in quickly, making it look very much like a halo askew.

Quade tapped one finger on his jaw and pretended to inspect her thoroughly as Meredith gently adorned Samantha's curls with the crown. "Not bad, Muffin, but it could use a little adjusting. Here, how's that?"

"Just fine, Papa. Do I look like a *real* princess now?" Randy swung her hips to and fro, making her petticoats swish and her crown tilt again.

"From the top of your crown to the tip of your glass slippers."

Randy looked puzzled as she pointed at one slipper. "It ain't glass, Papa, it's made of—"

"He was jesting, barnacle brain," Alex admonished. "You know . . . Cinderella? The glass slipper? That story he's read to you ten thousand times. You should have been a court jester, not a princess. When I rule the kingdom, that's what I'm gonna decree."

The six-year-old stuck out her tongue, then defended herself when she realized her father had seen. "She thinks she can boss me more now 'cause she's a real princess."

"That's because you'll be a royal pain now instead of an ordinary one," Alex countered, looking pleased with her suggestion.

Samantha giggled at her older sister's joke.

"Ladies!" Meredith clapped her hands to draw their attention, but the white gloves she wore muffled the sound. "Real princesses do not squabble with one another. Particularly when a gentleman has come to pay a call."

"Yes, and your carriage awaits you, m'ladies." Quade bowed and swept one hand extravagantly toward the staircase.

"Is it a pumpkin?" Randy raced ahead of them, not giving him time to answer.

"No, *Pumpkin*, it's not." Merry couldn't resist, loving the twinkle in Quade's eyes when he noted her cleverness.

Alex rushed down to join her youngest sibling. Though she no longer limped, Samantha descended the stairs more briskly than Meredith had expected. Quade and Meredith followed, she just as curious as the children to see what he'd planned.

When they reached the front door and she spotted the carriage, dual emotions battled inside Meredith. A fear that the girls would disappoint their father by refusing to ride, and an admiration that he'd gone to such lengths to please his daughters. She shaded her eyes to keep the wind from blowing sand into them and awaited the girls' reaction, wondering if any of them would be afraid to ride in the carriage after their last disastrous trip.

"Oooh, Papa, it's gorgeous!" Randy's frank admiration voiced itself as she fingered the garlands of white, yellow, rose, and purple magnolias that were draped in intervals around the carriage's frame. Even the driver wore a solid white frock coat and pants, his handlebar mustache curled and waxed to a fine sheen. Flowered garlands wove through the reins the man used to command the matched team of white Arabians. The breeze wafted with the scent of magnolias, giving the scene a dreamlike quality.

"Like Cinderella's coach," Alex whispered, awe replacing the usual sarcasm in her tone.

Tears sprang into Meredith's eyes. She glanced at the man who loved his children so deeply he had gone to such extremes to please them. Grief swept through her as she realized there would be no more moments to share with her own father. No exchange of ideas or knowledge. Yet he had given her memories. Just as Quade was giving his daughters a special memory now to treasure forever.

She silently thanked Quade for this moment. For within his gift to his children, he had also given her a way to come to terms with her sadness. Death might have taken the man, but it could not steal the past from her. Like buried treasure that had been unearthed, remembrance after remembrance washed ashore in Meredith's mind. Today, she would be a young girl again and relive what it meant to be loved and cherished, so that she might remember always. A very special man was this Quade Cameron she loved. A very special father indeed.

Quade glanced at the overcast sky. "We'd best be on our way so we'll have time for everything before the festival starts."

"Then they're not going to cancel it after all?" Alexandra allowed him to help her into the carriage, then scooted over.

"Let me in last." Randy backed away until her father had helped Samantha inside. "I want to sit on the end so nobody will squish me if they slide." Randy frowned at Alex. "Well, you nearly squished me when we turned over last time."

"You won't this time, Muffin. I've checked everything. Twice." Quade turned, offered his hand, and half bowed. "May I be of assistance, *querida*?"

"That means, *my sweet*," Randy informed them. "Miss Opal said so."

Meredith blushed, aware of just how little got past the imp. "*Sí, Señor. Gracias.*"

She slipped her hand into his and felt his other hand lightly grip her waist to help her into the open-air carriage.

Quade followed closely behind, taking a seat next to her and opposite the children.

As he spread a blanket over their laps, Meredith's gaze took in the Camerons in all of their finery and thought how exceedingly handsome and beautiful they all appeared. And for just one moment, she imagined what it would be like to truly be their mother and Quade's wife.

The image took hold and beckoned to her like a lighthouse pointing the way home to a wayward soul. And in that instant, she knew nothing short of her own death could prevent her from finding a way to convince the captain that Phillip would never again possess a piece of her heart.

"Ready, girls?" The captain eyed the trio, then stared at Meredith for confirmation.

She nodded.

"Driver!" he called over his shoulder. "To Belle Raven."

Though it may have only been the wind, Meredith thought she heard him add, "At last."

Quade waited, watching in anticipation as the children entered Belle Raven. His heart beat so fast he could hear it drumming in his ears, and his hands perspired inside his gloves. He watched as Randy ran up the staircase that took up half the foyer and swept down in marbled grandeur from the upper landings. The six-year-old straddled one banister and slid down to the bottom floor.

Meredith reached out to stop her, but the child had already slid to the bottom before she could react quickly enough.

"Oooh, it's dusty!" she exclaimed, dusting off her petticoats. "Didn't get my gloves dirty though."

"Of course it's dusty, silly. The house hasn't been opened in years." Quade looked apologetically at Meredith. "I didn't have time to have it cleaned yet."

Yet? Meredith heard the possibility in his voice. "Do you intend to have it cleaned?"

"Yes. After the festival and before—"

"Papa, who's that?" Samantha interrupted his answer, pointing to the portrait of a beautiful young girl who could have been the exact image of Sam, if it weren't for the difference in ages.

"That's your mother. When she was fourteen." Quade gently took her shoulders and swung her around to the left so she could see a portrait of the adult Katherine that hung yards away. "And that was a year before she died. I had the younger picture hung in the middle of the landing because I always wanted to remember how she was when I first fell in love with her."

"She looks like me," the child whispered in awe, facing her father. "I mean . . . I'm just like her. But she became beautiful, didn't she?"

Quade bent so that he could stare directly into his daughter's eyes. He lifted her chin and allowed his gaze to sweep over her features. "Just as beautiful as you're going to be one day, Princess. In fact . . ." He stood and made a sweeping bow. "May I have the honor of this dance so that I will at least get one before I have to fend off countless beaux?"

Samantha blushed and curtsied, glancing at Meredith for reassurance that she'd done it properly.

"My pleasure." She gripped the folds of her skirt in her left hand.

Quade encompassed her waist with one hand and waited until her right hand fit snugly into his. He began to hum a song he'd heard long ago, surprised that he still remembered its tune.

After a minute or two, Samantha brought an end to the dance. "I'm sorry, Papa. I didn't mean to step on your feet."

"That's quite all right, Sam. It all comes with practice. Just like your beauty will blossom in time. Besides, I should have thought about this being your first whirl around the floor with me. I like to show my partners how I prefer to waltz." He stepped back and let her go, hoping she would not take his instruction as criticism.

Holding his hands in the same position as if she were

still in his arms, he attempted to show her the waltz. "You take one step to the right, rise up on your toes, then go down. Take a step to the left, rise again and—"

"May I?" Meredith stood in front of him, with the folds of her dress in one hand and her other hand raised to fit into his. "I would like to learn your preference as well."

Challenge sparkled from her eyes and Quade accepted it. He took Meredith into his embrace and twirled her around the room, her body moving closer than required but in synchronized harmony with his own. She was a quick learner, his Meredith. And a worthy opponent. Her cheek resting against his, the perfume she wore, and the heat of her breasts emanating through the slim barrier posed by the dress's gossamer material proved a heady distraction. He stumbled, missing a step.

Quade released her. "Thank you for the demonstration, Miss Stanfield."

She winked! "Entirely my pleasure."

"Can I do it, Papa? Can I?" Randy raced up and held her arms out to him.

He laughed and told her to rest her feet on his, then waltzed her around the room until she was giggling too much to maintain any semblance of balance.

"How about you, Alex?" he asked, taking a deep breath and staring at his oldest daughter. She stood at the top of the staircase, frowning at the portrait of her mother.

"I've done it before. It's for babies."

Quade glanced at Meredith, who motioned him to go up the stairs. He complied and leaned against the railing that encircled the entire second floor. "What else do you remember, Alex?"

"Too much."

"Sam, Randy, let's the three of us go look in the next room, shall we?" Meredith encouraged. "I'll bet there are hundreds of things to see."

Quade glanced down and nodded his thanks. The other children were not old enough to recall much about Katherine, if anything at all. But Alex would have memories—

apparently memories she resented. After the others left, he reached out and touched Alex's shoulders.

"Why are you so angry at your mother?"

She jerked away. "Why do you care? She didn't love us enough to stay."

"Maybe she loved you more than you think." Quade recognized for the first time that he truly meant what he was about to tell his daughter. "Perhaps she knew that you would be safer here with me for the time being. The war was raging. Attempting to take children across enemy lines would have been difficult at best. And if she had . . . God, if she had taken you . . ." Quade realized the blessing he'd been given and only now understood its worth. "I would have lost you all."

Alex swung around. "You don't want us . . . so don't pretend you do."

"What?" Quade launched himself from the railing and grabbed his daughter's shoulders. "What do you mean, I don't want you?"

"You're always gone. Every time you get a chance. And if you are around, you hire some governess to take care of us."

Meredith's words came back to him. He had worked to earn their love. To prove himself worthy. To provide. But he'd deprived his children instead. Deprived them of himself. Deprived them of his love.

He tried to pull Alex close, but she shook her head, refusing to go into his arms. "Please, General. Forgive me. I had no idea I'd hurt you."

She shook her head again, tears brimming in her eyes.

"I'll change, General. Today is the festival. I won't ever take another night away from you girls. I'll send away any gov—I'll make sure I'm the one who shares your evenings. After the festival, we'll open up Belle Raven. I'll have it cleaned so we can move in. You can—"

"We'll move back here?"

She looked startled.

"Yes, blossom. That's what I was going to tell you all

a few minutes ago, but we got caught up in the dancing.''

Alex hesitated, then flung her arms around her father. She sobbed so deeply that her shoulders shook from the force.

''What is it, General? What's wrong?''

She stared up at him, question in her voice. ''Don't you see, if we move back here that means you don't want to get rid of us. We'll always be a family.''

''Well, of course we will.'' With his thumb, he gently wiped the tears from one cheek. ''Whatever made you think we wouldn't?''

She sniffled. ''Remember when you said that a warehouse was a place where you temporarily stored things that you would move somewhere else later? I thought because you made us move from here . . . and you made us girls live in the warehouse . . . well, I thought maybe we were just going to live with you for a little while, and you were going to make us stay with someone else.''

''Never, ever, ever, General.'' Quade clutched her, wishing he could take back the years of worry she must have suffered. Pressing a kiss atop her head, he vowed, ''We're in this all together . . . forever.''

''I'm glad, Father. I'm so glad,'' she whispered vehemently against his chest.

''Okay, can we come in?'' Randy asked. ''She looks like she's all right now.''

''You've been listening?'' Alex stepped back from her father's embrace and wiped her eyes.

''Yep. Every word.'' Randy grinned at her sibling, the missing teeth making her look all the more like the devilish imp that she was.

''We tried to get her to stay in here, but she wouldn't.'' Samantha shrugged.

''We certainly did,'' Meredith added sternly, but amusement lit her eyes.

Tiny hands tugged on one of Quade's pants legs. ''Papa, am I s'posed to be worried about something too?''

He chuckled, glad to be able to laugh off the sadness.

"No, Muffin. You don't need to worry about a thing, unless you just feel like it."

"Okay, I won't."

Quade laughed again, grabbing up his youngest and planting a kiss right on her chubby cheek. "You, Muffin, are a pure delight."

"And a voice of wisdom, if you ask me."

"How so?" Quade glanced at Meredith.

"Why worry about something until it happens?" she asked. "Why deprive yourself of joy because you fear the worst? Why believe that Phillip's arrival will change anything between you and me?"

❖ *23* ❖

"But, Captain, you have got to come!" Yori slapped his seaman's cap against his leg in frustration, looking at Meredith for support. "If he does not, they will change their minds and call off the festival, I am thinking. We will not climb the masts or do anything we have planned."

"I told Wisdom he was being quite absurd." Savannah's brows lifted in surprise. "But they wouldn't listen to me." She splayed her fingers across her chest. "*Why,* I have no idea. I've done nothing to make them believe they have the right to ignore me, I assure you."

Meredith's hand covered her mouth to keep from revealing her amusement.

"But they will listen to you and Meredith." Savannah's chin lifted, indignation glinting in her hazel eyes. "Both of you have a head on your shoulders they apparently value."

Yori looked upon Meredith's sister adoringly. "I like your head yist fine."

"Thank you, *kjere.*" Savannah patted him on one cheek. "I'm glad someone in this town thinks so."

"That means *honey,*" Randy informed him, tugging on Yori's pants leg and looking up at him as if he were a towering pine.

"Yes, I know, blossom." He tapped her nose and winked. "Remember, *I* taught you that."

"Oh, yeah."

"You said you would spend this afternoon with us."

The tone in Alex's declaration made Meredith shift her gaze to stare at the eleven-year-old who stood on the steps of the grand staircase. Alex had spent part of the afternoon showing her sisters every room and telling them of things she used to do in each. Meredith had never seen her so happy. Would whatever had been mended between her and her father now be shattered?

"I did, didn't I, General? But you do want the festival to go on, don't you, Alex?"

She stared at her feet. "Yessir."

"It would be selfish of us if we didn't at least try to persuade them to go ahead, wouldn't it?"

"I suppose so."

"You do want to enter the Little Princess contest, don't you?"

"I do!" Randy interjected.

"We all do, barnacle brain."

Quade ran a hand across his temple and shifted his attention to the Norwegian. "Then I guess that doesn't leave me much choice, does it?"

Meredith's heart ached for Alex when her shoulders shrugged in defeat.

"Then I say, we *all* go persuade them!" Quade smiled as Alex's head bobbed up and surprise filled her face. "Grab your things, and we'll head to shore. We'll show them the Camerons aren't going to let any old bluster scare us off!"

"Can I ride beside you, Father?" Alex grabbed the picnic basket that had stored their lunch.

"You'll have to ask Miss Stanfield. I believe she's laid claim to that particular seat and isn't likely to give it up." He winked at Meredith.

"Doesn't look like there's much hope." The banker shook his head sadly, talking to the crowd gathered around the kissing booth. "Lieutenant Mitchell said he wouldn't fire the cannons if it got misty. Ever since Grant pulled the troops out in May, Mitchell's been on a tighter budget. He says he would have to use extra pitch on them in order to shoot the fireworks up as high as we want. No cannons, no fireworks. No fireworks, no festival. Guess the Yankees whipped us again."

Grumbles rippled through the crowd. "Ain't fair," someone shouted.

"Trying to keep a stranglehold on us, them Yanks are," accused another. "Can't even fly ol' Dixie on the masts no more."

"Besides, we put up plenty of owls to ward off wind big enough to blow us clear to Montana," announced another.

Quade turned a full circle and tested the wind, spotting the wooden owls now roosting atop every booth and flagpole. The talisman was considered a protection against prevailing winds and unwise decisions.

"This is ridiculous." He licked his thumb and stuck it up in the breeze. *His* decision would be based on fact, not fancy.

"There isn't a drop of moisture in the wind. It's going to blow over, and probably long before nightfall," he told the banker. "You're going to spoil a lot of happy faces around here just because you're afraid of a little old bluster."

"*You* go talk to Mitchell, then." Wisdom pointed behind him. "He's over at the bank talking to Littlefield. I can't make him see reason. Maybe you can."

"Is he our only holdback?"

"I think I've persuaded enough of the citizenry to balance the decision in our favor, but with the provision that those damned fireworks be shot off."

"I'll see what I can do." Quade headed for the bank, waving to folks along the way. "In the meantime, you go ahead and get the games underway. The races, too. Let's act as if nothing's wrong, and I've already convinced the coward."

Quade wondered where Meredith and the children had gotten off to, then remembered she'd said something about touching up their hair and dresses for the Little Princess contest.

Delicious aromas blended to make a man's mouth water. Fried shrimp and oysters. Spicy gumbo and Mississippi corn fritters. Cinnamon and sweet cane. He passed the cake booth and spotted Yori standing next to Savannah, who was craning her head to see around a rather obese woman . . . and apparently having a difficult time of it.

"Any luck, Savannah?"

"How the fine fancy would I know?" Savannah frowned at the woman's back. "This barge won't move out of the way so I can see!"

"I beg your pardon!" The woman spun around, her three chins rising in indignation as she lifted a badge that had been pinned on her left collar. "But this *barge* is trying to judge the cake contest."

Yori hooted so loudly that Quade couldn't help himself. "Better watch that, Yori. The Stanfields are not known for their easy temp—"

A mermaid-shaped cake went flying upward, splattering the Nordic cheekbones with green and yellow icing that had once been a fin and hair. Several feminine gasps tore the air as Savannah Stanfield stormed down the promenade.

"Yist a minute, *kjere!*" Yori called after her, licking his lips and the tips of his fingers as he wiped a dollop of icing from his face. "It *tastes* better than the others, I am thinking. It yist does not *look* so good now."

The festival was getting stirred up, and Quade meant to see that there was plenty of opportunity for the Norwegian to resolve his misunderstanding with his sweetheart. He focused on his destination, ready to complete the talk with Mitchell and get the festival underway. All the colorful entertainers, musicians, craft booths, and food cafés in the world would be of no consequence if he couldn't get the lieutenant to agree to shoot the fireworks.

The bank was less than a block away on a site selected for easy access to the steamboat docks and, thus, trade. Unsure how long Littlefield had been told to keep the doors open today, Quade tested the knob and found it not yet locked.

"Good afternoon, Littlefield. Lieutenant Mitchell," he greeted, finding the two men huddled over a paper lying on the counter in front of the teller's booth.

"Heavens, you scared me!" Littlefield's writing instrument streaked across the paper, tearing a hole in the parchment. Retrieving a handkerchief from his back pocket, he mopped his bald head. "Now see what you've done."

The soldier in Union blue returned the greeting, his dark eyes studying Quade. "Good day to you, Captain Cameron. Or at least we hope it will be, if the wind ever dies down."

"That's what I've come to talk to you about. That is, if I'm not interrupting anything important." Quade nodded at the paper Littlefield wadded in his hands.

"Nothing that can't be discussed later, my good man. Mr. Littlefield was showing me—"

"It's about time I was closing." Littlefield appeared suddenly nervous. His hand shook so hard that he dropped the sheet of parchment. "Mr. Winkle expects me to be precise about my hours."

"—how proficient he is at imitating someone's handwriting." The lieutenant frowned at the clerk's rudeness. "I must say that could be quite calamitous if the wrong person were to learn the art. Quite calamitous indeed."

"I certainly agree with you, Mitchell." Quade stared at Littlefield, watching the man's neck retreat turtlelike into his shirt. The clerk's face was as red as the galluses he wore. "Especially if a fool directed the artist's hand."

He waved the soldier to the door. "Come, let me buy you a cup of *brûlot*. Let's allow him to close up and be on his way, while we discuss some business that I think will be of interest to both of us."

Once they were out of hearing distance from the clerk,

Quade tested the soldier's intentions. "I'd like to convince you of just how much we need those fireworks to go off tonight and start this festival with a bang, so to speak."

Lieutenant Mitchell grinned. "I knew they would send for you, and I also highly suspected you were a wise enough man to demand this talk. Now that we understand each other, Captain, we'll simply discuss the essential issues. *I* need a certain piano brought down from St. Louis, a circumstance to which I have not been able to apply funds . . ." Mitchell shrugged. "Ever since the majority of the troops left to go north, it's as if I'm a forgotten man and my post the last to . . . shall we say . . . reap the rewards of Reconstruction?"

"I understand perfectly, Lieutenant. A seafarer must always be open to the bartering system. It's the universal language, I'm told. I give you this. In turn, you give me that."

Quade dug into the inner pocket of his frock coat and pulled out part of the money he'd made to finance the repair of the docks. For just a moment he hesitated, remembering the long hours it had taken to earn the extra funds. But satisfying the soldier would keep the festival afloat and make a whole townful of people happy, including his daughters. He'd have to count on Meredith's meaning what she'd said earlier . . . that she would rethink her reasons for not awarding him the bid. "How much of this do I give you?"

"None of it." The soldier motioned to the boats anchored out in the lee. "Just next time one of your vessels sails to St. Louis, I expect my piano to arrive back here in one piece. Deal?"

Quade returned the money to his pocket and offered his hand to seal the bargain. "Deal. Feeling generous, are you, Lieutenant?"

He nodded. "I decided if Reconstruction is going to work, we'll have to work together a little better. I'll shoot those fireworks for you tonight, Captain. You bring back my piano."

"The townspeople will be grateful."

"See that they stay sober. I'm told the Paxtons are supplying security, and we'll have to count on them for the biggest part of it. My men and I will see that no one shanghais the fireworks. And have no doubt, they will go off on time. I give you my word."

"As I give you mine." Quade bid the man farewell as the lieutenant stepped into the skiff that had been tied to the end of the dock. He ordered the soldier waiting for his return to row them back to the island.

"Now who to tell first, I wonder?" Quade stared at the pelican standing silently on the piling that stretched out into the surf. The bird glared back with one eye closed before taking wing.

"That's it! One-Eyed Thomas." That man might walk more slowly than frozen molasses, but his gossipy tongue knew no equal. The yarn-spinner would get the word around.

Quade set off to find Thomas and almost instantly discovered his oldest daughter with Lazaro López. They were talking nonstop, and Alexandra looked absolutely enthralled. "Alex? Where are your sisters?"

"With Miss Meredith, Father. Oh—" She tipped her parasol and allowed her father a better view of the Spaniard's face. "You do remember Mr. López, don't you, Father? Meredith met him and invested in his—"

"I remember him. Good afternoon, sir. I trust you and Alex will join the festivities with the others *shortly*."

Lazaro nodded. "Indeed, we will, Captain. Miss Alexandra agreed to show me the docks you intend to repair. I'm afraid her ankle twisted on a raised board, and we had to rest here for a while."

"May I see your ankle, Alex?" Quade's gaze studied her hem, aware that she was deliberately attempting to hide her foot beneath her dress.

"It's quite all right now, Father. Really it is." She walked forward. "See? We'll be along in just a moment."

Quade examined the young man with a critical eye, as if sizing up a stalwart deckhand. He supposed it wouldn't be long until he must worry about suitors coming to call. But Alexandra had always been such a serious scamp. He must watch her more closely. She was growing up far too fast. Especially now, when he'd finally decided he needed to spend more time with her.

"All right, I'll leave you in this young man's hands. If you've not returned to the main strand in fifteen minutes, I will come looking for you."

"Yes, Father."

Quade hurried along his way, telling each vendor the news concerning the fireworks. He found Opal and Thomas listening intently to a medicine man hawk his wares. Quade wormed his way through the throng and whispered into Thomas's ear. Just as he had expected, the peg-legged man set to work informing the crowd. Several left to tell others.

"Have you seen the girls?" Quade asked Opal expectantly.

His housekeeper nodded. "*Sí*. They were trying to help *Señorita* Stanfield with the games. Savannah, I mean. I forget there are two *Señorita* Stanfields. There was *mucho* trouble with Dooley Duckworth and the frog-jumping contest. Ay-yi-*yi* . . . he sneaked up behind the lady and dropped a frog down the back of her dress. How could he know she had on ten petticoats and it would not fall through? It finally fell into her—" Opal blushed. "—unmentionables. Such a sight. Aieee! *Such* a sight."

He could imagine poor little Dooley now. Savannah would have him strung up on the yardarm of . . . oh no . . . he'd forgotten to tell Yori to test the paint on that last mast before assigning the numbers to the climbers! "Was Yori with Savannah?"

"I do not think so, *Capitán*. He was about to enter a race of his own."

"That's what I was afraid you'd say." Quade glanced at the line of booths down the boardwalk. "It looks like a lot of things are primed and running."

Opal squinted her eyes and shooed him on his way. "We knew you would convince the lieutenant. But the *muchachos* were getting . . . how do you say . . . fussy . . . so we did what you said and gave them something to do. Now we are *mucho* busy watching the *muchachos*. *Sí*?''

''Yes, I do see.'' Quade was glad they'd taken the initative. That meant the tide of superstition was turning.

''I'll see you later. Got to find Meredith.'' After he made sure everything was underway, he intended to find her and discuss what he'd discovered at the bank. If he was right and could prove it . . . then he now had some proposing to do.

❖ 24 ❖

MEREDITH WONDERED WHERE Quade had gone. She stood at the center of the grandstand and stared into the crowd. His speech to convince the town officials to hold the celebration must have been quite persuasive, for several activities were well underway. It was time to make the announcement, but she didn't want to do so until Quade could be there.

"Friends, neighbors, because Captain Cameron has been detained, I am going to delay announcing my decision until after the fireworks. By then, his duties will allow him to join us. I'm sure you'll all agree that we want both men here for the final announcement."

"He'll find something else to keep him busy. He always does," Nolan muttered as they exited the grandstand and people started moving toward other interests. "You're wasting your time."

Tired of the man's derogatory remarks toward Quade, she faced him. "No, Nolan, I'm not. What I regret is ever considering you in the first place and wasting precious time that could have been spent repairing those docks. The bid should have been awarded to the captain long before now."

Nolan grabbed her hand. "What else have you given him, Meredith? I'm sure Phillip would like to know."

She jerked away from his touch. "That is none of *your* concern, Mr. Richards. Nor is it any longer Phillip's."

"Then you don't intend to honor your pledge to marry him?"

"Not that *that* is any of your concern either, but no, I do not. For reasons I don't intend to discuss, I cannot marry him in good conscience. Now, if you'll excuse me . . ." She turned her back to him. "I have three children to prepare for the Little Princess contest. I cannot be detained."

Meredith sliced her way through the crowd, hoping to reach the children before they gave up on her. Shanty and Winifred had agreed to stay with them while she gave the brief speech, but the speech had been delayed the first time by the dull oration of one of the territorial politicians.

The boats that were big enough to hold several people, but not so large that they couldn't navigate the shallows, had been moored in an orchestrated sequence of protocol. Buoys were painted bright colors, while flags at the top of each mast fluttered its owner's insignia. Each vessel was to hold one of the finalists in the Little Princess contest, the biggest to allow the winner to lead the flotilla.

Meredith shuddered to think that the girls might be on those boats, especially with the wind whipping up like it did. But they all had assured her that each knew how to swim should anything drastic occur, and an adult was assigned to each boat in the event of disaster.

Hurrying through the crowd, she could see by the movement and rustle of skirts that hastily wove in and out of the throng that the contest was about to commence. Females everywhere rushed to the elected wharf where the judging would be held. Meredith hoped she had time to reach her wards, check them over, then deliver them to the judge without having them disqualified. Finally, she spotted Winifred and Shanty coming toward her with the children in tow.

She waved and moved as quickly toward them as the throng allowed.

"We decided you must have been delayed, Merry

dear.'' Winifred hugged her. ''Miss Shanty insisted that her leg was well enough to attempt the walk. I dare say she used her cane as if it were the rod of Moses.''

''Ye-ins would have been proud of me, gally-girl.'' Shanty hobbled to a halt. ''I didn't strike a single scalawag.''

''I'm always proud of you, Shanty.'' Meredith studied the children. Randy could hardly stand still. Samantha seemed a bit nervous. ''Well, I think we may have the very next Princess in our midst. Are you both ready for this?''

''We haven't seen Alex.'' Samantha raised on her tiptoes to look over a head or two. ''She's going to be disqualified if she doesn't return.''

''I did hope to keep you all together.'' Meredith searched each face that passed them, looking for a sign of Quade's eldest. ''I wanted us to be side by side when the fireworks go off.''

''Miss Stanfield! Meredith! I'm over here!''

Meredith finally spotted the eleven-year-old coming from further up the promenade, walking with that nice Mr. López. She should have known the two of them would find each other, even in this mob. Who knew? Twenty years from now Alex and Lazaro might be married and have a half-dozen children of their own to search for at Biloxi's summer festival. A sweet thought, but one Meredith envied. Perhaps one day she would still be chasing the girls and add a little brother or sister to the merriment.

Before this festival was through, Meredith was determined to make Quade want her so much that he couldn't possibly wait for her to make up her mind about Phillip. His resistance was weakening. She could tell. Maybe it seemed like blatant teasing to others, but she didn't care. Her heart knew what it wanted . . . who it wanted, and she wanted him forever. When Phillip returned, she would just have to explain to him that she'd fallen in love with the captain. Maybe she could steal a kiss during the fireworks tonight.

"Welcome, ladies and gentlemen, to Biloxi's annual Little Princess Celebration!" Wisdom Winkle's voice boomed across the boardwalk, drawing all to the raised platform where he stood. "The lucky belle who wins the title will represent our fair city in . . ."

"Go on, children." Meredith encouraged them to get in line to receive their official numbers. "Winnie, Shanty, and I will be out here cheering for you."

"Do you still think we can win, Miss Merry?" Samantha whispered in Meredith's ear as she gave the child a hug for good luck. "There's so many, and they all look so pretty."

Meredith backed away and studied Samantha's face carefully. "Yes, they do, Sam. And this will always be a fact of life. There will always be someone you think better than yourself. But that shouldn't stop you from entering the contest or from trying to do your very best." She caressed the child's chin. "Because *trying* is the real test, not winning. If you sat back and didn't enter, you never would know if you could have won. If you win, everyone will believe you were the best in that particular moment. If you lose, you know you tried your very best."

A round of applause broke out around them. Meredith blushed, not realizing that her words had been listened to by more than children. Embarrassed, her hand instinctively attempted to straighten the chignon at the base of her neck, but remembered in time that it was nonexistent. She'd worn her hair down as Quade preferred, in the hope that it would entice him.

"Yes, well. You girls do your best. We'll all be out here watching."

"Even Father?" Alexandra looked doubtful. "He promised."

"If your father promised, he'll be here. I'm sure there's something he must see to before he can join us. You go on up there, and before you know it, I'll have him wave so you can spot him."

She hugged Alex and Randy in turn, then reminded Randy not to leave the stage for any reason, unless she could clearly see Meredith and walk straight to her.

"I'm going to find me a place to sit." Shanty tapped Meredith's shoulder. "Ye coming?"

"I believe I'll stand right here. I want to be close to where the girls left me. That way, they can find me easily. If you see the captain, point him in my direction, will you?"

"Quit ye-in's worrying, gally-girl. If he said he'd be here, he will. Winnie, ol' gal," the mop-haired woman grinned at Meredith's housekeeper, "ye want to come sit by me a spell?"

Her mouth twisted to one side conspiratorily. "Ye never did finish telling me about that time they thought ye run that blackguard in with ye-in's kitchen knife. Seems to me if he weren't some fine duke, they wouldn't have even doubted ye word. Now, this here's what I woulda done if I'd been ye-ins."

Meredith stared after the odd pair—a lady of high society and an earthy woman—and found it incredible that they had become fast friends. The world was changing. North and South now one United States. Winifred and Shanty, Savannah and Yori . . . fine examples of Plantation Row and wharf folk blending in harmony. Now if only she and Quade could span the gap that separated them, the world would be as it should be . . . full of hope and promise and a bright tomorrow.

She decided to take her own advice to the children. She would do her best to make Quade understand how much she loved him. And if she had any doubts at all that she might not achieve her goal, Meredith offered them up to the one person who could make a difference—her Maker. Wherever Quade was at the moment, she hoped his heart was listening too.

In a quandary about whether to stay or leave, Quade shifted his position so his legs would quit cramping. He'd promised the girls he'd be there to see the contest, but he could only hope they would understand the reasons for his absence at the moment. An apology wouldn't be enough. He'd have to do something special to make this up to them.

Though large, the empty fish barrel barely hid him and smelled to high heaven. But the barrel had been a handy hiding place and had peepholes to look out from. He would have a lot of explaining to do when he caught up with Merry and the girls—if they allowed him anywhere near them.

The two men were up to something and every sense inside Quade warned him to keep alert and listen.

He had spotted the bank clerk talking to Richards moments after the Northerner left the grandstand. Though Quade had joined the crowd too late to actually hear Meredith's announcement, Richards's face was a mask of fury. The look the Northerner had given Meredith was enough to warrant Quade's concern. The man was up to no good, and Quade's every instinct told him it did not bode well for Meredith.

Now Richards and Littlefield plotted together, and Quade wanted to make quite certain that their scheme presented Meredith no cause for worry. If only he'd found somewhere else to watch that was a bit less confining. . . .

"I tell you, Richards, he *knows*."

The nasal whine and sniffle could only be Littlefield's. Quade tried to twist around to the correct opening to be able to see better. Moving was difficult without jostling the barrel and giving away his presence.

"You said you didn't tell him." The Northerner's gruff reply held a note of threat. "You weren't that stupid, were you?"

"I didn't say a thing. But he knows. And if he knows, then he's going to start asking questions. If he asks questions, I'll probably lose my—"

"Quit being such a simpering fool! I paid you well for your efforts. There's no way he can prove it unless you run scared and do something stupid."

"Don't worry. I've already done the other thing we agreed on."

"Good. I've almost got the investors where I want

them. I just need to reassure them that I, and no one else, will gain the Biloxi bid. They're getting tired of waiting, and I, for one, plan to see that they don't have to anymore." He stopped, his face turning toward the barrels. "Did you hear something?"

Quade froze, unaware that he had shifted to put his ear to the opening rather than his eye so he could be certain to hear every word.

"No." Littlefield's whine became a whisper. "Oh, God, do you think someone's watching us?"

"We've played it careful, you and I. But I think it would be safer if we talked someplace where it's less likely for someone to walk by and—peeuuw!—definitely someplace where it smells better. I hate the smell of fish."

Quade cursed his luck. He had to wait a few minutes before he attempted to free himself, in the event Richards was watching. The minutes ticked by, keeping time with the pulse drumming in his ears. Finally, he felt it was safe to appear.

With great relief, he flipped the barrel lid open and stood. "Lord, it stinks in there!"

A woman happened to be strolling by at that exact moment and shrieked with surprise.

"Pardon me, *madame*," he apologized profusely as he attempted to lift himself out of the barrel as easily as he'd gotten himself into it. But as luck would have it, he couldn't.

"Captain Cameron—" Her face paled. "What on earth are you doing in that thing?"

"Would you believe checking things out?" Quade's eyes closed as he saw disbelief set her lips into a frown. "It's really a very long, unpleasant story, and I promise if you'll help me extricate myself from this, I'll be happy to share it with you after my duties are completed. But I'm sort of in a bind here and need your assistance. If I move just so, I'm going to end up rolling myself into the gulf. Would you mind?"

"Certainly." Her nose wrinkled in disgust as she approached. "Is that you smelling so foul, Captain?"

"I'm afraid it is, Miss Prentiss."

"I do believe the gulf might provoke an improvement, sir."

Someone watched her from the dozens of people standing behind her. The feeling of a sinister intent forced her own gaze to sweep through the crowd. She found no one who seemed even remotely interested in her. All eyes were focused on the finalists. As should Meredith's be, since Samantha was among the select few.

Randy had made it past the first round, but got angry with contestant number four and kicked her in the shin. Both girls were disqualified for fighting. Meredith had asked Winifred and Shanty to keep an eye on the scamp.

Meredith promised to watch Sam ride on the flotilla until the parade was completely over. Randy wanted to join in the games Shanty and Yori were conducting, so she'd asked her housekeeper and friend if they minded taking the child to her sister for safekeeping at the moment. The women gladly agreed. Alex was eliminated in the last round and wanted to be comforted by Lazaro. The young man asked to be allowed to escort her to join her younger sister and their friends. Meredith readily agreed.

Anticipation and concern dueled within Meredith. Anticipation, because she knew how much this meant to Samantha. Getting this far was quite an honor for a young woman who only days ago doubted her own beauty. In turn, Meredith was concerned that the wind might cause difficulty in lighting the Japanese lanterns intended to illuminate the boats.

Twilight swept over the festival, darkening the gulf to a glassy sheen. The moon did not promise to be full, initiating concern as to how much light there would be for the floating procession. Meredith didn't like the fact that one of the children she had come to love so deeply would be out on that water in virtual darkness . . . no matter which adult swimmer had been assigned to be her companion.

"The judges' scores are now in and have been tallied!"

Banker Winkle's voice boomed dramatically for effect.

Meredith crossed her fingers and stared intently at Samantha's face, offering a prayer up into the evening sky.

"And the Biloxi Little Princess for 1870 is . . . Miss Samantha Cameron, daughter of Captain Quade Cameron and his late wife, Katherine."

Tears sprang into Merry's eyes as she saw disbelief, joy, and finally self-confidence blossom over the precious child's face. She shed the tears of happiness without shame, telling everyone around her that Sam was her charge, her friend, and for anyone who cared to listen . . . a child of her heart.

Samantha glowed as someone laced the royal robe around her shoulders, then handed her a bouquet of flowers and a scepter. The child had looked more beautiful only one other time in Meredith's memory . . . when she had fallen asleep with her own makeshift scepter and crown made of seashells.

"Where's the tiara?" Winkle demanded as several of the contest sponsors huddled at the corner of the platform. Something clearly was wrong.

"We can't find the crown. Someone's taken off with it."

"I can get a replacement!" Meredith shouted, instantly rushing to halt in front of the banker. "There's one back at the captain's quarters that the children use for play. I can get it, if you like."

"You do that. In the meantime, we'll take her to the boat and let her dress in the Princess costume." He straightened and grinned at the crowd, trying to reassure them. "Easily solved, folks. Miss Stanfield will bring Samantha another crown. Hopefully, we'll find the missing one before the parade starts. We want to thank you all for showing your interest in the contest and invite those of you who didn't win to . . ."

Meredith hurried away, eager to return with one of the tiaras Quade had borrowed from Savannah that morning. She needed to get through this crowd and back in time, before the boats were launched. But night slowly blanketed the seaport with darkness, indicating that the fireworks would soon be displayed. The parade of boats was supposed to be well out into the shallows so that the colorful presentation haloed the parade while the lanterns lit the space that linked boat with boat.

If only Quade had found her in the mob, Meredith could have shed this uneasiness that crept into her. She could have sent him with Samantha while she searched for the tiara. Though chaperoned by contest officials, Samantha needed someone she trusted by her side. Meredith hastened her steps.

A tinkling of bells drew her attention. Meredith turned her head long enough to see Gizelda exit the flap of a tent emanating an amber glow of lantern light.

"Danger precedes you. Trust another who has tread its edge many times." The memory of Gizelda's cryptic warning rushed back to fill Meredith with concern. *"Have faith in what has gone before. For this is the final test, and Destiny will smile upon the deliverer. Do not scoff at the Wisdom of the Ages."*

Reason told her it was simply her fear of the gulf that caused the apprehension churning inside, but instinct warned that there were, indeed, other dangers at play in the encroaching nightfall and the awaiting parade.

Instinct and a growing dread surfaced. She should not have dismissed the Gypsy's warning and taken it so lightly.

❖ 25 ❖

"GOOD *GUD*, YOU smell like a lutefisk, I am think-ing!" Yori batted away the captain's odorous presence, then held out his hands to Quade. White paint imprinted his palms. "You forgot to tell me the paint was not dry on all of them."

Quade closed his eyes for a minute, glad for a reason to laugh. "I'll bet going down was a lot easier than climb-ing up."

"*Ja.* Beat my record by two seconds, I did."

Savannah linked her arm through his. "You should have seen him, Captain. He put all the others to shame."

"I'm glad you two made up. Neither of you has seen Meredith, have you? I can't seem to find her anywhere, and the Little Princess contest is over."

"I imagine she went to the boat with your daughter." Savannah reached out a hand and lightly tapped Quade on the chest. "You do know you are the proud father of this year's Little Princess, don't you?"

Excitement filled Quade, glad that it could replace the concern that had been building since his visit to the bank. "Yes, I heard. I know she's thrilled."

Pride lit Yori's features. "The little blossom was al-ready a princess on the inside. Now everyone will know she is on the outside too. Meredith will be on the princess's float.''

"We're headed that way ourselves. Alex and Randy wanted us to watch them in the smaller floats. They've been asked to participate in the junior parade and told us it's supposed to be a surprise to you and Merry."

"As long as Yori's on hand." What Quade didn't add was, as long as Yori's on hand to dive in and help them if someone rocks the boat.

But Meredith on the water with Sam? Still, she'd walked the surf with him at the beach where they'd made love and had waded out to berate him the day he took the girls swimming. Perhaps believing Phillip intended to return had its rewards. It may have helped her overcome her fear. "Thanks, Yori. I'll go find her. In case I miss her and she walks by, tell her to meet me at the wharf where the parade will start."

What if his suspicions were true? What if Phillip was not returning and would never return to Biloxi? The reasons behind that actuality scared the damnation out of him.

Meredith braved the first deck, found no one aboard and decided the child must be dressing farther down the line of boats to seek more privacy. Glancing up at the flags on each vessel, she realized that the wind had died down as Quade had predicted. It was a small comfort when comprehension sank in. She would have to span the plank that divided the next vessel from this one. And without Quade's help this time.

"Well, I can't get there if I don't try." She reminded herself of the words she had offered to Samantha. Meredith raised herself to the plank and took her first tentative step. The waves cooperated and she crossed the distance easily.

She breathed a heavy sigh of relief as her foot touched down. "Made it!" Disappointed to find no one there either, she gathered her courage and dared the third.

"Something's wrong," she murmured. "Someone should be here."

"You're right." A voice behind her startled Meredith into spinning around.

"You!"

"Glad to see me?" Nolan sneered. "Or were you expecting to rendezvous with your lover?"

"I don't know what you mean." Meredith gauged the distance between herself and the plank. Nolan's malice exuded from him like an odor.

"Don't play innocent with me. I saw the way you looked after your little walk down the beach last night. You might try to convince poor Phillip you're lily-pure, but you and I know different."

"You are the foulest, most vile man I've ever had the misfortune to know!" Meredith took a step backward, a few inches closer to the plank.

"Don't do anything foolish, Meredith. I'm surprised you're even attempting to escape. Frankly, I thought you feared the water so greatly that you might not bridge the boats. But then you've had the big, brave seafarer to guide you to shore, haven't you? And I must say, you do seem to love that child dearly. You know the one—the pretty little freckle-faced girl I tied up?"

"Where is she?" Hysteria rose to consume Meredith. *Calm down. You've got to think clearly. Wait for an opening.*

"Tucked away in the cabin here . . . where I intend to do the same to you. And I wouldn't scream if I were you. It will only see the child dead."

Nolan delved into the inner pocket of his frock coat and produced a document. "You must blame yourself for this ill-fated turn of events, dear Meredith. You simply wouldn't allow me to handle this any other way. That carriage ride should have killed you, but the Stanfield luck took a turn for the better, it seems."

She eyed the parchment warily. "What is that?"

"The bid, of course. But all that's taken care of now. I've had Littlefield forge your name to this document saying that I now have the authority to proceed with the docks. Unfortunately, I can't let you live to dispute your signature." He waved the hand that carried the rope. "It really is a much easier solution, don't you think, and not at all as messy as it might have become?"

Fear pulsed in Meredith's throat, drumming in her ears. "I assume you're responsible for Phillip's letter, as well. But Quade is smart enough to see through this. Whatever you're planning, you won't find *him* such an easy target."

Nolan's mocking laugh echoed into the night. "I'll be far away from this place by the time your lover realizes what's happened. If he were as smart as you claim, I wouldn't have to rely on that frilly-sleeved Littlefield."

The man's duplicity sickened her. "You were my father's friend. *My* friend, I thought."

"That's just it, Meredith. You should have stuck with thinking. It's when you began to *feel* that you got yourself in trouble."

"What do you plan to do with me?"

He grabbed her and swung open the cabin door. "Nothing at all." His laughter rumbled over the deck. "I'm going to let the gulf decide your fate. Oh, but with just the tiniest bit of help from me. . . ." He threw her into the darkened room. "I'll merely cut us adrift, and you'll soon have to face that little fear you have." His tone became a growl. "Because this boat will be taking on water in a few minutes."

"Let the child go. It's me you want, not her."

"True, but you've left me no choice, Meredith. She's heard everything I've said and knows I plan to kill you."

Meredith groped in the dark, stumbling over something human. A muffled reply sent her heart soaring. She offered a prayer of thanks to the heavens that he hadn't killed the child, as she'd feared. Meredith clutched Samantha to her. *Please let me keep my wits about me. Give me a way to save her.*

"How touching. You make me sick." Nolan loomed in the moonlit doorway with something sinister dangling from his hands.

A rope and kerchief! He meant to bind her! Dread sped through Meredith, poisoning her ability to think clearly. Reality gripped her. The man's greed had ravaged his compassion.

"What's the matter, Mermaid?" His voice chilled her like a rush of winter air. "Afraid of a little water?"

"Some prankster unmoored the floats!" Wisdom Winkle complained, pointing to the drifting vessels. "None of the finalists or the Princess are aboard. We expected the fireworks to be shanghaied, but not the floats!"

"Have you seen Meredith anywhere?" Quade peered into the shallows, fearing the worst. Littlefield had confessed his forgery of the letter moments ago when confronted with what Quade overheard from the fish barrel. When he learned that the bank teller also had signed Meredith's name to a document that gave Richards the bid, Quade suspected that the life of the woman he loved was in danger.

"You know, as a matter of fact, the last time I saw her, she was headed for those boats." Winkle looked speculatively at Quade. "You don't think she would have . . . no . . . not Meredith Stanfield. She just went there to give your daughter a tiara. We lost the regular one, you see. I'm sure she's around here some—"

Quade dove, the icy grip of the gulf making him shudder. Long strokes propelled him toward the drifting flotilla. A loud *kaboom* overhead startled him, forcing a mouthful of water down his throat as he came up for air. He choked it out, realizing that Mitchell must have thought the parade had begun and assumed it was time to start the fireworks display.

Another cannon boomed and another, sprinkling the sky with color and matching the heavy beat of Quade's heart. He swam as hard as he could toward the vessels, knowing with all certainty who had set them adrift.

Meredith turned around so she could get into a better position. She rocked back and forth until she touched Samantha's hands. *Please understand—your hands. I want to untie your hands.*

The gag Nolan had secured tightly around Meredith's mouth prevented her from speaking, and she could only wiggle her fingers.

Moments ticked by as Meredith worked at the binds, hoping and praying that Sam would understand. Finally the rope loosened, freeing Samantha's wrists.

Water seeped under the door. The boat was swamping! Could she get Samantha out in time? Meredith screamed against her gag, commanding Samantha to untie her.

Samantha's hands worked madly, causing Meredith to wince. She strained to widen the space between her palms, but the rope cut into her flesh.

The water deepened, soaking her skirts to the thigh. She had to stand, before it got too slippery to do so. Meredith bolted to her feet, grateful that Nolan had not taken time to bind them. The rope loosened as she jerked upward, sending triumph racing through her. But the triumph quickly quelled, for Sam did not follow her up.

Like a madwoman, Meredith worked the knot until she freed the bandanna that he'd used to gag her. "Hang on, Sam. Hang on! I'll get you out of here."

She grabbed for the child, discovering that Nolan had not been as kind to Sam. The water level rose rapidly.

Meredith concentrated on working the rope that lashed Sam's ankles together. The binds were wet, making it difficult to unlace them. "Give, you monsters. Give!" Meredith's fingers worked deftly, though they trembled with effort.

Finally, the binds relaxed. The child was free! The two hugged each other.

"Oh, Miss Merry. I thought he was going to kill us."

"No, darling. Mr. Richards is a stupid man. He doesn't have any idea how much we want to live. Now, did you mean what you said about how being a strong swimmer?"

"Yes, ma'am. But my ankle hurts really bad."

Meredith raced to one wall, searching for what she knew must be here somewhere. Her fingers noticed the difference immediately, a cry of joy exiting from her as she touched the wall's indention. "I've found the port-hole!"

Samantha hobbled to her side and helped her open the doorway to their freedom.

"Let me lift you up here, and you wiggle through." With shocking realization, Meredith knew that her own life would depend on how well the child truly could swim and how quickly she could get help.

"I won't be able to fit through. It's too small. So, the moment you get on the other side, I want you to dive overboard and swim to shore as fast as you can. Find your father. Tell him I need him. If you don't see him any-where, get Yori. Anybody." She lifted Sammy up and pushed her through. "Don't look back. Don't think. Just swim for your life . . . and mine."

When the nine-year-old's feet tentatively touched the deck on the other side, she turned and whispered, "I can't leave you, Miss Merry. I know you're afraid of the wa-ter."

"Take that robe off so it won't weigh you down. Go on. I'm counting on you."

She watched as the tiny body shed its cloak, hobbled to the side of the boat, and dove into the dark waters of the Sound.

Quade saw the small figure dive off the vessel and come up for air a few yards away. He altered his direction toward the lead boat and lengthened his strokes toward the swimmer.

"Papa!"

Fear slammed into his chest. "Samantha!"

When he reached her, she cried, "Miss Merry's in the boat and it's sinking!"

Torn between assuring his daughter's safety and saving Meredith's life, Quade never knew such turmoil in his life. Fortunately, Samantha made the decision for him.

"I can make it, Papa. I'll get the others. You save Miss

Merry and don't let Mr. Richards get away. He tried to kill us!''

Quade rode the waves, paddling as he watched to make certain Samantha remembered the lessons he'd given her day after day for fear she might have a disastrous experience in the water. Her knowledge served her well, for she made steady progress toward shore.

He turned and swam as fast as his arms could propel him to the boat sinking ever deeper into the gulf . . . praying he would reach Meredith in time.

Wood splintered, startling Meredith. She'd thrust her shoulder into the door so many times that she could hardly endure another blow. She'd thought the heavy timber would never give way, but at last she was making progress.

"Stand back!" someone shouted.

"Thank God," she shouted back, rushing to one corner to get out of the way. The most beloved voice of all defined the identity of her rescuer.

A great ripping of hinges preceded a resounding *crackkkk!* that filled the cabin with the sound of freedom. The door jarred forward, crashing to the deck with a splash, soaking Meredith completely.

In a bound, they were in each other's arms, kissing, touching, assuring each other that their love for one another dared to defy Nolan's wickedness and the Gypsy's doomsaying.

"Nolan . . . he's responsible. He tried—"

"I know, love. I've got him. Actually, he got himself. He'd tied a dinghy to the boat to make his escape, but the rope got tangled up in the decorations along the rail. He was still trying to get them loose when I found him."

"Where is he?"

"We fought. He caught me off guard and managed to free the dinghy. But he won't get very far. I connected with that last punch."

The boat sighed and tilted, the stern dipping deep into the water.

Quade released his embrace and grabbed her hand, rushing her out onto the deck. "We've got to jump!" He searched Meredith's eyes. "Trust me?"

"Forever," she assured him, closing them to the reality of what she was about to do.

"Here we go!"

They plunged into the gulf, feet first.

Deeper, deeper, deeper she sank, her shoes, petticoats, and skirts weighing her down. She began to claw her way to the surface, flailing her arms, thrashing her legs as hard as possible.

Arms locked around her, pulling her upward until she thought her lungs might burst before she found precious air. She broke the surface, gasping, clinging to Quade's shoulders. But they went down again.

Her skirts and petticoats pulled at her, tugging her toward the bottom of the gulf. They had to come off, or she'd drown them both. She quit thrashing and let Quade grip her as she struggled to release the buttons of her skirt. The circulation in her fingers seemed to stop, making it difficult to flex them. Meredith willed them to move.

Finally, gratefully, she felt the first button give way. The second. A third. She offered a prayer of thanks that the petticoats were held together by lacing. Though it was difficult, she undid them. One by one, the layers sank, the weight no longer anchoring her down.

Like a fish that had sprouted wings, she broke the surface.

"Swim hard, Merry!" Quade shouted, gasping for air. "Swim for shore! You can make it!" Quade pressed his lips to her ear. "We can do anything together."

"Trust another who has tread its edge many times." The Gypsy's words came back to Meredith as she matched him stroke for stroke. *"Destiny will smile upon the deliverer."*

And so it had. She knew it with every wave that rushed past her, then returned to fight her forward movement. Quade had delivered her from the hands of fear, the manipulations of a rogue, and the promise of an erroneous love. She had taught him how to forgive and believe in forever. The past no longer anchored either of them.

As the glow from the lanterns along the promenade brightened and drew closer, they discovered dozens of friends and neighbors paddling out to rescue them— Thomas and Opal, Angeline and Winifred, all in skiffs that had not been set adrift. The children's dinghies provided buoys for the swimmers to hang on to as the people of Biloxi swam out to lend a hand.

Like a swamped scout sitting at the bow of the parade, Samantha pointed into the water. "There they are! I told you."

Quade and Meredith gladly accepted Yori's help into his skiff. As soon as they were both free of the water, Quade took Meredith into his arms and smiled at her with such love that her heart soared, knowing she had found what she'd been searching for all her life.

"I can't live without you, Meredith." Quade's thumb caressed the curve of her cheek. "A man never knows how many tomorrows he'll have. I want you to share all of mine."

His lips lowered to hers, pausing only an inch away to let their breaths merge. She could feel his heartbeat, keeping rhythm with the exhilaration surging within her.

"If you will stay with me, I promise you this . . . I'll never stop loving you as long as there is a single breath left in my body . . . and beyond." The light of his eyes beckoned to her like a welcome shore. "Marry me? . . . Love me?"

"Forever," she whispered, knowing she'd found true happiness in the three adorable children who had become her own and the man she would love for all eternity. "But only if you can give me the one thing missing from my life."

"Whatever it is, love, I'll die trying."

"A son," she whispered and winked, melding her lips into his.

"More than one, I am thinking," Yori mumbled, turning the skiff toward home.

DeWanna Pace enjoys hearing from her readers. .

DeWanna Pace
c/o The Berkley Publishing Group
200 Madison Avenue
New York, New York 10016

Our Town

...where love is always right around the corner!

● ●

__*Harbor Lights* by Linda Kreisel   0-515-11899-0/$5.99

__*Humble Pie* by Deborah Lawrence   0-515-11900-8/$5.99

__*Candy Kiss* by Ginny Aiken   0-515-11941-5/$5.99

__*Cedar Creek* by Willa Hix   0-515-11958-X/$5.99

__*Sugar and Spice* by DeWanna Pace   0-515-11970-9/$5.99

__*Cross Roads* by Carol Card Otten   0-515-11985-7/$5.99

__*Blue Ribbon* by Jessie Gray   0-515-12003-0/$5.99

__*The Lighthouse* by Linda Eberhardt   0-515-12020-0/$5.99

__*The Hat Box* by Deborah Lawrence   0-515-12033-2/$5.99

__*Country Comforts* by Virginia Lee   0-515-12064-2/$5.99

__*Grand River* by Kathryn Kent   0-515-12067-7/$5.99

__*Beckoning Shore* by DeWanna Pace   0-515-12101-0/$5.99

__*Whistle Stop* by Lisa Higdon (7/97)   0-515-12085-5/$5.99

Payable in U.S. funds. No cash accepted. Postage & handling: $1.75 for one book, 75¢ for each additional.
Maximum postage $5.50. Prices, postage and handling charges may change without notice. Visa,
Amex, MasterCard call 1-800-788-6262, ext. 1, or fax 1-201-933-2316; refer to ad # 637b

Or, check above books   **Bill my:** □ Visa   □ MasterCard   □ Amex _____ (expires)

and send this order form to:
The Berkley Publishing Group   Card#_____

P.O. Box 12289, Dept. B   Daytime Phone #_____   ($10 minimum)
Newark, NJ 07101-5289   Signature_____

Please allow 4-6 weeks for delivery.   **Or enclosed is my:** □ check □ money order
Foreign and Canadian delivery 8-12 weeks.

Ship to:

Name_____   Book Total $_____

Address_____   Applicable Sales Tax $_____
                                         (NY, NJ, PA, CA, GST Can.)
City_____   Postage & Handling $_____

State/ZIP_____   Total Amount Due $_____

Bill to: Name_____

Address_____City_____

State/ZIP_____